THE CEDRIC SERIES

The Oracle

KEEPER OF GAEA'S GATE

THE CEDRIC SERIES

The Oracle

KEEPER OF GAEA'S GATE

VALERIE WILLIS

4 Horsemen
Publications, Inc.

DEDICATION

Thank you to Mr. Justin Willis –my amazing, wonderful, super sexy, Mr. Fix-it-all Husband– who threatened that he better be in every dedication here on out by name... or else! I am not allowed to just say Husband! He also thinks that all my readers should thank him for not insisting I go to bed *every night by midnight.*

I LOVE YOU, JUSTIN WILLIS!

PREFACE

I t was brought to my attention that I should take a moment to talk to the readers and fans of *The Cedric Series*.

In this particular book, I discovered even I had misconceptions about Oracles and Sibyls. They were not a myth, but historical entities who practiced their rituals beyond the mythologies they became part of through the people they inspired and even humbled at times. My dive went so deep that I wrote an article for SciFiFantasy Network and was floored at the number of readers who dove in to see what I had uncovered.

Overall, I wish to share my inspirations for writing this story. This will explain a lot on how I came about creating these amazing ideas, characters, creatures, and events as a fictional work with heavy fantasy and romance elements in the mix. If one really wanted to drag out all its genres, I could label this a historical fiction, mythology, or even occult and paranormal. So far, Fantasy Romance has done this work the most justice for my readers' expectations.

Historical fiction can be applied to several parts throughout the series, whether it's a scene, event, or even a reflection of a character and their on-goings. What do I mean by this? Well a lot of you might get the Vladimir Tepes, or Vlad the Impaler references, but it dove deeper than that. King Frederic was the First King of Germans, the lepers in those times did indeed have to ring bells and seek refuge in colonies, Cerdanya was a real trade town, and so on. There are a ton of subtle hints here and there because I wanted to bring the unseen, untold side of the history during Medieval Times to a tangible state.

As far as the Mythology side of this series, I wanted to teach you all my version of forgotten lores, legends, and mythology. I did my best to not use anything that was newer than the 12th Century as I dug deep. Some of the concepts weaved in with my own perception was hard to obtain and justify. There was a lot of book buying, digging through a Medieval-age bestiary, and though I scoured the internet, it failed me often in my journey for research. As I created and developed each character, I did my best to tie them into one or more myths so that I may weave a wondrous story without limits. At the same time, I wanted some of you to get caught in a conversation or sitting in class and have that moment of, "*Oh! I know how this myth goes!*"

Let me enlighten you all on some of the tales, history, legends and myths stitched into some of these amazing characters you have experienced so far:

Cedric takes after a very forgotten and neglected epic legend from Medieval Times of the Russian Knight Hero, Ilya Muromets. Search him, check it out and feel free to compare what you unknowingly learned about this amazing legend. You'll be excited to see a red haired knight on a black horse as one of the images in the mix. Included in this was some really obscure Romanian beliefs involving early vampire-like stories. The off-shoots involving the strigoi showed less of fear towards these vampire creatures, but held a tone of sorrow and remorse. People who became these creatures had not finished living their lives (Including not ever getting married) and met the insane stipulations to come back as one of the undying. Truly interesting, and I can only hope to capture that same empathetic tone I had discovered in my digging.

Barushka combines a few tales as well, starting with his name drawn from the Russian Knight Hero tales. Other than that, I focused heavily on the Shag Foal lores. I was intrigued by the first few variants I stumbled on and found that the internet proved void of information. Amazingly, the hairy phantom horse tales started so long ago, there was no exact date as to when they began. The folklore was mysteriously always there. Adding to my wonder about this lore was the fact I stumbled on a 1927 Naturalist journal that devoted a section to them. Even this far forward, it was believed it may be an undiscovered species of horse! Despite that, the one thing I saw reflected in all the writing was that a shag foal approaches lone travelers and *scares* them so much that they run off to their deaths. Never once did the research say the horse actively killed someone.

Morrighan, Badbh, and Nemaine were derived from the tales involving the evil sorcerer Calatin. This was the older tale involving them that did not mix the three as one entity. There are no words to describe my frustration and disappointment at how many times that Badbh and Nemaine were labeled as alternative names for Morrighan. Especially when the story of the Legendary Cuchulainn made it clear that they were three sisters each with unique powers. Seeing that Badbh and Morrighan had earned the title of Goddess at some point through the passing of time, I felt the need to give Nemaine her own placement as a Goddess as well.

Romasanta is the most complex of all my characters. His name is taken from a man in history that is not as common as it once was, *Manuel Blanco Romasanta*. He was the first serial killer to be trailed and as you read book two of *The Cedric Series* you will see a lot of that history drawn upon. Feeding off the tragic aura, I pulled in both werewolf and wolf-related myths and lores, wanting to show a more accurate flow through a single entity. It was my intentions to bring in familiar aspects and add in the historically forgotten complications that modern book culture has failed to take into account. Those well-versed in mythology will be able to pick out elements on their own, but the amount of lore here is wide. Tales of Apollo and Daphne, Pan and Pitip, Fenrir, versipellis, Romanian beliefs of vampires were caused by a werewolf, Wolf of the Cemetery from Haiti, Romulus and Remus, and so on. There are deep seeds that I only give you teasers to the mythology that is mentioned here.

As for the monsters, you can say thank you to the Medieval Bestiaries. There are so many wild and crazy creatures in these that are no longer touched that I wanted to bring them to life again. Orms, Jidra, and Aitvaras were a few of the frightening things that travelers spoke of and warned each other about in their explorations. I can only imagine what they may have been based on, but there is a great sense of pride I take in including such monsters into my story. Granted, I have not followed their descriptions exactly and have embellished them with my own imagination, but I hope they make my stories more memorable.

In the end, I encourage my thirsty readers to explore what you've read in my *The Cedric Series*. Search the names, look deeper in the scenes, places, events and discover these in more detail. My goal is to introduce you to the forgotten lores and history while adding my own perspective and imagination into the mix. May this tale make its mark in your heart and open your world to the legacy our ancestors once talked about over the dinner table so long ago!

Happy reading and discovery!

VALERIE WILLIS

Acknowledgments

I cannot express how blessed I feel to have a great team and community who supports my writing efforts behind-the-scenes. From my Alpha and Beta readers to Racquel Henry's amazing Writer's Atelier to the fellow writers both close and far from home. There was a very amazing group of people who donated their skills, eyes, and thoughts to make sure this book was at its best potential throughout the whole process.

Here is a huge thank you and shout out to you all:

Racquel Henry
Kim Plaskett
Trudy Warman
Kim Adams
Joel Dunckel
Ryan O'Reilly
Karen Webster
Vanessa Valiente
Catherine Jones
Denise Mcgaha
Anthonie Burger
Ruth Burns
Brendon Burns
Troy Lake

TABLE OF CONTENTS

Chapter 1

Struggle

Sighing, it was a mixture of frustration and relief pouring out from Angeline. The intense aroma of cigarette smoke and spices did nothing to keep her thoughts from blurring her vision. Once again she found herself falling into the melting pot of images, feelings, and frightening memories. She was still struggling to accept she had escaped, that this place she found herself sitting in was indeed real. A shudder shook her shoulders. She had left the world and came back to something completely different. All of it in her eyes seemed surreal compared to the life she lived so long ago.

When Cedric first step foot on Avalon, his aura engulfed me, his soul embracing my own before our bodies dare meet. It wasn't any of my own emotions, I had lost them long ago by that point. It was Cedric's feelings coming to life inside my own heart, resuscitating my soul after an agonizing silence. He woke me from my undying nightmare where I was lost, wandering in darkness.

Her skin prickling at her thoughts as the air conditioning hummed to life overhead. The cool air made the sweat on the back of her neck icy, chills trickling across her spine. Taking in a slow inhale, holding it a few seconds, she dared her thoughts to continue.

I lost myself to the flow of time allowing the centuries to fade in and out. For a long time, I even forgot my own name. Those images, those fleeting moments where I sat there whispering to myself in the damp darkness. Over and over again, I told myself my name was, is 'Lady Angeline du Romulus.' My chant of desperation. Tears had stopped falling by that point. I became a bewitched husk of my former self. Praying to the shadows I would remember I was once a person, and even worthy of such a high title.

An old habit, Angeline found herself in a daze lipping her own name from where she sat leaning on the bar top. No one around her noticed how she was stumbling through her emotions. She couldn't tell which sensation was fear, sorrow, or even elation. A swirl of hooks grasping and pulling her deeper into her mind searching for answers, trying to come closer to discovering who she was, who she had become through all the pain and torture.

I had stopped counting the passing days, but then my fears gripped me. Cedric made it to Avalon, but would he be able to survive Merlin? My salvation, my only glimmer of hope would be shattered with Cedric's death. All this torturous hope would end and then I would have no more whims of pleasure, no more chances of knowing I wasn't forgotten, no one left to save me if he failed here. I would be nothing, no one, and not even remembering my name would have saved me after that point...

The feeling of their bond reconnecting again still stung in every joint and nerve within her body. Stunned, the torrent of Cedric's emotions jerked her out of her solitude. Thousands of years filled her memories with only the cold harsh touch of Merlin. The day she lost her freedom she never imagined feeling Cedric close ever again, not in the flesh. In fact, she had started accepting the torture as a monotonous chore. On occasion a sickening excitement would come over her when Merlin came to her cell door.

Shuddering, under the dim lights of the bar, she recalled the thrill of torture. It was the only moment when she knew Cedric was still out there, some place in the world. This was the one sliver of light which kept her soul from breaking into an irreparable state, from being swallowed by the void of nothingness. His determination to find her was so strong that pain never rattled her. It had all been replaced by Cedric's pleasure; a gift and a promise to her through their bond that was only possible through an incubus-moroi. His words echoed through her soul with each rapture, each slice and fillet of her flesh, *"as long as you feel my touch through our bond, know that I am still searching for you!"*

Peering down at her drink, the bar around her had faded further away. Huffing the stinging smoke from her nose, she was having a hard time with her newfound senses. It wasn't her first time there in Tony's bar with its neon sign out front blinking *The Lion's Den* through the dark tinted windows. Still, like the last visit here, the smell of smoke overwhelmed her. She had grown sensitive to smell, touch and even her sight looked into dark corners as if lit by an unseen torch. Most of the bar was dark with nothing more than yellow-toned bulbs, her ears hearing them buzzing as they casted shadows on the patrons who loitered under them. It wasn't very busy, but they had come long before the main rush. This was her way, Cedric's way, of slowly helping her grow more comfortable with this new world she knew nothing about.

Everyone had told her their own version of what had happened the day they found the entrance into Avalon. The bar had been destroyed when the portal opened and they leapt in, magic lashing out in angry swipes like a wild animal. Tony insists Badbh the Battle Goddess had been the front runner in wiping out most of the place. She had destroyed the bar top with the pool table and then the rest of the furniture afterwards impatiently waiting for Avalon to return to its former state, eager to join the battle. None of that damage could be seen. The bar top was glossy black with her reflection staring up at her doe-eyed. The long countertop came off the wall in a large 'L' shape from the entrance to where it protected the office door. A new pool table lay under a long fluorescent light and spiraling out from there were several tables and chairs until your eyes hit the walls adorned with booths hugging around them.

The Lion's Den had become a meeting place for creatures and demons alike. It was a much needed hub for the rebuilding of a community where they no longer fought for the top of the pyramid of power in this new age. Many hadn't a clue they were weighed on these imaginary scales, but there was no mistaking they were frightened by those who dominated the top: Lillith, Cedric and

Romasanta. Merlin had taken down some of the strongest nonhumans in the world. With the Eye of Gaea keeping Merlin safe from recoils and even curses, he had dwindled their numbers to the point where humanity was choking out the remaining populations to near extinction. Many of these hid within barriers which were unknown, unmarked. Even then, it was up to the Guardian of the Barrier to allow you to enter or leave.

Angeline wasn't sure if she was relieved or sad over this fact, this struggle Cedric and those like him found themselves living with. Before all of this, she had been a human girl married off to a demonic knight. This was not the world she knew, nor could begin to decipher what anything witnessed meant or what purpose it served in everyday life. It might as well be an encrypted dream, with foreign names and purposes that felt unnecessary. Her days of camping on a route travelling horseback had been discontinued centuries ago. No signs of a horse to be seen in the few months she had been living in this place of square castles and mechanical transportation. This was not home, this was not her world, whether human or demon, she belonged nowhere.

Closing her eyes, the conversation between Cedric and Tony was no longer audible to her ears. Allowing herself to remember the horrific events, something she still fought over whether it was a good or bad to urge any of it. Her mind stretched back to the beginning of her torment. It wasn't her time with Cedric that had rotted her soul, but one twist in fate she had failed to see coming. The frightening turning point wasn't the fight where Cedric defeated Boto and became the new King Incubus, but the appearance of Merlin.

At first glance, Merlin seemed like nothing more than a bald old man with a long white beard. A few layers of long-sleeved tan robes and a rope belt with a satchel added to his sage-like appearance. Powerful and wise, yet the sensation of good judgment faded in an instant. Merlin had placed the Amulet of Avalon, the Eye of Gaea, into one of his sleeves after snatching it from Morrighan when he turned to address them. Cedric was still in his incubine form. Horns black and curled like a rams at the sides of his skull. Glaring at the wizard, Cedric clenched his fangs tight with contempt. Hands and feet were clawed and massive, while he was three times larger in overall bulk and muscle in this form. A smooth thin tail swished with anger and his massive bat-like wings adorned with two fingers at the main fold were still held high in alarm.

I stood there, painted crimson from the bloody war waging around me, my nostrils stinging from the iron smell. Boto's first strike ripped into Cedric's side, encouraging red rivulets to gush forward. Drops of blood shattered on the black marble floor, blooming like rose petals at Cedric's feet. My chest ached from the fear clawing at me. To think, he could feel that emotion screaming through our bond.

Cedric had slain Boto only minutes before, claiming the title of King Incubus for himself. Angeline witnessed the harsh reality of a bond breaking, the outburst of magic's harsh whiplash rattling through Morrighan. The amount of pain ripping through the souls of Boto and Morrighan was unmistakable and never-ending. Her breath caught in her throat as Cedric's fear slammed into her and she mirrored back her own. This could be them someday. She tried to voice her concern, wanting to ask if this is what he would face due to her own mortality, but his green glare silenced her. The wave of dread retreated back into him, letting her know it was not her place to worry. She was a human bound to a demon, married to *Lord Cedric du Romulus the Demonic Knight*. In this world, she had no right to voice her thoughts. The world of humans was the extent of her knowledge, while his world was a cruel place somewhere between demons and gods.

But now, I have no knowledge of any world... no place to belong...

Morrighan had fallen victim to the recoil of her sins. Years of curses had been waiting for an opening to exact their revenge for her abuse of necromancy and other black arts against magical beings and creatures. Taking the stone away was like stripping her of her shield and armor. She had been left naked and exposed to Gaea's Law and the lashing for hurting children of Gaea; those who were made by her, descended from her or carried her magic within them. Morrighan's punishment unfolded at incredible speed and she took on a gruesome and beastly appearance. Spending decades, possibly centuries making chimeras had made her into one as well. She fell, passing out across Boto's lifeless body, exhausted from the sudden physical change. Cedric and Merlin had stripped Morrighan of everything she'd held valuable in her life.

Merlin had materialized before them, his power resonating through the air. He continued his casual conversation with Cedric while eyeing her at every chance. Goosebumps prickled across her skin and she involuntarily held her breath, hoping it would make her less visible.

"You see, I have been digging through a century's worth of time trying to find this particular bloodline, but I see you have spoiled it with your own blood." The eyes of the wizard were growing brighter as he scowled. His tone of voice towards Cedric was as if he were a child who broke an expensive vase. "This is going to delay my work. I will have to find a way to undo the damage you have done to her witch's blood. I despise demons and the work they do on the human body. Worse off, you have gone as far as binding yourself to her, it's degrading."

Cedric's wings flared out in response of the wizard making it known Angeline was his target. Her heart had been pounding, leaving her chest aching. Anger waved out of Cedric, the heat of it physically flowing from him. She could feel the scorching fire of his ire and his muscles tightened as if they were her own.

"Don't touch her." Fear shook her core at the sound of Cedric's growl, a deep demonic tone pouring from him.

Her thoughts tightened their hold on her. *Am I afraid of Cedric or the wizard?'*

"You will not take her!" Cedric roared.

"Ah, but I will, demons are such poor thinkers, tsk." A smile crawled across the old man's face.

Angeline stood, watching it unfold. *'No, not Cedric, but the wizard has every part of me shaking with fear. Those glowing eyes... he will leave here with me... I can feel it...'*

"She will be making her new home on Avalon, without you, of course." Scoffing, he continued to patronize Cedric. "It never shocks me to see how easily demons fall for humans. The wolf never sleeps with the sheep for a reason."

Cedric snarled, "What do you want from her?"

'I can't run, he'll get me.' Looking down she saw her enchanted bow and a sparkle of hope fluttered in her heart. *'But if I can land a hit with Wylleam's bow, I can't help but wonder if its magic might allow us to run.'*

"Her magic is dormant, there is nothing you can get from her." It was more of a plea coming from Cedric.

"Ah, but you see, I have been pulling such deep magic into my own blood to gain immortality. With the ancient line she holds, I will be able to achieve this as well as the power to clean the rest of the demon powerhouses off this earth. I will become supreme ruler of mankind, not Beelzebub, or any creature of such spoiled lineage." As Merlin continued his rant with Cedric, she gripped the wood of her bow tight, sweat rolling down her cheek. "Feh, but unfortunately, I got here far too late and will now have to cleanse her of your filth and try not to kill her in the process. Bindings and transformations are difficult filths you hellish dogs have plagued mankind with."

She froze. The wizard took a step towards Cedric, sending him into a charge. Her stomach knotted as she watched the distance between them grow until she was out of Cedric's reach.

'NO! He'll get me! I know it! I can sense it! CEDRIC COME BACK!' If only he could hear her thoughts!

His claw swiped, but it met a swirl of wind. The illusion broke, nothing more than a breeze. It had served its purpose, pulling his focus away from his goal, Angeline. She watched Cedric struggle to catch his balance. A burst of wind from behind her knocked the bow from her hand, the wizard had seen her attempt. Merlin grabbed a fist full of her hair, firm and harsh, her scalp stinging. She was jerked back against the wizard, his breath hitting her shoulders hot with anger.

"You are mine!" Hissed Merlin in her ear.

Her brown eyes locked with Cedric's own, both wide and full of fear.

"CEDRIC!" The shriek echoed in an unnerving manner across the great hall, muting the war waging outside.

"LET HER GO!" Another yank of her scalp sent tears down her face, a dagger digging deep into her neck.

"Watch, girl, as your demon panics over the smell of a drop of your blood." The tip stung at her throat and a warm crawling snaked down her neck. "You feel his fear, don't you?"

All she could do was cry. She could tell Cedric was struggling to hide the emotions unraveling within him. Her own terror had sent her heart racing, each piece slipping through their bond, driving him further into a panic. A searing heat within her soul struck her like Death's bell revealing what had went so horribly wrong. Her own voice laughing, whispering an echo of a promised heartache from so long ago over a campfire. The heat of the tears on her cheeks were self-indulged anger sliding down her face.

'I cursed us... that night at the fire, I left the door open for Merlin. This, this is my fault.'

"Oh, what do I see there?" The dagger's point pulled away, but his grip tightened and pulled at her further as he glowered at Cedric. "You can't be serious? A wedding band on a demon's hand is improper and insulting. Let me fix that."

Merlin called forth his magic, she could barely breath. Her lungs felt squeezed and her blood boiled in reaction to the magic being summoned from her captor. It was hard to say if it was the smell of searing flesh or the red hot glow of the golden wedding band which called her attention back to Cedric. In horror, she watched him scream. With ease the molten metal burnt through his ring finger. Gasping, she was overwhelmed with breathtaking arousal as they stared into each other's eyes. Droplets of melted gold continued to dig into the marble floor around the fallen finger. Paling, dread swallowed her. There was no hope for him to be able to save her against power like this. Cedric panted, the stump of a left ring finger smoking still. He demanded her to not look away from his fiery green stare.

"Angeline, remember that sensation well!" It was the first time she had seen tears fall from those sharp eyes.

'He knows he can't save me,' her heart was breaking.

"I promise you that no matter what, you will never feel pain again!" Cedric's look of desperation and the bitter reality in his words stabbed deep in her soul. "And know that I am still searching for you!"

'No! I don't want that! Don't do this to me! I'm not as strong as you are!' Her lips trembled, unable to scream the thoughts, unable to respond to those green eyes embracing her for the last time.

Grunting, Merlin pulled her closer, the wind rushing around them. "Sorry to disappoint you so soon, but only Lillith would be able to keep a promise like that."

CHAPTER 2

A PROMISE

Merlin was wrong. Not once did I feel my bones break, my skin slice, or even the pull of the twine sewing my mouth shut when he had grown tired of my rebellion. All of it had been blissful moments of feeling Cedric somewhere beyond Avalon still searching. He kept his promise and never wavered.

Pausing from her thoughts, she took a sip of the drink Tony had made for her. The flavor was sharp and sweet thanks to the pineapple juice added into it. There was so much she was clueless about in this new world, so many new flavors. She was raised in a time without electricity, without the technology which made up the everyday life she was surrounded by. Now, what once was believed to be only plausible by magic, was happening in daily routines such as communicating across the world or flying from region to region. These habits seemed meaningless compared to what she recalled in a world where storing food for winter and tending to your horses were high priorities. Looking back at the glass door, there were no more horses and food was anywhere and everywhere.

Cedric gripped her thigh, a playful wave of arousal coming from his touch. He gave her a forced smile and she knew he had felt her fear and panic while recalling her last time outside of Avalon. Taking in a slow steady breath, she returned her own obligatory grin. She took another sip of the overwhelmingly tart drink, reassuring him she was having a good time. His smile faded. Huffing at her, his jaw muscle twitched and she knew her deceit had failed.

Leaning over to her, his breath tickled at her ear. "We won't be staying here for much longer. You're doing good, my Angel."

Nodding, she looked away from his sharp green stare. Her fingers fidgeting with one another while keeping their hold on the rocks glass between them. He continued his conversation with Tony and she dove back to her thoughts, drowning herself once more into the past.

Merlin. He called himself Kronos more times than not. Whoever or whatever he was, his real power only came through with the help of the Amulet of Avalon. Several times he called it Mother's Eye or Eye of Gaea in such an affectionate manner it sent shivers through me. So much of my memory has holes. Most of all, I am missing the first year I was there. Everyone insists that I was in shock, but something grips my soul when I try to remember it. There was something horribly important in that first year as his prisoner. Even now my heart aches to remember even a droplet's worth.

Swallowing, her attempt to break her thoughts failed. She was thrown to a time of when a needle and twine was pushed through her lips once again. Kronos had tired of her chatter, but even now she forgot why she had fought so hard to continue her verbal rebuttal. His look of disgust and terror of her flashing fangs for the first time had given her the small chance to be more brave, and her time of leaving the dungeon dwindled shortly after. Those cerulean eyes were cold and cruel, the magic from the red stone wicked.

Was he afraid of being bitten? Or was it the fear I had inherited some of Cedric's abilities? If so, if I had fed on anything, would I have had a chance of escaping?

"Here try this." Cedric slid away her half empty glass and gave her a shot glass full of a clear liquid. "It's vodka, and unlike the mixed drink, straight liquor. You might like it better."

Looking down, she stared at her own reflection with disdain. Her eyes were tired, even empty from her ordeal on Avalon with dark bags reflecting how she still had trouble sleeping. Worse, her hair tickled at her chin, forced to cut it only added to her sense of losing who she once had been. Cedric had scolded her for cutting it so short, but the amount of tangles and years of being unable to bathe herself had destroyed her long brown locks. There was a phantom-like essence about her reflection, her skin pale from not seeing the sun for so many centuries. Her stomach twisted. She hadn't aged at all but her hardships had changed her appearance. The person wavering in the vodka was once human, and now, not even Cedric could answer the question of *what am I?*

Taking in a deep breath, she gulped the sharp liquor down, eager to rid herself of the broken girl. She grimaced as it burn down her throat and warmed her belly.

Cedric laughed. "It's got a bite, but I like that warm sensation at the end."

Again, she mustered a smile. "Indeed, warm."

"Cedric," Morrighan's voice caught their attention as she approached. "Romasanta is calling a meeting for tonight."

He scowled, protesting. "What for?"

"His past with the stone."

Cedric's eyes widened and he stopped himself before he dare lock eyes with Angeline. "The old man has more secrets than I care to acknowledge." He wasn't sure how much of this would pull Angeline's connection with Romasanta into the light.

A smile snaked across Morrighan's lips. "Agreed, but he has very good reason for it all."

"I never said he didn't have a good reason for it all..." Mumbling into his rocks glass, Cedric finished his drink.

Morrighan turned, leaving out the door and Cedric caught the amber glare of Romasanta from across the room. The old man nodded, a discreet motion for him to come and talk out his frustrations in private.

Cedric's jaw tensed and he squeezed Angeline's leg to call her back to the present yet again. "I'll be right back, I need to ask the old mutt something."

"O-ok." She blinked, his tension not only visible, but she could feel Cedric trying to hide his panic. "I wonder what has him so worked up?"

"Ugh, I never know with those two." Scoffed Tony, watching Cedric march off. "And it's a hundred times more intense when Lillith shows up."

"Lillith..." Flashes of the Queen Succubus' toothy grin filled Angeline's mind.

Chills made her shoulders shudder. The arrow hitting its mark, the smell of the decaying land in Williamsburg were sharp. Lillith's face turning, eyes gripping her soul with a wicked smile. The sense of arousal she had released over the distance between them as she pulled the shaft out, licking her lips. Angeline bit her own lip, her eyes out of focus as her hands balled in fists.

Tony blinked. "I'm sorry, I didn't mean to upset you..."

"No, it's just." Shaking her head, clawing herself back out of the memory. "I only met her once."

"Oh, that time she fought Cedric?" Tony had remembered Cedric's story well, especially after being hurdled into being his descendant. "I am fortunate to have never seen that side of her..."

A wave of frustration from Cedric brought her eyes in his direction. "I wonder what they are discussing. Cedric's not happy about it..."

"I'd rather not know." Tony replaced the shot glass with a glass of ice, filling it from a strange hose-like contraption. "Here, some water to wash away those drinks."

"T-thanks." The cool water was a refreshing burst, something more familiar and welcoming to her taste buds. "What is *she* like?"

"Lillith?" Angeline nodded and Tony rubbed the back of his neck, wanting to answer the question with the greatest of caution. "Powerful. I suppose it's a given for those who are aware of what she is, but even then, the way she walks and talks is unmistakable. You can't help but feel she could take over the world. I can also say from a man's point of view, she's sexy. Again, it's not just her looks, though they help, but she's the epitome of confidence. Every move seems graceful and planned. It's, it's terrifying to watch from behind the bar at times."

"I see..." Another gulp of water and she continued her own confessions. "I've avoided her. Or rather, Cedric might be keeping her at bay for my sake. I feel bad since I know we are staying in her apartment but the thought that they..." She shook her head, swallowing and asking what it was she was more concerned with. "Do you think they have feelings for one another after that?"

Tears were welling up in her eyes, no one had hid the fact a new brood had been produced between the Cedric and Lillith. Worse, the reason solely for the purpose of gaining access to Avalon in order to rescue her. It was a bittersweet fact, leaving her mind numb and pained all at once to think Cedric had made that decision for her sake. A shot glass dropped from Tony's hands, his face paling.

"Oh God no!" Tony could feel a heated glare from Cedric as he peered over his shoulder. There was no doubt he felt the panic and sorrow boiling out of Angeline. "I think he would kill her before he would allow it to happen again. He only did it in desperation to find a way to get to you. To be honest, I think there's something between her and Romasanta. And please don't repeat that... I pray he couldn't hear me say that."

"You think so?" She sniffled, the notion baffling to her. "Why Romasanta?"

"I, I just know that look people get in their eyes, the one that says *I'll see you later on tonight*. Comes with bartending for nearly ten years. They may not be affectionate in public, but I have the feeling there's a behind closed doors love affair that's been going on for some time between them." Sighing, Tony realized he was failing to calm her down, though he did pull her attention from her worries. "Just don't repeat that suspicion. I'd end up as wolf food for sure..."

Tony looked to Cedric and gave him an apologetic shrug. Grunting, Cedric hurried to finish his discussion with Romasanta. It wasn't the first time Tony had failed at calming her since Angeline had come back to the world. She had a long hard struggle ahead, far as anyone could see in regards to adjusting and accepting things, physically and emotionally.

***

"So you do plan on leaving out her connections to you?" Sweat was running down Cedric's temple as Angeline's sorrow pressed down on him ever heavier. "I just need to know that this secret will still hold until she's, she's ok again."

"You're ever annoying, pup," snarled Romasanta. "You do realize the sorceress sisters already know. I am sure by now Nyctimus' nose has revealed the truth and as for Lillith, she has her own secrets to track, but I am confident she too is aware of the circumstances if not more than all of us combined. The only one not aware of this secret is Angeline herself. No one will tell her willingly, at least not in her current state."

"Fine." Cedric's jaw twitched, annoyed so many could easily let it slip that Romasanta was her blood relative. "Is there something I should be aware of? Any secrets still kept from me, perhaps?"

"If there is, you'll hear it at the meeting." His brown eyes gleamed amber, addressing the condescending tone Cedric's voice carried with it. "Now go take care of her. She is not invited to the meeting anyhow."

Cedric snorted, no longer patient enough to entertain the banter any longer with the old werewolf. Angeline was sobbing audibly at the bar top where Tony failed to calm her down, losing her in his final attempts to simply change subjects. Marching towards them, Tony flinched with each angry stomp. Cedric's green eyes ripped through him and the ice cold sweat of Tony's fear trickled down his back.

"What did you say to her?" Hissed Cedric.

"She asked a question and I, I." Tony tripped over his tongue and decided nothing he could spit out would appease Cedric. "I don't know what to do, honestly."

Cedric reached down, gripping her upper arm. Yanking her off the barstool with a commanding jerk, his jaw tight and he remained silent. Dragging her still sobbing out of the bar, the bell clanked loudly overhead as he flung the door open. Wincing, she tried to dig her fingers under his own, but he refused to budge. He hadn't even glanced down at her, his muscles taut and anger waving out of him calling her attention, making her ever more alarmed.

"Stop it, you're hurting me!" She fussed, bewildered by the aggressive actions unfolding.

Angeline's heels skidded across the concrete, unable to slow his momentum. Cedric was dragging them between the buildings, away from prying eyes. Around another corner they met a dead end, all three sides of it nothing more than windowless backsides of commercial buildings. Her chest ached, heart pounding in her ears. Desperate to break free, she tugged, attempting to jolt pass him. His grip tightened, twisting her around, pushing her against the cold concrete block wall. Her head rung from banging against it and she glared up at him, the fear washed away. Anger was pouring from her, cheeks red with frustration. Huffing she opened her mouth to argue, but his lips locked onto hers. His tongue pushed playfully into her mouth, skillful and alluring her own to come join. Waves of arousal flooded into her from their bond, leaving her breathless and wanting. The sting of his grip eased, his hand gently caressing her jaw. He pulled away and her heart swelled. His green eyes sparkled at the wave of sorrow. Grinning down at her, he was satisfied he had broken her out of her panic attack.

"Feel better?" He cooed, relishing in the emotions stirring within her, thirsting to feel more through their bond. "I couldn't think of anything else to do but to drag you out here."

"And kiss me?" She knew he could feel the excitement it brought her, but part of her was still infuriated. "Wasn't there a better way to do this?"

"Not exactly." Nuzzling her ear, whispering with the heat of his breath flowing over her neck and shoulders sending chills of euphoria through her. "But you got so angry that it reminded me of the woman I lost and hope to bring back…"

"…I'm sorry." She mumbled. "So sorry…"

Leaning his forehead on her shoulder, he continued whispering to her in a delicate tone. "Sorry? For what? Shouldn't I be the one to apologize for taking so long to get you back?"

"I broke my promise." She leaned her cheek against his head enjoying the oaky musk of his cologne. "I'm not supposed to cry over you anymore."

He laughed, "Not this again…"

Her arms wrapped around him, fingers clinging to the back of his black hoodie. Burying her face in his shoulder, he froze. The sorrow she let lose in that very second had left him stunned and breathless. She was struggling to talk, feelings knotting with one another as the echoes waved through them both along the ropes of their bond. The core of their emotions ached with such ferocity within his soul, Cedric found himself lost in her emotions. Biting his lip, he held in his own sorrow, fearful of only adding to the storm raging between their souls.

"I was crying over losing you." Gasping, she squeezed into him tighter. "Why did you come back for me? You could have anyone, even Lillith."

Blinking, he wrapped his arms around her, trying to keep her from shaking. She was too deep into her panic once more to see his smile.

So true, my Angel. I could have had anyone in this world, even taken them against their will, but you, you are something special. Despite the rage and hate you held for me in the beginning, you accepted me for what I was, a monster, a devil, an abomination. No one before you, no one after you has ever loved me for what I saw myself as the way you do, and still do. To think you even feel jealousy in knowing I can be with someone else only adds to my desire to never let you go, never let anyone bring you harm, never let pain rattle your soul. You are mine and mine alone, my pet.

He cuddled her, indulging in the jealousy which bit at her. When silence washed all her sadness away and shifted into a level of fear, he took his chance, confident his words would reach her soul.

"Don't cry about what you think I might do," Angeline stilled, her fear melting as Cedric's words hit her ears. "Be angry at the choices I made."

She took a long inhale, her emotions muddled and losing their peak, dulling with each second as she fought with the words echoing in her mind.

"I did some very dark things to get you back," His arms tightened around her. "And if you think I would let you go so easily, you are mistaken, my pet."

Gasping, a wall of affection slammed into her from Cedric through their bond, something he had never allowed to seep through ever. It was an emotion he hid deep within him, never truly letting her know it even existed. Realizing he had failed to let her feel this protected part of his inner self, he let it flow freely into her, hoping to tear down any lingering doubts. Tears of joy washed away the ones left behind from sorrow. She began laughing as they held onto each other in the back alleyway.

"What's so funny?" Pulling her away, she was wiping the last of her tears away.

"I cannot tell you how relieved I am to hear that." Another giggle rippled through her, watery brown eyes looking up into his own eyes.

Raising a brow, he questioned, "That I'll never leave you?"

"No." Sniffling, she sighed. "For once, I am happy to hear you call me *pet*. Never in my life did I think I would prefer such a ridiculous nickname..."

Bursting into laughter, he took her hand. "Let's go home, my pet."

CHAPTER 3

RISKS

"**C**edric, is everything ok?" Romasanta repeated, his voice snapping Cedric from his thoughts as he paused at an empty chair. "Is Angeline-"

"She's fine!" Cedric barked, sensing the abnormal level of concern radiating from Romasanta, Lillith, and the Sorceress sisters all aimed at Angeline. "Are we going to cover this new fascination you all have over her?"

They all flinched. His sharp green eyes slicing across each person in the room. Jaw twitching, Cedric refused to sit at the conference table with the rest of the group. Romasanta had called them there to share his life's story, but as the tale progressed, the parts involving Angeline or her Ancestor Artemis were vague and left unspoken. He had been tense about Angeline discovering those parts, but the fact Romasanta was still shielding the information from everyone spoke volumes. Indeed, he had entrusted Cedric with much more than he had originally assumed the old wolf. Still, the faces and shifts from the other patrons at the table told Cedric they were aware of the missing chunks, instances, and even mentioning of Artemis' or Angeline's relation to Romasanta. The old wolf was painfully aware the group knew and kept secrets about each other and themselves.

Angeline was overwhelmed, not just by the incident at the bar, but adjusting to the modern world. All of this was exhausting both mentally and emotionally, even for Cedric who desperately took the edge off where he could. With her asleep in the bedroom, he aimed to pry secrets from the elder demons and gods he leered over. He was tired of feeling like the last one to know anything about his own life, but the unusual worry over Angeline irked him. They needed to work together or they wouldn't be able to face the enemy who still lurked in the shadows. It was only a matter of time now before they would have to take up arms yet again.

"I want you all to spit it out." Cedric growled, the pounding of his fist on the glass table making them wince. "She doesn't need to know, but I do. I'd be a fool to think you all didn't have your own needs for her survival, even for my own survival. Spit it out!"

All eyes fell on Romasanta and Cedric turned, the muscles in Cedric's arms visibly tightening. Romasanta's docile brown eyes turned yellow in response. It was Romasanta's choice to allow him to know anything more, meaning he had known more than previously let known. They glared at one another, but soon a sigh broke from Romasanta's lips, looking over his audience. Secrets were only part of the dilemma he was working over inside his mind.

"I suppose I keep giving each of you a small part of the whole problem." Snorting, Romasanta returned Cedric's green glare with his own amber stare. "As some of you all know, Angeline's ancestor, the old witch, is actually my sister Artemis. We were twins raised in an ancient village whose name I have even forgotten over the thousands of decades. I was born without magic and Artemis had acquired all of it, possibly absorbed my own in the womb, but one could only guess. She was strong, but even I did not know how deep her own involvement went in my own life let alone yours and Angeline's, Cedric."

Leaning forward, Romasanta had everyone's attention at the table, even earning an eyebrow left from Lillith. Satisfied with no further interruptions would be unfolding, he continued the secrecy he had held to himself since the start of his curse.

"Growing up, I felt like a little brother years below the intelligence and understanding she possessed. To say she was a genius in the arts of magic would be an understatement. If I recall, she served Gaea directly in those days she served as the village shaman." Closing his eyes, Romasanta saw memories of the hut burning, the smoke still stinging in his nostrils. "What I recently learned, thanks to the sisters, is that she was the creator of Avalon itself. Worse, she intended for me to inherit control of the island, but I cannot do that. An immortal can only hold a key to one barrier at a time. I am bound to the Black forest and refuse to tear down the barrier that protects not only Daphne, but many forgotten magical beings. Only someone from our bloodline has the rights to claim Avalon."

"Then Angeline..." Tension broke and Cedric allowed himself to sit down and ponder. "So, Angeline is the heiress to Avalon."

"Yes." Morrighan's whisper joined the conversation. "We realize allowing her to even know this much would be damaging to her current mental status. I don't think any of us would be capable of absorbing the idea we were the rightful owner of the very place we spent centuries being torn apart and put back together. Merlin had access to some unfathomable practices... the idea that any of herself was still there in her head is... impressive."

"Does the girl show any signs of having access to magic?" It was the first time Cedric had heard Nemaine speak in a serious manner. "Even accidental? Surely you, my dearest little brother could sniff out the difference between dormant and active magic in a human's bloodline, no?"

Cedric paled, closing his eyes to recall the memories he had held. "It was her curse that gave Merlin the opening he needed to steal her away. That alone signals there was magic before I was able to really acknowledge it. I have also tasted the magic there in her veins before but... now... with the change..."

"You haven't drank her blood since you've reunited?" Nyctimus lifted an eyebrow, pushing his eyeglasses up on his nose. He looked like a model doctor with his hairstyle combed over wearing a business suit and clean shaven. "Not to be rude, but why haven't you?"

Cedric rolled his eyes. "None of you understand how my body works at all. Before Vladimir awakened the moroi bloodline in full, I drank from Angeline as a means to keep the magic in my system intact." He shot a nasty glare at Nemaine and Morrighan who both chuckled. "I only fed on her in order to keep myself from dying. Before her, I was taking advantage of the ability to suck the souls and power from demons to do essentially the same thing. Since then, I have found more sufficient ways of healing myself. So no, I have not thought of drinking from her, it's not something I do in leisure."

A coy grin crawled across Lillith. "A more sufficient way? Is that so?"

"I am stable and have no need to suck her blood." Cedric scoffed, ignoring Lillith's teasing. "From my experience, when magic is dormant, the sensation is like it has something heavy covering it. With Badbh, there was no mistaking her magic was active, it pulled with the blood much easier than with Angeline. I suppose I could tell the difference if I had taken any from her..."

"Merlin's goal was to access Artemis' magic. There is a chance he managed to flip the switch somehow." Morrighan tapped her lips, thinking on the facts laid before her. "Would you be willing to-"

"No." Cedric's voice was stern and he glowered over at Morrighan. "Until I fully understand what she has become, I refuse to tempt my luck or hers. No offense, but it also involves an unknown factor of how I would react. I am sure Lillith, Romasanta, and even Nyctimus would understand the complications of being a demon of animalistic tendencies. Developing a blood lust is a hard habit to kick once you start one, the last thing I want to ensue now that she's become something... else."

"He has a point." Romasanta raised his eyebrows, impressed Cedric was thinking things through for once. "We won't need to know until the time comes for her to decide to take Avalon over as its possible protector."

"Protector?" Cedric was back on his feet again, Chair screeching and his fangs clenched. "You've got to be kidding me! She hasn't told me one thing about her time as Merlin's prisoner. To ask her to protect the place where she has spent centuries being tormented! You've got to be kidding!"

"Calm down!" Snapped Romasanta, his golden stare placing Cedric back into his chair. "Don't you think we already took this into consideration, pup?"

"Sometimes I wonder why I am still sitting at this table." Cedric sneered over at him. "Why are we having this story time session? I imagine there is a matter to be resolved."

"Glad we can get back on topic." Grunted Badbh, her arms crossed with her feet propped on the table. "So I know this involves going to Mt. Parnassus and battling the Mother of dragons."

"Y-you can't be serious?" Nyctimus knotted his brow, looking over at Romasanta's unmoving expression. "You don't intend to face her alone to get to the Oracle, do you?"

Laughing, Romasanta smirked. "I know I've been a fool in the past, but please give me more credit, my old friend. I called this meeting to see who here would join me. There is no way I can carry this out on my own."

"I will." Cedric's voice cut through the room and Romasanta's smile fell away.

"And what about the girl?" Scowling, Romasanta's eyes flashed their golden color. "Do you intend to leave her behind so soon?"

"Where I go, she follows." Cedric snorted. "This is a chance-"

"Are you trying to get her killed?" Snapped Romasanta. "Do you realize we are facing dragons? Have you ever battled a dragon?"

"No." Cedric's brow folded, angry at the demeaning tone. "But who else do you have willing to go?"

"In that case, I will go." Nyctimus removed his glasses, tossing them on the table. "After all, I owe you and Fenrir for taking down Aitvaras and gaining me the Lykoan throne."

"Badbh?" Romasanta lifted a brow, pleading for someone else to join other than Cedric.

Sighing, she removed her feet from the table making her chair slam on the floor, groaning out her words. "I can't."

"My apologies, but our barbaric sister is needed on Avalon as a stand-in guardian." Nemaine frowned. "Needless to say, she blames us for this missed opportunity. Come now Sissy, have more faith in our little boy toy."

"Don't blame me if I get restless on Avalon…" It was a cold tone from Badbh's lips. "Regardless, I will give you my blessing and perhaps some parting gifts can be arranged under my guidance. This will not be an easy fight. Unlike Aitvaras, his mother is the one to watch when it comes to trickery, let alone the sheer power and size she possesses will be overwhelming when she takes her true form."

"I see." Nyctimus peered over to Lillith at this news. "I don't suppose the Queen Succubus has time to spare for this matter?"

"Romasanta already knows this is something I cannot aid you in." She lit a cigarette, smoke puffing up from her hands. "My hands are tied."

A devilish smirk crawled across Cedric's face. "We both know that two werewolves aren't enough for this, old man."

Snarling, Romasanta continued his refusal. "And what good would it do two werewolves and an idiot if the fourth is unable to join the fight?"

"She can, and will, fight." Cedric's smile dropped, replaced by a serious expression. "You know I would not offer this if I had any doubts in what Angeline could or could not do. If we go with you, that gives you the Incubus King and a Demonized Sorceress in your ranks. This is as good as having Lillith and Morrighan on board, is it not?"

Closing his eyes, Romasanta huffed at the term *demonized sorceress*. "What good will a medieval bow user serve us? Angeline is stuck in the past, what good could she do-"

"Actually…" Lillith interjected, blowing a long thin line of smoke from her pursed lips. "Mt. Parnassus has a very unique barrier.

Delphyne is not one to leave herself vulnerable by allowing certain items to exist within the barrier she is the keeper of…"

Badbh leaned forward. "That's right! The Mother of Dragons has it where certain things get destroyed when you pass through. Technological advances are useless. Electricity not created via magic will not work and gunpowder will not ignite within that barrier. You will literally have to depend on your own brute strength, melee weapons fused with silver, or a magic wielder."

Romasanta's face reddened and veins visibly pulsed on his head. Cedric was grinning like a fool at the news. He knew what Badbh and Lillith were both saying. Not only were they agreeing, but insisting Romasanta needed them. Silence took over as all eyes fell on the angry golden-eyed man who refused to meet the excited green ones next to him.

"Romasanta." Cedric started in a softer tone. "If something happens to her, know that it falls on me. I do plan on asking her, she will have a chance to say no."

"Fine." Romasanta caved, having no other options among those he trusted. "We will meet and prep at Lykoan Tower. Before we head to Mt. Parnassus, you will have to prove to me she still has the will to fight, or even remembers how to fight. I'll have her take care of the nuisance Busse buck in the Black Forest."

"Busse?" Cedric blinked. "I thought they were extinct?"

A smile came to Romasanta's lips. "Not under my roof. I have a large bull with eighteen or more points on his horns that is terrorizing other wildlife. Plus, a kill like that should provide enough leather and horns for tools for the trip to Mt. Parnassus. Considering we will require some older gear fashioned to accommodate the circumstances."

"Fine." Cedric rubbed the back of his neck. "We'll take it down."

"You misunderstood me, pup." The tension in the exchanged glares sent shivers across those watching. "Angeline will have to prove *she* can fight, without you or me or anyone to save her."

Jaw tight, Cedric turned and left the conference room without another word. His wave of anger had escaped him and he could feel the reflection of worry from Angeline. Whether she was still asleep, he would not be able to tell until he made it to their bedroom where he left her. No one in the conference room dared to stop him. They were still dealing with Romasanta's frustration and rage with the idea of putting Angeline in the line of fire and having to be dependent on Cedric. Pausing in front of the bedroom door, his hand gripped the cold handle. He could feel the struggle of emotions coming from her, a mixture of fear, anger and pleasure. Sighing, Cedric knew Angeline was dreaming about the countless times she had been tortured. Opening the door, the room dark, he blinked a few time before he could see as clear as day.

Standing at the edge of the bed, Cedric stared down at Angeline with overwhelming sympathy. He had been hard on her, but the fate she had led without him had eaten away at his own soul. The covers had been kicked off and she continued tossing and turning in her sleep. Her skin prickled as an ghostly chill from her past made her body shiver. She was wearing one of his t-shirts, but her sweat soaked it, making it cling to her skin. Panting, she shifted, her eyes tight with sleep. Struggling with her nightmare, flinching from an unseen action, he could only grimace. She had wiggled to the point the shirt which normally reached midthigh had bunched up under her breasts. Smirking, he soaked in the site of her laid across his bed.

Her lips still reminded him of a rose pedal, but her once sun-kissed tan was now a ghostly white. Despite her torture, she was in the same physical condition he remembered when they last laid together. The cotton shirt clung to her, exposing the curvature of her breasts in an enticing manner. They seemed fuller than he had recalled, but she was also much older. The flashing memories in his mind made her feel like a girl by comparison. She had become a woman in her time spent imprisoned. If only she realized how beautiful she had bloomed in the darkness. So much time had gone by that even he felt older. Looking back to his days with her during the Medieval age, he had changed too. His shoulders were thicker, muscles stronger and harder from his excursions through the centuries, his eyes more tired, and he couldn't remember the last time he recalled worrying about keeping his fangs hidden. Still, his trademark blood red hair with its black tips had not faded and the ferocity in his bottle green eyes still stung those they hit.

His eyes moved on to the one scar that had not faded on Angeline. Most of her injuries and marks faded away after she dug her fangs into him in that first embrace. A long purple scar distorted the flesh across her abdomen just below her belly button. It stretched from the top of one hip over to the other like a grisly grin teasing him for his failure to keep her from harm. Looking down at his left hand, he sneered at the scar on his ring finger. Stomach knotting, he knew some place deep in her subconscious she was preventing this one scar not to heal. Many times he caught her frustrated stare in the mirror. Even she felt there was something important she was forgetting. Looking back to the ragged scar, her hands gripped it. Teeth clenched, tears rolling down her temples from her sleeping eyes. Terror and rage slammed him so heavily he felt nauseous from its weight. Paling he reached out to shake her awake but stopped. Panic rattled him.

She insists she cannot remember her first years on Avalon. Would waking her kill a chance of remembering a sliver of that time?

A scream broke free of her lips and a wave of pain emitted from her. Dropping to his knees, he watched her nightmare shake through her. Gripping his own stomach, he involuntarily did what he had done so many times before. Replacing her pain with pleasure was merely an instinctual reaction for him. Sweat poured over him as a haunting and familiar sensation shook him. This was the same as the time he was at the monastery shortly after he lost her. The jagged ripping that matched the grim scar across her stomach was playing out its beginnings again. He felt the muscles under the slice tighten and release in excruciating waves. Folding himself into a fetal position, the pain tearing through him made him lose his focus on Angeline. He was failing to keep himself intact. With his heart pounding in his ears, his thoughts exploded in a flurry of questions and memories.

When had this happened? This is the moment scarred across her body that she is so desperate to remember. I was at the monastery. This pain made the monks think I was possessed. I lost consciousness, I was weak for a long time after. How could I forget, it was the first time I had experienced illness, fevers, shivers, and every part of me ached without reason. What could this be? Where did the pain come from to lash out at even me through our bond...

His mind raced to recall where in her timeline her abdomen had received the mark. Muscles tightened yet again, her voice was moaning in pleasure but her pain was now his. Grinding his teeth, it was up to him to help her overcome these moments and if she woke not recalling any of it, at least he could give her the information that was fleeing her grasp. He owed her that much for his failure to get her back sooner. Folding over slightly, the pain erupted in a cold sweat across him and he swallowed back his fears of experiencing the sensations for a second time.

The pain was peaking. Angeline's back arched with pleasure while Cedric fell on his side to the floor. Flashes of his own past drowning him, holy water plashing across him and the chanting reverberating in his mind. Eyes rolling in the back of his head, shaking on the floor, much like the first time, he faced pure agony. Tears were welling up in his eyes, his jaw clenching to keep in the roar he wanted to release. He had lost focus on his environment, everything blurring to black. At his core, his soul was being ripped apart in waves of fire and ice.

Squeezing his eyes tighter, harrowing thoughts crept forward, *Why does this hurt so much more than the first time? I remember it was ungodly, but I'm stronger now. Why does this feel like the throws of death I have felt so many times at the tips of my own fangs?*

He felt himself jerked to his feet, dragged across the floor and into the blinding light of the hallway. Gasping, his pain was washed away by a chilling amount of arousal. His pupils adjusted and he stared up at the befuddled faces of Lillith and Romasanta. Enraged, he jumped to his feet ripping Lillith's hand from his wrist.

"What do you think you're doing?" Hissed Lillith. "Are you daft? An incubus can die taking on that type of pain!"

"It didn't kill me the first time!" He roared.

"What the hell is going on?" Romasanta looked to Cedric then to Lillith. "You rushed back there so fast... exactly what was happening?"

Lillith's maroon eyes were fiery and her voice full of ire. "You are such an idiot! The fact you don't acknowledge the kind of pain she's reliving at this very moment! How can you call yourself an Incubus King if you're going to be so oblivious!"

Pushing between Cedric and Romasanta, she slammed them against the walls of the hallway. Her face had mottled, eyes watery as she marched away. Nearing the end of the hall, Cedric's own anger faltered seeing her horns crawling out before losing sight of her. The apartment was filled with loud bangs as doors slammed shut in her wake. Lillith was leaving in a fit of rage. Never had any of them seen her lose her calm, always a stronghold of confidence left in an unstable fit where she failed to even hide her own demonic appendages. Romasanta and Cedric exchanged wide-eyed stares. Angeline's dream had ended, but sweat dripped from Cedric's chin from the feat. Romasanta's expression filled with wrath before he closed the gap between them. Gripping the front of Cedric's shirt, they both growled at one another.

"What were you doing to Angeline?" Fur sprouted from his skin, clothes ripping as his face distorted grimly before reaching its final form of a wolf's head. "Spit it out now!"

"None of your business!" Cedric shoved Romasanta and his shirt ripped, chunks of it still in Romasanta's clawed fists. "But if you think it was wrong to take on the pain a dream was bringing her then go ahead and kill me over it!"

Romasanta blinked, snorting from his massive nostrils in frustration, "Is that all?"

"Well I was on the fucking floor! What do you think!" Cedric reared up on him, nose to nose.

"Then why was Lillith so pissed?" They were huffing from the adrenaline filled moment. "Is it not what you do for her all the time?"

"Y-yes." They paled in confusion. "Or I thought I was doing the same thing?"

"Do you always do it for dreams as well as the real thing?" Romasanta pushed Cedric back, pacing over to the cracked bedroom door where Angeline whimpered in her sleep.

"W-well, no." Cedric rubbed the side of his neck, thinking deeply. "It was different. Before it was always the actual pain. I realized she was having a nightmarish memory and instead of waking her, I thought I could pull the pain from her so she would have a chance of remembering something she had forgotten. A moment in her past she's desperate to recall, in fact."

Romasanta let Cedric pull the door close, whispering. "Why on earth would she want to remember any time there on Avalon?"

Cedric headed down the hallway after Romasanta. "She can't remember the first few years there. It's safe to assume Merlin took them from her, but she seems determined to remember that first year in particular. When her dream started I realized it was from that time period. What right did I have to deny her what she has been trying to recover?"

"Then you had experienced the pain once before?" Shuddering off his wolf form, they continued to the kitchen. "Did you have that hard of a time with it the first time?"

"That's what concerns me..." Cedric's jaw muscles twitched with anxiety. "And if Lillith hadn't interfered..."

"She flew from the conference room like the place was on fire. Whatever happened to you, she could sense it." Romasanta grabbed a bottle of vodka from the liquor cabinet and took a long draw from it. "I've known her for well over a thousand years and I have never seen her face mottle or turn red or look as pissed off as she was when she put us against the wall."

"I've seen her that mad..." Cedric motioned with his fingers to give him the bottle and he followed with his own long gulp of vodka.

"Oh yea?" He had Romasanta's attention as his eyebrows raised high over his brown eyes. "When did you manage that?"

"That time you left me at Vladimir's castle." Another hard slug of vodka sent Cedric's throat burning. "Let's just say I would have rather repeated my fight with my grandfather. There will never be another brood made between us. There was no love, no lust, it was purely-"

"Cedric! CEDRIC!" Angeline came running into the kitchen.

The two looked over in alarm when she stumbled to a stop at the entrance of the kitchen. She was covered in sweat, still in the cotton t-shirt panting from running down the hall. Her eyes locked with Cedric's and a wave of relief snuffed out the blast of fear she had sent out. Her eyes fell on the other person who stood between them. Romasanta crossed his arms, his clothes nothing more than a pile of scraps in the hall. Angeline's eyes fell below Romasanta's belt line and a wave of embarrassment hit Cedric through their bond, making him grin.

"Why are you naked?" She turned on her heels, blushing as she covered her face, squealing. "Where are your clothes, Romasanta!"

A roar of laughter exploded out of the men over her reaction to Romasanta's unwarranted nudity.

"What on earth is the matter?" Cedric was struggling to catch his breath.

"I opened the door and saw the hallway smashed up and pieces of your shirt and I thought, I thought..." Her voice was trembling.

Handing the vodka bottle back to Romasanta, Cedric came up behind her. His arms wrapped around her, his lips kissing and suckling at her neck and shoulder. Pausing, he watched as her damp skin prickled in response to his warm breath, something he missed so dearly about her. Leaning back into him, she sighed, enjoying his warmth and relieved nothing had happened. Reaching up, her shaking hands gripped his arms, a silent plea for him not to let go.

"I'm sorry. We were rough-housing and got carried away." Cedric nuzzled at her neck some more, knowing she could smell the liquor on his breath. He hoped his lie would suffice, she didn't need to know what had sparked the fight in the hallway. "We drank a little too much."

"I need a shower anyhow..." Grumbled Romasanta, disappearing through the living room with the vodka bottle still in hand.

"Why is he naked?" Angeline was trying not to giggle, her nerves still tingling from her fright. "Who wrestles with a naked man?"

"In my defense, he started as a werewolf..." Cedric began walking her back to the bedroom, tugging her hand lightly behind him.

A chuckle escaped him when they passed the cracked drywall. Pausing, he let go of her, looking down at the two holes in his shirt. His bare chest was unharmed underneath as he inspected the damage. Smirking, he tugged off the ruined shirt and tossed it to the floor behind him. Turning his attention back to Angeline he grabbed her hand. Pulling her once more, he led her into the bedroom, slamming the door behind them as if shouting to leave them alone.

CHAPTER 4

NO MORE SECRETS

She broke free of his reach and sat on the bed. Her mouth bending into a frown and her eyes falling to the floor with a sense of shame. Leaning his back against the door, he marveled over his sad Angeline and how quickly she shifted emotionally. Angeline's eyes carried a haze at times, making it known she found herself lost in her own mind, yet again. The sweat soaked shirt made her cold, her nipples pushing through the cotton that once hid them. Unwilling to hide it, Cedric let his arousal slam her. Gasping, her eyes shot up to his own where he grinned from the door. A shiver shook her and she hugged herself for warmth. Her lips let out a heavy sigh yet he waited patiently. Both of them could still feel the stinging sensation of her nightmare. He opened his mouth, but he didn't know which question to ask first, *Did you remember something from Avalon or do you blame me for taking away your humanity?*

A tightness struck across his chest. Anxiety was a new emotion that had started to push forward inside him now that he had her back. His mind no longer filled with plans of chasing Merlin down left gaping holes to be filled by feelings he once deemed distractions and even unnecessary. A new wave of fears were working their way into his mind and heart. Though it was exciting feeling her fangs in his neck during their first embrace, it brought a heavy sensation of dread. She hadn't ended up like Yvette and Lord Romulus from his past, but still, there had been no more signs in months since her return. Not even the fangs that had made their reunion intoxicating had shown themselves to him. The daunting sensation of terror lingered in the back of his mind, wondering if she would fall victim to this hidden demon dwelling some place in her veins. She cursed him so long ago over a campfire only for him to return the favor. Both moments unintentional, a reminder of how naïve they had been. Swallowing, fear was digging its claws into his racing heart.

"Are you," She paused and he realized he had failed to hide his terror from her. "Are you afraid of me?"

"No…" He frowned, whispering tenderly to her. "I'm afraid for you. I took your humanity away, even if I had not realized it back then…"

"But if you hadn't," Tears were building up in her eyes as her voice shook. "Merlin would have gotten what he wanted from me. Worse, I would be dead."

Sighing, he leaned his head against the door. "At least you wouldn't have lived through hundreds of years of torture. That much is my fault."

Standing to her feet, she ran to him. Her cheek slapped against his bare chest and her arms forced themselves around him, pushing him off the door. Stunned, he petted her head as she sobbed against him. Sorrow flowed from her, drowning his own to the point he felt a tear crawl down his own face. They shared a sensation of guilt, neither of them able to figure out who it belonged to while they stood there adrift in the sea of sentiments. Desperate to free them both from their emotional abyss, he pushed her away.

Dumbfounded, she looked up and he pressed his lips to hers. Their terror, their grief, their guilt all shattered from the rush of provocation. All he could do was rely on the incubine powers which had set their relationship in motion one faithful night in King Frederick's castle. His tongue playfully licked her own, chasing her back within her lips. They were stumbling towards the bed. The warmth of his fingers wiggling under the cold wet shirt sent goosebumps across her skin. He delighted in sliding his hands up her sides. The way her hips fell inward before they rippled into her ribs was a thrilling rollercoaster ride. To know he could hold her again and bring her pleasure by a simple touch was intoxicating. His hands slid under her arms and on command she lifted them. Breaking their kiss he pulled the shirt off, dropping it to the floor at her feet. Angeline was breathing faster, her exhilaration building louder across their bond. Her fingers fumbled with his belt and then the button on his jeans. Both were proving difficult. His hands grabbed the panicking fingers, a smile crawling across his face.

"You have no idea how much of a turn on it is to see you struggling to get into my pants like that." Feeling defeated, she tried to pull her hands free, but instead he pulled them up onto his shoulders. "Because I started this, it doesn't mean you have to do anything for me. I'm more than happy to do all the work..."

Her fingers gripped his shoulders, cheeks red with frustration. "I've missed you so much... but sometimes I look back and feel guilty for not returning the love you have shown me... being more affectionate, more willing to act, more willing to... to..."

Nuzzling her head into his chest she had lost her confidence and words.

He finished undoing his own pants, musing over the panic twisting with her vicarious wants. "Have I ever told you what it is an incubus desires most?"

Shaking her head against his chest, she muttered into him. "No, I know nothing about what you are... or even what you want or desire... I know nothing..."

He froze. *I had been so secretive about my true form before she was taken from me... But then again, was it really me being secretive? Even now, I don't understand what I am. Isn't it the reason why I was afraid of myself for so long? Is it not why I'm afraid for her? Could I ever confess I don't even understand what it is I do? Regardless, this woman has accepted me, it is only fair that I show her what I do know about what I am... and possibly what she has become...*

"What's wrong?" Pushing back, she stared wide-eyed at him. "Cedric?"

"I've never shown you what I really am..." Swallowing, he gathered his nerves to ask the one question his former self would have never dared. "Do you want to have me as I am or lay with the demon I truly am?"

No matter the answer, both are just as painful as the other for me. I'm an abomination... and in that form my passion is unbridled, though she wouldn't know unless she could uncloud the dreamlike memory of that first night together. Which is the lesser of two evils? For her to say no and lay with the man she remembers or yes and see me as the thing I am most ashamed of being?

There was a long silence between them. The thumping of his pulse was deafening as he waited for her response. A shudder shook her shoulders and she pressed herself harder against him. No tears were falling, but he could feel the struggle of emotions he stirred in her. Fear, excitement, and sorrow were smashing into one another, but this was her choice. No longer did he fear losing control like before. In her absence he had grown powerful, but had become aware of the fact he was truly a demon. All the mixtures of blood and the conditions of his very creation only added to what he was capable of doing and expanded his options to feed and thrive. For now, he took his earned title to heart. To the world, he was and is the Incubus King, nothing more or less.

"What is it that an incubus desires?" Blinking he looked down into her doe-like eyes. "First, tell me more about what you are..."

"An incubus craves pleasure generated from their chosen partners. The greater amount of euphoria experienced by our prey, the more power that is generated as a result of our meddling. Your sexual sensations, not my own, create an invisible essence which is absorbed into me like air into my lungs. Just so you understand, this becomes even more intense and efficient for me when I allow myself to be in my real form. Regardless of this, there is no advantages of me being the sexual focus." He stroked her hair, missing the long locks from the days when she was a Lady of the Court. "We work like a mirror. The more aroused and lustful you become, the more I do too, my body matching it tenfold. Incubus can be overpowering once this vicious sexual synergy starts to unfold, it's addictive for both sides. Even without our bond, I would be echoing the euphoria into you, ebbing your own desires to blossom. It's not uncommon for us to lose ourselves, drunk in the moment... anyhow, it's a monstrous form we take on, muscular, horns, wings and tails."

Another excruciating silence passed before her next question came. "That fight with Boto, that form, is it, is that..."

"Yea, that is what I am." He took in a deep breath. "Even being half incubus, that's the form I take on."

"Then that first time, when we bonded..." She bit her lip.

"Yes, in order to bond with you I took that form." His forehead creased, *I need to let go of all the secrets, we've lost too much time for me to hide myself away from her.* "But I was afraid of what you would think of me and I tried to mask it all as if it were a dream."

"I, I want..." Her heart was racing and her naked body shivering against him.

"It's your choice, my Angel." Rubbing her cheek, he sighed. "To be honest, it terrifies me to know what your answer might be."

Her hands slid off his shoulders and wrapped around him, her breasts pressing against him ever-increasing his desires. "Cedric, I want you. All of you. You are my Demon and I am your Angel... be who you truly are, because I know who you are under it all and that's the person I love without fault." She squeezed herself into him harder as he marveled over her words.

"You say that with so much certainty, why?"

"Because no man on this earth would have kept the promises you have made me." Eyes locking with his, her hands framed his jaws as she steadied her voice. "You have shown me more love than I had ever hoped to have received from a man. If I had understood the depths in which your love could survive, I would have been a better bride..."

The guilt exploding through their bond into him only broke the damn holding back the tenacious want building between them. Shoving her back onto the bed, he hungrily kissed her. Lips locking, breaking away to gasp for air only to dive back into the fray. Her words had flooded him with passion and now all he wanted is to drown her in its waves. It was her tongue that pushed through his lips this time, playing with his fangs, rubbing at his own tongue. Her hands still held the sides of his face, his hands fumbled to slide her panties off her thighs. Both of their bodies were feverish and glistening with sweat under the darkness of the bedroom. Pulling away from her, they fell into each other's eyes. She sat on the bed, panting while he took a few steps back. They ached to touch, but he stilled himself to shed the last of his secrecy, to build this bond back into its proper place with this moment of renewed bedroom vows.

Stretching his arms wide, he let his horns curl into existence. Arm-like wings crept out from behind him as if they had merely hid themselves in his shadow. They were folded, but at the bend two long fingers shifted downward to grip the corners of the bed. These appendages were made for flight and to be used as a second set of arms for whenever they were needed. His thin prehensile tail rocked playfully behind him. Long and slender, it was far less intimidating than the muscular, long fingered wings which had qualities reminiscent of a bat's. Despite it all, a thrilling amount of arousal exploded from Angeline. She had seen this form in Morrighan's castle, but it was the memories unfolding from her mind. From under the static of the pain and torment a flash of light gripped her from their first night together which had created their soul bound connection.

Her body ached to have it all unfold again. A rush of reminders of how powerful her sense of touch had become, driving her sexual desires to places she didn't know existed within her. Though the moments together with Cedric had been breathtaking after the necessity of that night, she still hungered for his touch and affection. She had no way to describe the addictive flavor his affection left on her soul, bringing to light the haze of their first time together. Her body trembled in the wake of pleasure from her past and she physically ached to have him take her there again.

"I... I remember." She mumbled and he moved closer, towering over her. "Our first time, I wanted, I've wanted this from you, like in that moment from so long..."

Her words melted away the last of his barriers. The amount of lust exploding from her, screaming through him through their bond was a rush he hadn't experienced before. He began crawling back onto the bed, hovering over her as she laid down, knees rubbing against his ribs on either side, unafraid of the beast she saw before her. Kissing Angeline's lips one more time, he began working his way down her body. All he wanted was for this delicious fountain of power pouring from her to never end, to nurture its intensity knowing she would be besotted with his every touch. Chills and shudders followed the heated breezes of his breath and the silken warmth of his licks. He worked from her neck, across the hill of her collarbone and traversed the curve that led his ravenous lips to her nipple where he suckled with vigor. Her muscles tensed, encouraging his playful gesture to be more aggressive. A moan came from her, a hand gripping one of his horns. Fingers curled tight yet did nothing to pull him away from his object of interest.

He felt the erogenous feelings overflowing from her as the rough texture of his horn met her palm. An erotic wave escaped her and he gave a devilish grin. Nibbling, he sent her squealing, her back arching only to press her breast firmer into his lips where he responded with more suckling. Satisfied he had teased her enough, he licked and suckled across her ribs, pausing to kiss her scar. He ran his tongue from the top of her hip slithering across her lower abdomen where he dove between her thighs to seek other adventures. Her back arched, panting and moaning, smitten with his work on her body. Blindly her free hand met his other horn, but again, she did nothing to push him away as she held on, screaming in the overwhelming wake of pleasure. Heat and sweat increased across her body, legs shaking.

With each wave of ecstasy from her, he felt more intoxicated. The fingers of his wings gripped her thighs, freeing his hands from the task of keeping them apart. Gliding his palms back across the valley of her stomach and ripples of her ribs, his hands squeezed her breasts. The onslaught earned him an exhilarating yelp and quiver from her. Thighs tensed, unable to close them to gain reprieve, her back arched until she sat up, hands still clinging to his horns. She started to shudder, desperate to catch her breath. He could feel she was on the edge of another orgasm, but he wanted to tease her longer. Releasing his hold, letting her breathe, he pulled away leaving her throbbing and panting. Their bodies were on fire and he panted looking down at the state he left her in with pride. If it had been colder in the room, steam would have rolled off his shoulders from the rate his incubine blood boiled in his veins.

Breathless, she hummed to herself. Closing her thighs, her hands rubbing across her own body encouraging the waves of pleasure to continue. She didn't want it to end, fighting not to lose the high he had left her riding. Once again he leaned over her, pulling her towards him by the edge of the bed. Pushing her thighs back open, he teased with the notion of the next act of their rendezvous. Her legs hugged themselves around his hip, pulling him closer and adding to the aching he felt to take her. Refusing the plea, he leaned over her, close and nose-to-nose. Falling into her soft brown eyes, he smirked down at her flushed face. Even in the darkness, sweat sparkled across her cheeks, her hair clinging to her wet forehead. She tugged again with locked ankles and he laughed. Refusing to give her the climax she was visibly pleading for took every nerve to appeal within himself. Looming over her like this added to the waves of pleasure pouring from her and he enjoyed it. Now he wanted to hear her beg to be taken by him in this devilish form.

"Take me..." She whimpered, still struggling to catch her breath from feeling his own arousal growing heavier with each passing second. "I can't stand it... I want you... please take me."

A smile crept wider across his face. Wrapping his arms around her, another rush escaped her to feel the muscles in them hard against the divot of her lower back. It broke the last of his restraints and he pushed himself hard and deep against her. Squealing in delight, she trembled with each thrust. With each lustful stroke, his wings flared wider, moaning as their euphoria peaked as one. His fingers dug into her hips, pushing hard against her with his back arching. He never felt so invigorated. Every muscle within him resisted the want to roar in delight. Waves of their orgasms mingled with one another for several minutes before he managed to pull away, both exhausted from the overload of shared sexual climaxes.

Breathless, he laid beside her, scooping her up in his arms. Kissing her shoulder, he waited until she caught her breath. A chill ran across her and he wrapped a wing over her like a blanket, then he panicked. Freezing, he wasn't sure if he had gone too far. Feeling the moment of fear, gentle fingers pulled his wing closer, soothing his panic. She had accepted him in this form, there was no more reason to question anything between them. Nuzzling the back of her head, breathing in her scent deep and slow, he allowed himself to sleep.

CHAPTER 5

THE COWARDLY BARTENDER

"What's wrong with you?" Tony was wiping off the bar top when he realized Lillith was sitting there, silent. "Normally you make a grand entrance."

"Just don't ask about it." Huffing, she paused before exhaling a long sigh. "Can I have something strong? Maybe that stuff Badbh drowns herself in..."

"One Johnnie Walker coming up." Peering over his shoulder, it was hard to ignore the fact her horns were visible for the first time since they met. Like Cedric's description had noted, they curled like ram horns, one broken. "No pun intended, but you seem rather *horny* tonight."

He managed to get a smirk from her. "Glad you found some humor from it, but honestly, I'm *very* upset."

"Oh?" His muscles tensed at the news. "And who on earth would be crazy enough to piss off the Queen Succubus?"

She took down the shot, her glass clomping loud against the bar. "Cedric."

He held his breath, choosing his words carefully. "Exactly what did he do?"

Her maroon eyes pierced him, making him physically flinch. "I said don't ask."

Nodding, he glanced around the room, seeing it had emptied out in time for closing, or because she had marched in looking pissed off. "Well, you can sit and drink there while I close the place down."

"Thanks." She scoffed, pouring herself another shot. "This stuff burns..."

"Yea, but it doesn't slow Badbh the Battle Goddess down to keep her from guzzling it straight from the bottle." He turned the latch at the door, pulling the chain to the neon sign to announce *The Lion's Den* had officially closed. "I've had to start ordering a larger stock of the stuff since you guys started coming in."

"Cedric can be such a child." She fussed, her mind still wrapped around her anger. "I don't know how anyone could be so blind to his demonic abilities and instincts to the level of being so reckless as to nearly kill himself."

Tony paused, placing a chair on its adjacent table. "Nearly kill himself?"

"Let me ask you this, Tony." She took another shot, she was indeed upset. "Do you believe yourself to be human or part demon?"

Releasing the chair, he rubbed the back of his neck. "Human."

"Why?" She turned in her stool, crossing her legs as she leaned her elbows on the bar top. "What makes you think you're human?"

Wide-eyed, his heart thumped against his chest, her voice echoing in his mind before he shook it loose, answering with confidence. "Because I'm weak. There's nothing special about me. I live in a dive apartment, I've gone nowhere in life besides bartending for ten or so years, and besides being handed ownership of the bar by you, I don't have anything to my name. Not even a love interest in my life right now."

"Why would that only apply to being a human? What does being human even mean? Is it what you are on the outside or what you want to be on the inside?" She lifted an eyebrow, her lips stern, neither frowning or smiling as the words dug into Tony. "You think because we have special abilities and powers that we don't make mistakes? That I don't have a complicated and shitty life? It amazes me so many of you are clueless and lack the ability to be self-aware. It's as if you all assume I don't suffer, it's insulting to me."

"No offense." He grabbed another chair and started stacking again, the bang loud as the muscles in his face tightened. "You seem pretty well off. Hard to imagine you not being able to get what you want. Let alone have a means to resolve your problems. The rest of us, people like me, we are doomed to crawl on our bellies in the mangled mess of life while others walk across our backsides. People like me just settle with the fact-" He swooped his arms out before the next chair. "-this is as good as life will ever be."

Her head tilted back, staring at the ceiling, her voice barely above a whisper. "What good is it all if you are cursed to be alone all your life..."

He stacked the last chair with a loud bang. Silently he walked back behind the bar, pulling out another shot glass. Lillith spun around, curious of this new side of him. Tony's face was stern, his eyes sad as he grabbed the bottle of Johnnie and poured them both a full shot glass. Picking his glass up, he sighed, waiting for her to do the same. She brought hers up even to his glass, their eyes meeting as she waited to see what he intended to do next.

"Here's to the true nature of the world." She blinked, his voice strong and unshaken. "Where no immortal is beyond the ailments of man."

Snorting, she clanked glasses with him. "It's the truth."

Exhaling from the burning liquid, he smiled at her. "You must be feeling better, your horns are gone."

Pushing the bottle and empty shot to him, she blushed. "Didn't think I'd calm down so easily. Thanks for the talk, Mr. Bartender."

He placed the bottle back on the shelf behind him and added the glasses to the dishwasher. With a few beeps of the buttons, the machine roared to life. Working his way over to the first cash register, he punched in codes and using his key, accessed hidden areas of the machine. She watched as he printed a receipt and ejected the cash drawer. Tony did the same for the other two registers and carried them into the office, like a programmed robot, every motion a reflex. He left the office door open as he counted the money, continuing their conversation from within.

"If you want, I can walk you home." He offered, shoving the first register's contents into a blue bag and noted a number on his notepad.

"You're joking?" She ridiculed, leaning on one arm watching him count the huge wads of cash. "Do I look like I need to be walked home?"

"No." Tony replied, moving on to count the last cash drawer. "But, I want to know more about why you asked me that question a moment ago."

"Huh?" Lillith straightened herself as his eyes glanced over at her for a second before he leaned away to lock everything in the safe. "Which question?"

He grabbed up his keys, his face hadn't lost the firm expression. Locking the office door he came around the bar top and waited at the door in silence. Curious, she followed his lead as they exited, the lights flickering off as he flipped the switches. She watched as he locked the door, then pulled down the metal guard and locked it as well. He motioned for her to start her walk and followed close beside her. Glancing over at him, her maroon eyes watched his brown stare observing her own face. Looking away from her, his face reddened, as if she had seen something she wasn't meant to see in them. She could sense the tension building in his muscles, the flutter of his heart.

"Why did you ask me that?" He was avoiding eye contact with her.

"Ask you what?" She felt lost watching his body language. He was tensing, as if preparing for a fight. "I threw out a bunch of questions, none of which I meant to have answers."

"If I thought of myself as human or part demon." His jaw muscle twitched as he turned to stare her in the eyes, this time he made her flinch. "Why even ask me if I thought I was part demon if there wasn't some underlying truth there in your words."

Lillith burst into laughter, halting in her steps. "Are you offended?"

He frowned. Her laughter stopping as she stared him in the eyes, fascinated with this new side of who she thought as only the cowardly bartender. Sighing, a smirk came to her lips. His confidence and boldness toward her appealing to her. A hand on her hip, she looked him over, gauging the look on his face once more before she spoke.

"I suppose you are more like Cedric than I had thought." Avoiding the question, she marched away, leaving him behind.

"Lillith." The commanding tone in his voice made her standstill, her back facing him. "That's all I needed to know, thank you."

Winching, she looked over her shoulder, not expecting him to take her words in so easily. He had started to head the other way towards the subway. It was unclear what assumption he had made from her moment of silence just now. Regardless, she found this hidden side of him interesting, even arousing. She started her walk back to her apartment, her mind reeling over Tony. Her only regret was not slowing down to have discovered more about who he was as a person before the events to come. Tucking her hair behind her ear, she smiled at the thought of toying with this Halfling that had some elements of Cedric in him. It would all have to wait until after the King Incubus arrived within the barrier of Mt. Parnassus and made his way into the Otherworld.

CHAPTER 6

NIGHTMARES

A ngeline woke from her nightmares filled with the echoes of
Avalon. She was gasping for air, longing to go back to the lustful
events, the point before she had fallen into the deep abyss of
sleep. Sweat drenched the sheets under her as she sat up, desperate
to break away from the phantom sensations of pain and torment.
Cedric's arm wrapped around her waist pulling her close. He was
still in a deep sleep as he nuzzled her hip, kissing it with his drunken
grin. Her heart raced staring down at him. His hair still the blood
red in tone she remembered in their first days together and the black
tips were slipping out of the hairband.

Sighing, she shoved his arm off, sliding out of bed. A shiver
shook her shoulders as she looked about in the dark for where her
clothes had fallen. Reclaiming them, she was relieved to be wrapped
in their warmth and reminded that she was here and not in a dark
dungeon. Approaching the bedroom door she paused. Aching in
her chest and throat told her she was too anxious to venture out just
yet. Biting her bottom lip, she turned her attention to the desk and
a large pile of journals. Picking one up, she peered over her shoulder
to confirm Cedric was still asleep. She felt like a child doing something bad as she dared herself to open one.

Much to her surprise, it was handwritten notes all dated from
centuries ago. A memory flashed before her, the night they were
attacked by the horde of werewolves he had pulled one out and
taken notes of sorts. Smiling, she remembered the sharp glare he
had given her and the excuse he had grunted: *"I'd be an old fool to
think I could remember everything."*

Scanning over the desk, she realized there were even more on the shelves above the desk. All of these journals were his memories, his thoughts, even his feelings. Eyeing the open book in her hands again, she rubbed her fingers across his beautiful script. The date on the top left ledger was *December 1476*. It was strange, before this section and after it, he had marked an exact date, but for some reason he had lost track of what day he was on at this point. Intrigued, she found the start of the abnormal entry and the first line frightened her.

I have devoured my grandfather Vladimir.

THUD!

The sound of the book falling heavy onto the desk echoed in her ears like gunfire. She covered her mouth, hands trembling. Tears welled up, her memories of Vladimir and his wife Catherine flashing across her mind. She had been somewhat happy in the short time they stayed with them. It was one of the few calm moments in her life and she had wandered back to that time often during her imprisonment. Cedric had changed there in their home, but this, this was heartbreaking. The searing heat of a tear trickled down her cheek and she gritted her teeth, caging the wailing scream squirming in her throat.

What happened while I was gone? Is this what Cedric meant by 'be angry at the choices I made?'

Warm arms wrapped around her, adding to her terror. Her flood of emotions had woken Cedric, there was no hiding how she felt seeing the journal, open haphazardly on the desk. Shaking in his embrace, her panic sent her mind spinning in confusion, thoughts and feelings wrestled one another. He pulled her hands from her face, shoving the book back into them.

His breath washed over her shoulder and he demanded, "Read."

Forcing her eyes back to the pages, she did as he commanded. His arms tightening, he rested his chin on her shoulder as if preparing himself for a hard blow to the gut. Failing to focus on the letters, she rubbed the blurring tears away with a hand and started again:

I have devoured my grandfather Vladimir. In the absence of Catherine, he turned to destroying everything around him. Outside this castle lays the snow-covered bodies of innocent lives to prove how far he went in his grief and rage. Children and women weren't spared. I am here under the request of the current vampire lord, the Sultan, to end the madness. Vladimir even declared war against his own kind, knowing his only blood relative left would be me, the current Incubus King.

How far does one's soul break when the one you love is no more? Looking at him, here in this decaying castle with its field of crimson red, I couldn't help but wonder if this could have been me. I have been without my Angeline far longer than he from his Catherine, yet here I stand with an absolute resolve, sound mind, and aching heart. Is it only because I know she's still alive?

Hundreds of years have passed, but I feel her torment and the excitement waving from her as my pleasure reaches her through our bond. I may not know where he keeps her, but everything I do is aimed to get her back. If she dies, I fear I will become the murderous shell Vladimir became in his last days. During our fight, I felt the agonizing moment of her lips being sewn shut...

Tears splattered across the page. Swallowing, she flipped the page and read on.

...and in that moment, when he showed he cared not to help even his last remaining connection to his wife and daughter, I knew the man I admired had been lost. In the end, I am the monster who devours monsters, as it has been intended since the day of my conception.

I took in the legacy of power destined to be mine, but even that was not enough to take the chill of my coming death from my body. It cost me part of my own soul for what I had to do to keep death from taking me. Angeline's pain was still ravaging me as I sat in that chair bleeding out. If it weren't for her connection with me, I would have left this world. Somehow Romasanta found me and he brought Badbh the Battle Goddess with him. The regret I felt to drink from Badbh was

nothing compared to the largest sacrifice I would make shortly after-
wards. At least with Badbh, it was a mutual friendship, an exchanged
of repayment had occurred in that dreadful moment between us. I am
thankful for her willingness to provide me with her blood so that I may
live another day to continue my search for my Angeline.

It was when Lillith...

She closed the book. Her heart racing and terror on high again
at just reading the name. With his chest and abdomen pressing
against her back, she couldn't run away from it. He reached over,
opening the book again. The same commanding plea fell over her
shoulder, "Read."

It was when Lillith arrived that I realized what needed to be done.
Merlin was merely a man who wielded magic. Even then, a demon
possessing a human would cave to desire eventually. Lillith needed a
brood and I needed a way to gain a means of accessing Merlin's blood-
line. I was willing to wait for the moment he would fail, I was willing to
commit any sin to get me that much closer to getting her back. The key
to Avalon was in the blood, but what was blood? Mere genetics, some-
thing inherited from your forefathers, from your father and mother
and maker. If Morrighan could make something like me, a fucked up
melting pot who has all access to everything running through my veins,
then what were the chances my blood could find his?

What happened to me, to even Lillith, in this exchange made it
clear it would never occur again. There was no lust or even pleasure in
the necessity of the actions. I lost myself...

As she turned the page, hands shaking, his arms tightened. He
wasn't comforting her, but relying on her as a means to support
himself. A wave of pain and sorrow flowed from him and she knew
this was something he could never physically tell her. He wanted
the truth of the biggest secret between he and Lillith to be told to
her in the moments after it happened so she could not, would not,
ever think anything different about his feelings.

...to rage. There have only been two times I have ever fallen into the depths of the incubus' nature to the point of becoming an animal, angry and hungry. The first was the fall of Williamsburg. The second was when I laid with Lillith. My hatred fueled something I never want to experience again; losing my soul to the demonic instincts that this body keeps in the shadows of my heart.

I remember the sensation of my claws digging into the back of her neck as I shoved her down. A shudder shakes me recalling the unearthly intoxication I felt feeling her flesh tugging on my fingertips. Inside my own head I watched, unable to stop as I unraveled into a real devil. Never again. Drool foamed from my mouth like a rabid dog as I gave her the seeds she needed to sow. I would have taken death instead, but blood was the key to Avalon, blood was the key to getting Angeline back. There was no mistaking that in this state I even frightened her, Lillith, Queen Succubus and a demon said to outlive the Gods of old. Her waves of lust did nothing to stop the overwhelming fury that took over.

When she managed to break away, she made it clear it would never be asked of me again. Besides the hope of my blood finding Merlin's through my offspring, I now could only watch time pass me by. After laying with Lillith, I could feel my incubine powers fully blossom, much like Vladimir had done with my moroi bloodline. Sitting in that ice covered castle, I knew I would never find myself in need of drinking blood to keep myself from falling apart. Lillith has many abilities she does not speak of, and looking back, perhaps the pressure to make a brood had an alternative purpose. Regardless, it was an act I truly did not want to commit. I have had no desire to lay with anyone since Angeline came into my life, and being forced to do so released something dark. If I fail to get her back, I can only wonder if it will eventually consume me, much like Vladimir.

She paused. This was what she had been afraid to ask directly. Instead, the answer was there, in his writing the very moment after it had happened. Strangely she was calm, but he had only made a brood with Lillith as an act of desperation in some small chance to gain access to her. All he had done was make decisions based on what was needed to achieve one goal: to hold her in his arms again. His breath pounded over her shoulder with each exhale. He was waiting for her to give him some sign of how she felt now that she knew what had happened.

Her chest ached, remembering how terrified he was to lay with her in fear what was written on these pages would happen between them. When Lillith approached, he hadn't even considered the notion he would lose himself to the hidden and dark animalistic demon within his soul. She opened her mouth, but no words came to mind. Swallowing, she focused her thoughts and tried again.

"I... I'm so sorry..." She leaned back into him and he kissed her shoulder. "To assume... this is all my fault."

Anxiety squeezed her lungs, but his words freed her. "I love you, Angeline. The moment I saw you on that balcony, I wanted you, though I fought my feelings at the time. For the longest time, after lulling you back to sleep that night in the castle, I sat there, not sure what to do. I marveled over every detail of you, and when you became my bride, I felt like I had cheated. I can't help but look back and laugh at how childish I was. Lashing out at you because I did nothing to earn you. Beating up five guys horribly weaker than me was laughable. So sorry I took you from your life because I was greedy."

"I am glad you took me from it. They only used me as a servant girl for my so-called cousin." Goosebumps rippled across her skin as she recalled that very first fierce stare from him. "You taught me to live, to fight, and more importantly, what it means to say you love someone..."

Grabbing the book from her hands, he closed it, setting it on the table. His arms still engulfed her, swallowing her within himself. No words could take back those horrible moments, those necessary evils that had transpired while she remained shackled in a dark dungeon. Tears were sliding down her cheeks faster with each second. Her heart twisted, a stinging sensation burning this chapter of Cedric's own life to her memory. He didn't commit a sin, but sold his soul to get her back into the world of the living as far as she could see. A man could never live up to the sacrifices this demonic knight was capable of doing. How could she accept such undeserving love?

Chapter 7

The Lion's Den

"So, why are we doing this in my bar again?" Tony was leaning against the countertop.

Cedric and Romasanta were pushing tables and chairs off to the side, clearing a large spot between the pool table and booths. Tony scowled at the crowd before him. Angeline, Cedric, Romasanta, Nyctimus and Lillith were all present in the early hours before he opened his doors for business. Tension was building in his chest knowing the trouble he'd seen from this group. Worse, today was his busiest night, Friday, when an above average amount of creatures and humans mingled behind the security of his doors. Before he met Cedric, he had thought these regular weekender's had been *normal*. After a shock to his system, he no longer allowed his mind to reinforce naïve thoughts of comfort. Now, he simply envied the ability to sense who was what, like the vampress bartenders he found himself managing.

"Because I refuse to allow them to do this in my apartment." Lillith winked, sitting at the bar top beside him.

Tony paled as a flashback of the aftermath from the portal to Avalon raced through his mind. "Is this anything like the *first* portal?"

He could still hear the jingle of shattering glass and the screeching of the wooden legs on the pool table as it slid violently across the floor. An ache tingled in his biceps and lower back. It was a reminder of how long it took to mop up the sickening melting pot of liquor and beer that painted the floor for weeks. Even now, his shoes made it known the floor was still sticky despite months of nightly mopping. The copious amounts of cleaners failed to disperse the layer of tacky sludge. Eyeing his wall of liquor bottles, he wondered if he should start stacking them in the office for safety.

"No." Grunted Romasanta. "This is my portal, so there's no friction or spells trying to repel us."

"Oh." Pondering this information, Tony continued his flood of questions. "You can use magic, Romasanta?"

"No." Another grunt.

"I'm afraid he's void of all magic. What he possesses is a key generator of sorts." Lillith crossed her legs, amused by Tony's curiosity as she continued to explain. "He was gifted demonic powers by Fenrir, which makes him the guardian to the Black Forest Barrier."

"Barrier?" Rubbing the back of his neck, Tony was being answered in riddles. "What's a bar–"

BANG!

A chair slammed to the ground, still rocking on its legs from the force.

"Ask another question," Tony tensed, his eyes meeting the annoyed expression on Cedric's face as he snarled. "And you'll be eating this chair."

"I suppose I'll learn more about this stuff another time." With a sigh Tony started his rounds of powering on the cash registers and popping open the tills. "Don't mind me, I'll be doing my thing..."

Lillith snickered, lifting an eyebrow at him. Tony's jaw tensed a moment, but he phased her out, ignoring her completely.

Romasanta walked in a circle, staring at the clearing they made in the floor. After about three rounds, he slumped his shoulders. He looked over to the bar top, first eyeing Lillith who greeted him with a devilish smirk. Her excitement for what she knew was coming next tingled in Romasanta's chest and he caught himself from rubbing the mark. Acknowledging it only added to his ire and her arousal. Shifting his glance, he watched Tony finish the last register. Being his bouncer, he knew he would be fading into the office and he would finish the process then. There was no need for the boy to ever see a transformation as swift and violent as his own.

"What are you waiting for?" Scoffed Cedric, annoyed at the unusual pause in Romasanta's actions. "Did you forget something?"

"No." Snorting, his spine tingled as he heard the register close and then the office door clicking behind him.

It was like a marathon flare firing as he exploded into black fur. The snarl and stare he had on Cedric did not break once while his face distorted, crackling into its canine shape. What clothes he had on fell away in shreds at his clawed feet. Another huff and he stepped forward, shaking off the last painful throbs of his shift. With another step forward, he found himself standing in the breeze and shade of the Black Forest. The ruffled fur on his back fell flat, his muscles going lax. He hated not being able to be human here, for Daphne, but he felt free when he set foot in the forest. The sounds, the smells, and even the arching roots diving in and out of the ground were all nostalgic of the days when he lived a farmer's life. Closing his eyes, he inhaled deeply, cherishing the moment of peaceful bliss.

Footsteps coming through behind him made his large ears flick with annoyance. Reluctant, he opened his amber eyes to glare at Cedric again. Taking on the Mother of Dragons was a task in itself, but he and Nyctimus would have to prep both Cedric and Angeline for what was to come. Cedric's pride and overconfidence were once more drowning his instincts, but then again, it seemed a mistake most incubus make. Regardless, he already knew that one or more of them would not make it to the end of this mission alive. His eyes shift to Cedric's side to the frail framed shoulders of Angeline and his chest ached, *One of us will die trying to save her. There's no way she's going to hold her own in a battle like this. Nyctimus and I were lucky to have Fenrir's guidance and fervor against Aitvaras, but we're on our own.*

"I'm worried about it too." Nyctimus' voice cut his thoughts short and he flattened his ears as he glanced over at him, envious to see him still in his human form. "But, are we really going to send the girl out on her own after that Busse?"

"I need to know if she can hold her own." He waved a clawed hand and a gust of wind filled with the smoke and liquor scent of the bar rushed past, signaling the portal closed. "I also need to know how Cedric will handle her being beaten to a pulp. In fact, that's what concerns me more than what the girl can or can't do."

"I see." Nyctimus took off his eyeglasses, tucking them in his shirt pocket with a grin. "You want to stick him in your old cell?"

A toothy grin came across his wolven face. "It did hold me in while beating myself into the door in a blind rage."

"Are you okay with this, Angeline?" Cedric's whisper broke her daze off the forest from her memories. "Y-yes."

He could feel the confusion tangling with panic, his confidence in her response falling flat. "Did you even hear what I asked you?"

Forcing her eyes from the forest, her heart racing as she looked into those sharp green eyes. "N-no."

He smiled at the confession. "I said, you don't have to come with us, you can back out at any point if you want, pet."

A wave of anger made his blood boil with excitement, her words sharp. "Where you go, I go."

"But you do realize you are hunting a Busse, right?" He lifted a brow, trying his best to hide his feelings from her.

"Is it as big as a chimera?" They were making their way down a well laid footpath.

"Yes, but less of a nuisance if you ask me." He paused, thinking about the last time he had encountered one. "It's an overgrown deer with obnoxious antlers and will mow down anything in its way."

She looked down at her hands while following them through the streams of sunlight that speckled the pathway. It had been centuries since she last touched a bow. Balling her hands into fists and opening them again, she looked questioningly at them. Would the skills she worked so hard to gain even exist anymore? She was a good hunter before her marriage with Cedric, but the training he gave her took her to a new level. That day, with Morrighan's chimeras, made it clear she had become like the legendary Lady Ranger Ann that he often shared stories about. Fear was sending her heart racing as her mind flashed reminders of her fangs and undying state in Avalon. Tears were dripping down her cheeks, her hands covering her mouth as her tongue frantically searched for the still missing fangs.

Slamming into Cedric, she looked up wide eyed. He had stopped and faced her immediately and, in her panic, she hadn't noticed. His face was taut, his lips straight and his eyes stern as he glared down at her. Her hands were gripped firmly by his, pushing them down and away. She bit her bottom lip in response. Leaning in towards her, she flinched, awaiting the scolding that was sure to be following. Instead, the heat of his breath on her neck and shoulder sent shivers through her. He nuzzled her ear a moment, inhaling her scent before his voice delicately whispered into her ear.

"I can't wait to feel your fangs digging into my flesh again, my pet." She nearly suffocated under the weight of his arousal, but it lifted as soon as her terror waivered. "But first, there's someone here who's been waiting to see you again..."

He pulled away from her, leaving her breathless. Sweat trickled down her temple, her fears washed away but her heart was still racing. Cedric turned, releasing an ear-shattering whistle that echoed through the forest. Nyctimus and Romasanta both growled in response, shuddering off the pain it brought to their sensitive ears. Birds were fluttering up out of the brush, closer with each wave. Angeline's eyes widened, a familiar sound thudding ever louder towards them. Her eyes searched the brush, and graceful as ever, a horse of flames erupted through them. Steam burst from his nostrils as he cantered around them once and came to a stop by her. Barushka nosed her cheek, pawing with one hoof as his flames receded.

"BARUSHKA!" She hugged his neck, tears of joy washing away the ones left from her frightful thoughts. "I thought I would never... last I saw, you were, you were dead!"

Neighing in response, the large hairy horse nibbled at her shoulder. Looking to Cedric, he flared his lips, snorting. He had failed to tell the old steed his beloved friend was back.

"How about you ride him to the castle?" Cedric gripped Angeline's hip, lifting her onto Barushka. "You always looked better riding the stubborn beast, anyhow."

"O-ok." She was wiping the tears from her cheeks, but more were still falling. "I'll see you there."

Slapping Barushka's rear earned an annoyed side kick in his direction before he took to a playful canter once more. Cedric stood watching as they faded down the path, the brush swallowing them from view. He was far too tense about her test, and turning to Romasanta, he aimed to settle the stipulations of said-test. Romasanta's golden glare never wavered as Cedric came to a stop, making his ears pricking forward. Crossing his clawed arms, he snorted as a way of asking, *what now?* Cedric took one more look over his shoulder, gauging if she had made it out of earshot for even his ability level. Satisfied and unable to hear the heavy thuds of Barushka's hooves, he glared back to Romasanta with anger written across his face.

"Will she have time to train before you send her out alone?" It came out more like a demand than a question at the tone of Cedric's voice. "She hasn't touched a bow since, it's been hundreds of years."

Romasanta glared at him a moment before stating what should have been obvious. "And I assume she needs a bow too?"

Cedric's jaw tensed and he knotted his brow.

"Stop it." Nyctimus sighed. "You two should be aware that Badbh has already insisted we train with the new weapons she has waiting for us. Going into battle blindly for any of us would be naïve and ignorant. Plus, we don't know what sort of creatures we will face inside the Mt. Parnassus' barrier."

"I'm starting to feel like you're in charge of this, Nyctimus." Romasanta flattened his ears as he glance at the hazel-eyed man.

"Currently, I am." Both Cedric and Romasanta flinched. "You two are so wrapped up in this private silent war of pride that I took it upon myself to be in charge. Not once have either of you considered where you were getting weapons or thought to research what we are walking into."

Cedric's face reddened and he turned on his heels. "I'm going for a walk, I'll see you two back at the castle."

Waiting for Cedric to disappear, Romasanta's arms fell to his side. "I should be telling you thank you, Nyctimus."

A smirk crawled across Nyctimus' face. "You're welcome."

CHAPTER 8

HUMAN OR DEMON

Tony couldn't stop shaking, a bead of cold sweat tickling his spine from the fear created by what he had just witnessed. Lillith's grin was wild as he looked pass her arm that had slammed the office door closed. It had startled him when the door suddenly shut before he could go through. As he turned to express his disapproval, his eyes had locked onto Romasanta, not her. In horror he watched as the room filled with the sounds of cracking and snapping. It could only be described as several bones breaking all at once. The already broad shoulders of Romasanta exploded into double the mass within seconds. Fur as black as night erupted in a blink of an eye. The sheer massive size of Romasanta's neck and wolven head were a shock to his system to see protrude from what once was human. He knew Romasanta was something else with those gleaming amber eyes, but to hide something like that was unbelievable. No one had looked over their shoulder before disappearing into the invisible ripples. As a gust of wind brought the smell of flowers and fresh air through the bar, he felt his muscles relax. The portal had closed without any further disruption to Tony or the bar.

"What's wrong, Tony?" Cooed Lillith. "Did you forget Romasanta was a demon?"

Finally feeling like he could breath, he locked eyes with Lillith's maroon stare. "What was the purpose in making me watch that?"

Her eyebrows lifted. "You seemed so smug the other day. I figured showing you what a man turned to demon looked like in his true form. Thought it would clear up things in that silly head of yours."

"That wasn't what you meant at all." He gripped her arm, failing to shove it off the door. "I am in no mood for your games. Weren't you suppose to go with them?"

"Me? Play games? Go on missions?" Looking to where he gripped her arm, she furrowed her brow. "And aren't we rather brave today?"

He pulled on her arm, failing yet again. "I have a business to open."

"Tell me how scared you were to see Romasanta change." She licked her lips, Tony's grip tightening in response. "I see..."

A wave of arousal shot up his arm and he let go, gasping. "Dammit!"

He found himself holding his arm, panting as his body heated up. Something wasn't right. Lillith was far too interested in him and the instinctual panic building was alarming.

"Feeling warm are we?" She chortled.

"Were you waiting for them to leave just to toy with me?" It felt like his blood was on fire, the sensation only building momentum, his heart racing. "They'll find out sooner or later, Lillith."

"Oh?" She pulled herself up onto the bar top, sitting there, watching the sweat drip from his chin. "You still don't get it? All this heavy breathing and sexual desire isn't coming from me, my love."

Tony's eyes widened. The sensation that rattled through his arm, which way had it travelled? A sickening twist in his gut whispered, *from your shoulder through your palm and into her.*

"Here it comes! The revelation!" She mused. "Did we forget what blood runs through our veins after we were told?"

Closing his eyes tight, he sunk to his knees in defeat. "But why now?"

"That was what I was wondering." Sighing, she waved her hand to dismiss the unknown. "It seems rather odd and I can't help but wonder why your blood is wanting to shift now of all times. I think Mother Gaea is playing games again..."

His heart thumped louder in his ears, his concentration on her words failing. The shirt on his back was soaked with sweat and the heat building from his core wasn't slowing down. It was a conflictive sensation; painful and pleasurable; frightening and exciting. An icy hand gripped the back of his neck, but he was too lost in the sensations overwhelming him. Tingling started to pull away the burning sensation in his blood that was sending him into a lustful rage. His heart slowed, he could take in deeper breaths. The heat was flowing away into the harsh grip at the back of his neck, nails digging into his flesh felt intoxicatingly wonderful. This was the power Cedric had struggled with in his past. Catching a full breath, he opened his eyes. Lillith was no longer on the countertop. His hands flew to the hand at his neck, but it had pulled away too fast. Spinning around, he saw a frown on Lillith's face.

"W-what did you do?" He stammered, both terrified and relieved.

"You should know, I have given only two other men that mark." She paused, looking off to her thoughts before speaking again. "I don't know who is pulling the strings, but no man deserves to be forced into becoming a demon. Not without consent."

She started to walk away, but he pleaded for answers. "Why did you help me?"

Her steps came to a halt, and without looking back she whispered. "I like you, Tony. Consider yourself lucky."

He fell onto his back, his neck tingling as he stared at the dropdown ceiling above him. The bell on the door signaled she had left, but he found himself playing the last several minutes over and over in his head. His thoughts repeating, *am I human or demon?*

Chapter 9

Nostalgia

Barushka and Angeline came out into a clearing and before them stood a magnificent castle of old. A smile crossed her face, the scene making her feel more at home, more like herself. She tightened her knees on Barushka and he trotted happily across the bridge. The sound of hooves on cobblestone made her heart flutter. She had missed the sights, the smell, and even sounds of her life from so long ago. Much to her surprise, there were quite a few people walking about as they drew near. Many were tending to the stables or coming in and out of the castle's open doors. Blinking again, she realized that they were all *women*. In awe, she twisted about jumping from one person to the next, each girl as beautiful as the last. If it weren't for Barushka's muscles softening under her legs, she would have been alarmed by it.

A blonde-haired woman approached them, her movements graceful. "You must be Lady Romulus!"

"Y-yes." She was still taking in all the commotion.

"Welcome to Lykaon Castle!" Bowing deeply, Angeline's face mottled at the formality. "Please, come join us inside."

"S-sure." Slowly she slid down Barushka's side, who nudged her back, reassuring that it was indeed ok to follow the girl. "Where am I going, exactly?"

"The Battle Goddess has brought a gift for you before you carry out Romasanta's test." She smiled, though her maroon eyes reminded her of Lillith's own. "I heard that you were studying to be a great archer?"

"Y-yes." Again her eyes fell to her hands and doubts crept forward. "But, it's been a long time since I've touched a bow. I doubt I am any good..."

The girl stopped and Angeline looked behind her at the towering wooden doors with carvings of forgotten animals from so long ago. Swallowing, she nodded to the girl who pushed the doors open in response. It wasn't her first time meeting Badbh, but being in a place that reminded her of the days she served as a Lady of the Court brought back humbled feelings. As the doors crept open, she saw a mahogany long table with its scattered items sparkling from the brazier in the center of the table. Walking in, she made herself stiffen, her posture tall as she had been taught to do so in the presence of the king. Part of her smiled, that even after so many years in a dark prison she would still remember to react this way.

The doors thudded closed, echoing throughout the grand war room. It reminded her of the armory in Cedric's mansion with walls of weaponry, tapestries and banners reflecting royal houses that fell even before her time. Badbh was standing in front of the largest banner, her thick black hair falling down her back failed to hide her muscular shoulders. Angeline took in the scars that ripped across her skin. They painted her arms, the skin on her back and even her hips. She could only assume her legs were no different, but they were hidden by a skirt of white leather with an underskirt full of raven's feathers. The fire torches danced in the reflection off the brass armlets and she turned to face her. As always, she wore her headdress of brass, silver, and gold that resembled a bird's head.

A smile came across her face, but it did not soften the ragged scars across her chin. Marching with authority Badbh approached the table, grabbing up a magnificent bow. Angeline gasped, the silver bow magnificent in design and balance. As she took in the near glowing piece, she could see the decorations and curves made the image of a raven on a branch. The tree branch twisted from the bottom of the arc and in the middle the Raven's claws gripped it.

Flowing up the raven looked as if it were screaming to the heavens and its wing become the top arc of the bow. All in silver, it nearly blinded her even in the poor light of flames. As Badbh came closer, offering it to her, Angeline winced. Her hands jerking back to her side, she furrowed her brow, refusing the gift.

"I can't. That bow is far too much for someone so unskilled." She closed her eyes, refusing to see the expression on Badbh's face. "You would understand that..."

Badbh's laughter boomed through the room. "Are you that worried of losing your skills?"

Opening her eyes, she pleaded with the Goddess. "I can't possibly accept such an elegant bow as that!"

"First off, let's fix this sense of doubt." Badbh's sudden burst of speed only allowed Angeline to stumble one step back as she flicked her forehead.

"Ouch!" It felt more like a punch.

Angeline's ears were sent ringing as she folded over, holding her forehead where Badbh's finger had hit her. The ringing soon sounded like murmuring, which turned to whispering, and then she realized what those words were. Astonished, she froze, no longer worried about the pain. Closing her eyes, she listened more deeply, taking in the lessons, the experience being given to her. In her mind she felt the ebony skinned girl, her white hair tightly braided under her black hood. She hunted alone and swallowed her fears the instant her opponents appeared. Chimeras, Hellhounds, Jidrah, even Wyvern fell at her feet. Rarely was she ever harmed thanks to her abilities to hide. Her heart fluttered as she went dagger to sword against a very young Cedric. This was all the skills and experience from Lady Ranger Ann, someone who had sent even Cedric down to the ground with ease, one of the few who outclassed demons with her prowess.

Eyes still closed, she stood straight, her visions shifting. Before her stood a mysterious woman whose face was hidden under a headdress made of a deer's skull. Her exposed lips smiled at her as if she could see Angeline. She too carried a bow on her back and she approached Angeline in her mind. She gripped her shoulders, her fingers both icy and hot. Angeline was panicking. Her heart racing as she failed to open her eyes. She had felt this grip before. Flashes of the time a skeletal witch cackled and prophesized her union with Cedric shook her core. Looking into the eyes of the deer skull mask, she felt anger replacing her fear now. With Lady Ranger Ann's influence, she bottled her terror and replaced it with something more useful, her rage.

"You." She huffed, frustrated to be facing the witch again. "What do you want?"

A toothy grin sent chills across her soul. "Do you know who you speak with, child?"

"My ancestor." She flustered. "The old witch that I inherited magic from."

"True." The smile faded. "Do you know my name?"

"N-no." She confessed. "No one has ever spoken it."

"It does not matter then." She smirked. "Did you not come here for aid?"

Angeline looked at her hands, her skills with the bow burning in her palms loud, as if they had never left her. "I reclaimed my skills from Lady Ranger Ann, that's all I need."

"Oh?" The witch's grin grew wider. "And do you know who gave Ann those skills?"

Angeline's heart sank.

"But, for you, I will relinquish all that I have. You have earned the right to receive your birthright in full. I pray you learn to master it, quick, for time is unfolding faster these days." She went to let go, but Angeline gripped her arms.

"What if I refuse?" She glared coldly at the witch. "I have more than enough to face my enemies."

"You're stubborn, and more importantly, fiery." She laughed. "But for you, child, Artemis' gift is in your blood. This will be my only chance to unlock all of it without *her* knowing. The enemies you see are not the same I know that you will come to face. Let's keep this exchange a secret. They can't know I was ever here."

"*Her?*" The witched yanked her arms out of her grip, and like Badbh, she readied a finger. "Wait, who can't know?"

"That will be revealed in a later fight. Oh, do tell Badbh, *Artemis is in her debt for sending you to me.*"

The finger slammed her back. She felt herself falling backwards, her eyes wide in surprise as the power shot through her. Warm arms caught her from behind as the bright light from the flick faded to stones and wooden beams. Blinking, her ears ringing, she paled. Trembling the information soaring through her mind and body swelled in her soul. Looking to her hands, she realized she was gripping the silver bow. Confused, her ears focusing on the sounds around her, she realized who held her there on the floor.

"WHAT DID YOU DO!" A wave of anger made it through the ripples of magic still working through her body. "Dammit, Badbh!"

"That wasn't my magic on that back half!" She roared back. "I simply aimed to recover her skills and then someone took over. I just wanted to help her, before she was sent out there solo!"

"Then whose magic followed yours?!" Panic waved from Cedric and it startled Angeline.

"C-Cedric?" Looking up, he squeezed her tighter. "I'm ok! I saw her!"

His forehead folded with worry. "Saw who?"

"Lady Ranger Ann! I, I saw how she trained you, her dagger against your sword! You only bested her once!" His eyes widened at the information only he could have known. "But then, she showed..."

"Who exactly interrupted my spell like that?" Badbh's pride had been dented and she demanded to know who dare tread across her in such a backhanded manner.

"The witch... my ancestor." Angeline swallowed, gathering her nerve to dare speak the name of who had gave her so much knowledge. "Artemis is in your debt, she said."

"Artemis... sly as ever." Badbh looked pass them to the wide-eyed werewolf. "She owes me for this. I wonder what she could possibly be up to jumping into a spiritual knowledge spell like this. She was always good at finding loopholes, but this is beyond me..."

Still standing at the doorway, Romasanta's fur prickled from his head, down his massive neck, to the tip of his tail. Even now, his sister was meddling with his life and even Angeline's own. Snorting, he turned, marching down the hall and out to the castle. He had to see Daphne to pry what he could from her. If anyone had connections, a deep understanding of what was unfolding with his sister, surely Daphne could.

Angeline wobbled to her feet with Cedric's help. The concerned expressions she was receiving from him and everyone else in the room only made the encounter with the witch more unnerving. Gripping the bow tight, her confidence back with the bow in her palm, she marched to the table.

I need to do something for myself. Romasanta is testing me to see if I can fight still, but if I can't act on my own what good am I to them, to Cedric? While travelling with Cedric, never did I ask or wait for him to tell me to go hunt. Why am I doing it now? I have my skills back and knowledge I lacked before. If I want to stay by his side, I have to be able to protect myself.

Her eyes fell onto a quiver made of leather with silver embroidery of vines and ravens. Gripping it, she paused a moment. For the first time she could feel it was a magical item and she glanced to the bow she had set down. Scanning over all the items, everything on the table had been blessed by Badbh in some way, but her ability to feel it was new.

Was this something Artemis gave me?

Swallowing, she felt the warm tingle of the magic vibrating off of everything and tasted its benevolence as if something sweet had been laid across her tongue. Shrugging the sensations off, she refocused her thoughts. Slinging the heavy strap across her chest, she took a moment to tighten the buckles, making the quiver tilt in a way that she could reach behind her lower back to grab the shafts of the arrows. Another item on the table made her pause as her eyes met it. It looked like a finely tailored archer's glove with an embellished '*A*' embossed into the back of the hand. Blinking a moment, she looked to Badbh.

"Is this for me?" It was more than she had expected to get.

"Oh, yes." Nodding, Badbh waved her fingers to imply *take it*. "I'm not the type to not fully equip my warriors."

"T-thank you." Cedric was standing on his feet as she strapped it on her hand. "I appreciate everything you've done for her, Badbh."

Satisfied, Angeline started for the door.

"Where are you going?" Demanded Cedric. "You can't possibly be considering to go after the Busse after what just happened?"

"Why not?" She threw the bow across her chest, marching pass him. "This is my test. I rather do this on my own... I need to do this on my own."

His jaw twitched, anger and worry struggled with one another and he held it in the best he could. No one there could deny that something more had happened in that instant the spell had been cast. Even the way she walked and carried herself had shifted drastically. The wave of ire boiling from within her though, told him she was very much the same girl he had snatched away from the King's court. Still, Artemis had caused so much chaos, back then and even now. After her last round of meddling they both found themselves targets of much darker entities. The thud of the castle door echoed down the hall and into the room was enough to send him marching after her. Nyctimus stepped in his way.

"Move." They were about the same height, but he hadn't ever faced Nyctimus in battle. "You're in my way, four-eyes."

"You don't intend to go after her, do you, Cedric?" A smile crept across Nyctimus' face, his hazel eyes never faltering. "It would defeat the purpose of her test."

Cedric opened his mouth, but swiftly shut it. If she ended up being in danger, he had several advantages. Here, she was under the protection of a barrier. Another point was the fact he could feel her emotions and physical pain. *Angeline can do this, but still, I hope Romasanta is out there to watch over her.* Taking in a deep breath, he calmed his anger while still glaring at Nyctimus. A smirk crawled across Cedric's face.

"So where exactly did Romasanta go?" He crossed his arms.

"I imagine he went to see Daphne." Nyctimus looked unamused by the question. "Normally he would have seen her first before coming to the castle."

Irritated, Cedric walked back to the table, flopping into a chair. They were treating him like a child confined to his room. He watched as Badbh paced the floor muttering to herself. It was the first time he had seen her fuss over something in all the centuries he had encountered her. Even that day, when she offered her blood to him, there was no inkling of fear or concern. She paused, waved her hand in the air as if to shoo away a thought, muttered some more and began pacing again.

Exactly what went wrong in your spell, Badbh? What did Artemis do to my Angeline?

"So what has your feathers so ruffled?" Scoffing, Cedric peered over at the items still on the table: a silver sword, a wooden box laced with silver, a couple of daggers and various leather gloves and bracers. "I don't think I've seen you worry over something so much."

"Artemis." Badbh held her breath a moment. "She normally doesn't intervene like this unless she has a very good, and often, frightening reason. I am pretty sure Angeline tried to refuse what she was offering, but for some reason it was forced into her."

"Exactly what was offered?" He raised an eyebrow, picking up the sword and looking it over as nostalgia tingled at the back of his mind.

"Experience, skills, talent…" She flopped into a chair across from him. "She was in there under the spells agenda. So the only thing that was transferrable would be battle worthy abilities and knowledge. It's bothering me since she could have given Angeline that knowledge any time, any place, but waited for me to cast my spell. I'll have to seek Morrighan's guidance on the matter. If any of us understands loopholes in spells, she's the expert of backdoor deals."

"I see…" His voice trailed off as he took in the markings etched into the blade, every line familiar to him, something he spent his childhood admiring. "And where did this sword come from?"

"Romasanta." Nyctimus was still at the doorway, watching their conversation from afar. "He intends to give it to you. He doesn't plan being a human when facing anything that might be on Mt. Parnassus. The sword is useless to him in his shifted form."

"But, is this not the heirloom weapon of the House Romulus?" His sharp eyes came with a heated air as they hit Nyctimus. "Was this not the sword the last remaining member of the House of Romulus wielded to his grave?"

The smell of aged dirt and the blood of those he beheaded centuries ago in Williamsburg still lingered on the blade. If he could tell, he was certain Nyctimus' wolven nose could also sense the putridness.

"And do you know who the original owner of that weapon was before the first Romulus was born?" Retorted Nyctimus, pacing closer as his eyes glowed. "Tell me that."

Blinking at the sudden shift of aggression, Cedric looked back at what he always labeled as *his father's sword* with more awareness. "I suppose with such archaic writing, it didn't belong to Romasanta either."

"No." Nyctimus grabbed the sword up, holding it with familiar skill. "This was my grandfather's sword. When Romasanta killed Boreas, he took it for his own. He had every right to, after what that vile man did to even his own flesh and blood."

"So it's true, you're as old as Romasanta?" Cedric lifted an eyebrow, intrigued to learn more about the mysterious man who served the old werewolf.

"No. He had been made a werewolf long before me." He offered the sword back. "But apparently you weren't listening to his life story the other day. Did you fail to even capture the fact he's *Romasanta, father of werewolves?*"

"How could I listen to it all..." Setting the sword back on the table, Cedric grunted. "They should put it in a book and I'll read about it later."

Nyctimus smiled. "Come, follow me. I want to show you something that wasn't shared in great detail."

Sighing, Cedric looked over at Badbh who shrugged. Pulling himself out of the chair, he followed Nyctimus further into the castle until they met with an old ragged door. Taking the torch from its nearby holder, Nyctimus opened the door and started leading Cedric down the stone spiral steps. With each loop the air grew colder, even dryer as the smell of dirt and sawdust came somewhere below in the deep abyssal of darkness. He remained unmoved by Nyctimus as they finally hit the bottom. It opened up to a cellar room with stockpiles of goods and wine bottles. Following him deeper, Cedric realized this was more of a wide hallway as doorways would appear in the playful light of the torch to the right and left. They reached near the dead end, one last doorway remained their right.

This one actually had a heavy oaken door with encryptions carved and seared into it and along the doorframe itself. Cedric looked the details over, none of it in a writing he was familiar with and most of it reflective to what the silver sword had engraved into its blade and hilt. Nyctimus motioned for him to go in, but Cedric frowned at the idea. Snorting, Nyctimus entered the room, walking to its center and waited for him to follow him in. As Cedric came close, he nodded back to the door, the inner side of it still visible. Holding the torch higher, the light fell on the battered wood stained with blood. All around their feet the dirt here had large claw marks dug into it and Cedric furrowed his brow.

"I thought he didn't come back to the Black Forest until after this..." Cedric could still smell Romasanta's blood in the room.

"He had no idea we brought him here when we were trying to calm him from the prison until afterwards." Nyctimus sighed. "We weren't sure that the magical barrier on the door here could even hold his rage, but if it came to it, Daphne was willing to be the one to put him down. He was so far gone, so broken away from being the guardian of this place he wasn't forced to be a werewolf in those moments."

Cedric tensed. "Exactly why are you showing me this?"

He turned to face Nyctimus and found himself watching the torch falling to the ground. For an old man, he was shockingly fast. Spinning back around, he saw the light from the hall snap close and the bang of the door shutting. Running, he slammed into the wood, gripping the door. With all his strength, he pulled. The magic scrawled on the other side was beyond strong. Another tug, putting all his weight into it. Still it did not budge.

"NYCTIMUS!" Roaring, Cedric slammed his fist in the door, blood snaking down between the grains of the wood. "What is the meaning of this?"

"Do you think we would only be testing the girl?" There was a long pause before Nyctimus continued, confident that Cedric was calm enough to listen. "We need to know if you are capable of letting her be harmed at all. You're the only one in the group who seems to not understand that our greatest threat in battle is your temper and your obsession of coming to her rescue. We are facing dragons, and they will take notice of that. She is going to get hurt, possibly be mortally wounded, but we cannot fail reaching the Oracle."

Another angry punch signaled he understood. Glaring at the split wood under his punch, the splinter biting into him red with his blood, coaxing drips to snake down the grooves. Gritting his teeth, Cedric knew Nyctimus was right. She wasn't the frail human girl he married so long ago. He had made her into something more, something fearsome. Though no one would ever know exactly what it was until it revealed itself. Regardless, she was an excellent hunter and even against her first encounter with a chimera, she held her own before he could reach her. This was one Busse, though larger and more aggressive, it was dumber than a pack of hunting chimeras. Badbh not only returned Angeline's own knowledge and skills, but she gave her access to Lady Ranger Ann's own. He slid to the floor, leaning his back on the door smiling.

The woman who taught me how to fight has become my soulmate in a way. His smile fell away, his thoughts reminding him of the one thing that did matter. *Can I really not react to her pain? Sit here, level headed, and allow her to fight alone?*

CHAPTER 10

HUNT FOR THE GOLDEN STAG

arushka was excited to see Angeline had a bow and quiver drawn across her back. He nuzzled the items, begging her to take him along on the hunt. Smiling, she patted his thick neck and then gripped the saddle. At least she would be in good company and not alone in the forest. Huffing, she kicked her leg over the saddle, took a deep breath and she closed her eyes.

This is the first time I've felt like my old self again...

"Lady Romulus!" A maiden with short black hair waved up at her. "Here's a pack for you! We didn't want you to leave without food and supplies."

"Oh, uh, thank you." She threw the pack into the saddle bag without further delay. "I completely failed to consider how long I'll be gone. Thank you so much... I'm a little out of practice, I suppose."

"It's ok, we understand it's been a long time since your last hunt." Angeline's eyes darted to the ground. Nyctimus must have informed the others of her situation. "We are praying for your safe return."

Angeline's cheeks heated at the thought of everyone staring at her, knowing she was lost in this new world and timeline. Embarrassment, frustration and shame muddled at her core. Clicking her tongue against the back of her teeth, she signaled Barushka into a canter, eager to get away from them. As the cool shade of the forest covered them, she sighed in relief. Releasing the reigns, she rested her head into his mane and wrapped her arms around his neck. Snorting with delight, Barushka trotted with a sense of pride, allowing her this moment of reprieve. Sitting up, she took in the sights of the ancient forest, remembering the days spent riding, taking in its natural beauty, desperate to find a cure for Cedric after Nemaine had attacked them. Every leaf was a marvelous green, the trunks massive like the buildings of the city. Barushka weaved around roots, bowing in and out of the ground like sea serpents.

"So where on earth will I find the Busse?" Barushka bobbed his head, picking up speed. "I see, you know where it is. If we can get close enough, I can use the trees to my advantage and get a clear shot of him."

Every surface of the forest was starting to look the same as more time passed. They must be moving in circles. Yawning, she rubbed the sleep from her eyes. She continued to look and listen to the area around them. Glancing over, she did a double take, pulling the reigns to signal Barushka to stop. Her eyes noticed something different, and turning Barushka around, they trotted closer to the side of a tree. Blinking, she realized she was looking at scrapes dug into the bark. Sap dripped down to eye level from the fresh markings and she started searching the ground around them. An animal taller than Barushka had made these, therefore she should be able to see footprints to reflect the same. Shifting her weight, Barushka backed up and she locked onto one massive depression in a patch of moss. Not only was the Busse horned and taller than Barushka, but it was clear he was far heavier.

Sliding out of the saddle, Barushka snorted his disapproval. The sky was turning peach through the holes in the canopy of branches, a warning of the sun sinking into the horizon. Standing by the imprint in the moss, she searched for more footprints, but there were too many to keep track. Some sap twinkled in the light on another trunk of a tree, but it looked no different than the one behind her. Feeling flustered of the dying daylight, she took in the trees and towering roots. One archway of roots looked climbable, and with the arch at the top, it may prove a safe place to even rest for the night. As she gripped her fingers into the gapping grooves, she was thankful they were wide enough for the toes of her boots to catch.

Sweat trickled down her cheeks. Barushka paced and circled in worry far below her. She looked over her shoulder, pausing to see how far above the scrape marks she had climbed. Movement in the distance made her refocus, squinting in the dimming light. Her heartbeat raced in excitement. Branches were shifting in the growing shadows about a hundred yards away, spurring her to climb faster. Another glance made her realize she was seeing not tree limbs, but the outer points of antlers. Flashes of the Orm devouring horses made her pull herself to the peak of the arching roots. Panting, wiping the sweat off her forehead with her forearm, she stared back through the towering trunks. Something shifted, but with the fading light, she lost focus, unable to make out the creature. Cursing the night as it took its hold on the sky, her chances of seeing far away died with the last sparks of daylight.

A whisper of a neigh hit her ears. Peering down, she felt dizzy. At this height, Barushka appeared tiny. He circled around, his flames projecting a gentle blue tone like a wisp. Sighing, she sat there, her legs dangling off the edge while trying to steady her beating heart. Waving down at him, he stopped in his tracks, his head bobbing making the flames on his mane flicker.

"I'm sorry, Barushka. I guess we're spending the night here after all." Yawning she turned and gauged the width of her platform. "I'll stay up here. We can get our bearings in the morning before I climb down."

Much to her relief, there was a groove deep enough in the root to make a bed. The tall edges kept her safe if she were to roll too far on one side. Removing the bow, she unbuckled her quiver, laying them within reach. Exhausted from her day, the night sky and twinkling stars were lulling her to sleep. Something about this moment gave her a sense of security, a sense of normalcy from her past.

I guess my quiver can be my stand-in Cedric for the night. As long as I don't panic, he shouldn't have any reason to chase after me. I have to do this myself...

***

"She is settling in for the night it seems." Daphne's wooden hand stroked Romasanta's arm, stirring him from his nap. "You should head back in case Nyctimus needs help."

"I'm sorry you ever had to see me like that..." His eyes were still closed as he nuzzled her arm.

"Like what?" Her face was barely visible, but her expression clear with worry. "Are you talking about the time they brought you here, unknowingly?"

"Yes..." He sighed, his bright yellow eyes shining in the moonlight as he glared down at his claws with disdain. "Still, what bothers me...how did I become human?"

"Lillith is older than this forest and her magic is that of a titan." The thought made him shudder. "Even I don't know what she's capable of. She may be Queen of the Succubi, but she's not one of them."

"She's not a succubus..." His heart ached and he could feel the slight tingle of Lillith's mark on his chest. "Her touch has the power to change me back into a man. She can control the feelings of those around her and her ability to see into the future is impeccable... Perhaps she is a titan."

"Perhaps she can only expose your true nature?" Two wooden arms wrapped around his massive neck. "Romasanta..."

"Yes, my love?" Tears rolled down his wolven face, regrets and frustrations echoing in his mind as he soaked in Daphne's cursed form, nothing more than a wooden statue bound to a tree. "What is it?"

"Don't go..." said the whisper in his ear, making his heart thud against his chest. "Don't go. Delphyne is sure to kill you..."

There was a long pause and then with a heavy sigh, he rumbled, "I have to do this, for you and for myself. Remember, *it's not your fault*."

He tore himself from her, tears of sap flowing from her color-less wooden eyes. She didn't try to convince him. They both under-stood what it meant. She had foreseen his death, but he owed her his life and her freedom. As long as Daphne lived a normal life, his death would not be in vain. He had lived for over a thousand years, squandered it off and on through the decades. At least she would be safe. At least she had people by her side if he fell in battle against the mother of dragons. He hoped that his whispers haunted her like her own had done to him so long ago.

***

A flock of birds startled Angeline from her sleep. The fluttering of their wings made the morning light flicker. Flying close to the tree, she could feel the gush of air on her cheeks and hear the air ripple through their feathers. Rubbing her eyes, she sat up, yawning. Her back and hip ached from sleeping in an awkward position nestled in the grooves of the tree root. Light filtering through the canopy made the forest floor glow.

She could continue tracking the Busse now. Barushka had disap-peared from his spot under the tangled roots. She could only assume he had wondered off for food or cool water to drink. Regardless, he would return the moment she called out his name. Dark shadows flashed across her face as more birds burst out from behind another tree in the distance. Again, she caught movement at eye-level and she held her breath.

Eyes wide, the moving branches were in sync with the *skid-skud* sound invading her ears. Her heart fluttered. A realization gripped her; these weren't branches, these were the antlers of the Busse gouging marks into another tree trunk. Like any other stag, he was marking his territory and sharpening the points. The morning sun-light made his fur shimmer like gold, the muscles twitching with the efforts he made to mark the trunk. She could only see a shoulder, but a slight shift would bring him into targeting range. Scooping up her bow, she pulled an arrow from the quiver at her feet. Instincts made the hair on the back of her neck stand on end. She drew the arrow back, the string biting into the tips of her fingers. Every nerve screamed for her to stop, to get her quiver buckled on before letting her arrow fly.

"Shit..." She eased the string back to a resting position, placing the arrow back into the quiver.

Cedric had warned her that a Busse was known for charging at potential threats. Already at a disadvantage, she was unsure of the speed, strength, or the tactical capacity of the beast. Calming herself, she refocused her plan of action and took another look at her opponent. The golden stag's height alone was impressive, at least two stories high. Scanning the beast from its exposed cloven hoof to the shoulder, she took in what information she could gain.

Glaring down from the wooden arch, she measured the impact of the deer charging the root she stood on. The massive creature would be capable of knocking her off the top with ease. If a chimera could shake her off a tree branch at half the size, then the Busse could topple the roots under her feet. Swallowing, her fingers fumbled to buckle the leather straps of her quiver. She struggled with the last clasp, while keeping a steady eye on the raking antlers. From here, they were like two oak trees banging into the side of the archaic black trees of the wood nymphs.

The last buckle slid into place with a clap and the Busse froze. The antlers pulled away from the tree and she held her breath. A flash of gold broke the drab brown and green backdrop of the forest as the colossal beast stepped further into view. He made Barushka feel like a miniature horse at best. The antlers added another ten feet to the length of its head. Dense muscles curved along its legs and body, bulging out like a Charolais bull. The Busse swiveled its enormous deerlike face and neck, ears poised in her direction. Flicking one ear around, he listened for surrounding noises. Plumes of steam puffed out from each nostril as the beast continued to stare.

She remained still as a tree, hoping for the Busse to divert its gaze or shift further into her view. Considering he heard her buckle, he surely could see movement from this distance and without hesitation, would charge towards her. The head spun in the opposite direction, birds speckled the air behind him, calling his attention away. Her lips parted, releasing a suppressed breath. The fletching on the arrow shafts tickled her fingertips as she reached behind her. Pulling an arrow free, she lay it on the resting notch of her bow across the engraved raven's feet.

Taking in another deep inhale, she pulled the bowstring as far back as she could, fingers aching from the tension. Her eyes locked on a spot behind the golden stag's elbow. If she could get an arrow into its chest there, it would pierce the heart and slow the creature down. It will take several hits for a beast that size to bleed to exhaustion. Once the arrow hits its mark, she will be in a struggle to dodge and aim for more vital points. Everything depended on this first shot or the battle would fall in the Busse's favor.

Holding her breath, she raised her aim above her target to compensate for the arrow's fall. The distance was large enough between them, which would give her time to land a second shot if he charged in her direction. At once, she let go of the string and her breath. As the string vibrated, humming in her ear, she watched the arrow snake through the air.

CLACK!

Antlers collided with her line of sight, the shaft of the arrow shattering. Jumping to her feet, she stared at the angry glare of the Busse. With a twitch of muscles, he leapt in her direction with alarming speed. There was no time for a second shot. Dropping onto her belly, she wedged herself into the groove, gripping the roots tight. Her body tensed as she felt the vibrations of the galloping around her. The Busse rammed the archway, sending it tilting. Her feet lost their grip and she found herself dangling. Frantic, searching around, desperate for an escape. A screeching bellow rang out of the Busse's outstretched neck. He backed away, prepping for a second ram. She pulled herself up, hugging her arms around a vining root. There wasn't time for anything else. Vibrations from the hooves reverberated through the root and her arms. Wincing, she prepared for the next smash. Her legs swung violently from the force of the second hit while the root dropped down further. She was low enough for him to attack directly.

CR-CRACK!

Screaming, the root broke away and she found herself falling. The curve in the root sent it swinging, slamming against a nearby colossal-sized trunk. Her arms failed to hold tight as it hit, sending her flying. Midair she balled herself up, preparing for the inevitable slam to the ground. Her right shoulder hit first, another scream ringing out. She bounced, unravelling with each blow. Another smack against the ground sent her left hip ringing in pain.

The world spun around her, body skipping and rolling across the dirt and patches of moss. By the time she stopped, tears were streaming down her face over the amount of pain she felt. Panting, her mind raced to figure out how bad of shape she was in; her right shoulder dislocated, hip and ribs on the left sore, possibly fractured, shins both took a beating, and blood dripped from her bottom lip as her tongue bled. She had bitten it on one of the rolls, but she needed to get up, she needed to move. Her life depended on it.

Why isn't Cedric taking this pain away? Her panic was climbing as she wobbled to her feet. *Is he not allowed to intervene in anyway? C-can I really handle the pain...*

The ground shook under her feet. Turning around she saw the Busse bashing the root she had fallen off of where it lay between them, blocking him. Gripping her shoulder, she searched the ground for her bow. The silver shimmered in a stream of sunlight, calling to her. She ran for it. Tripping, she hit the ground on her bad shoulder. Another gut wrenching scream left her lips, but she was already clamoring back onto her feet. Grabbing up her bow, she twisted and ran for the closest tree to her. Cringing, she pointed her bad shoulder to it. A pop rang in her ears as she slammed her shoulder against the tree. Leaning there on the trunk, she cried, blood dripping down her chin from her bleeding tongue. Her shoulder was in place, her fingers moving, meaning she could still fight. Yanking out the clomp of moss clogging the top of the quiver, she pulled an arrow and aimed it at the Busse. It glared at her through the gap, bellowing at her in rebuttal.

Her fingers opened, the arrow flying, hitting an eye. The Busse screeched in pain, rearing up. In a fit of rage, he lowered his head, shredding at the root away with its antlers. Pulling another arrow, she only had one chance once he busted through. One more hard slam and the root burst apart, pieces falling all around the forest. The heavy thuds were approaching, but all he was showing her was a wall of antler points. She wouldn't be impaled, but torn apart with the amount she saw there. Her side stung as she wheezed, the ginormous stag drawing near. She stood patient, unmoving. As if confused at hearing nothing from her, the Busse looked up to make sure its aim was true. The arrow flew in an instant, hitting its mark within the remaining eye, blinding the stag. She ran for it, weaving as close to the roots and tree trunks. The hooves were becoming staggered as the muscled beast bounced off one tree only to slam into the next.

Panting, the stag stopped running, ears flicking about, searching for her. She too was huffing, her injuries still aching their disapproval. Leaning against a tree trunk, the Busse was in the opening on the other side. She searched her thoughts as what to do next. Climbing was out of the question with her injuries and the animal would hear her. Peering around the trunk, she watched as blood dribbled down its cheeks. She had indeed managed to blind him, but now she needed a better angle to get in a kill shot. Leaning forward, she misjudged her first step and a branch underfoot snapped. The ground quaked under her, making her fall forward. An antler point ripped through the trunk of the tree where she had been seconds before. Scrambling to get away, she managed to stand and look over her shoulder. Had she not fallen forward, she would have been impaled.

Luck was on her side. The antler point was stuck in the tree. She had to hurry if she wanted to take advantage of the Busse's misfortune. Running in a wide circle around her opponent, she aimed to have enough trees between them in case he broke loose. Pulling out another arrow, she aimed behind the elbow and took the shot. The arrow hit its intended mark. Antlers twisted, shattered the tree trunk. Glancing, she realized her arrow stuck into the ribs too far back from the heart. Regardless, her new threat was a tree falling in her direction. Crackling of limbs warned she still wasn't out of harm's way. Her breath and legs were failing her, she was losing speed. Debris fell all around her, a booming sound ringing in her ears. The tree bounced off another tree, it felt as if it were aiming at her!

A flash of blue flames caught her attention, "BARUSHKA!"

He galloped next to her. Tears streamed down her cheeks, she had a chance!

Landing a foot in the stirrup and gripping the saddle tight, she roared, "GO!"

He made a hard turn in direction, dodging between a small break in the trees. She yelped, bark scraping her back and shoulder blades. Clenching her jaw, she looked back. Blue flames were left on the tree on the other side as well. Barushka had taken a hit as well. The falling tree bounced, taking out their escape route and boomed to a stop. A massive gust of wind slammed into them and Barushka turned to shield her. She was clinging to his side. As the wind died down, she pulled herself further onto the saddle, pointing him at the fallen tree. It was like someone had lain a castle wall in the way. The stag's bellow could be heard echoing from the other side.

Chapter 11

Final Test

Cedric was pacing in the darkness. *Something isn't right.* Glaring at the wooden door, marching from one wall to the other, he was growing impatient. Night had passed and they were drawing ever closer to noon. He hadn't felt anything come from Angeline. No emotions, no panic, not even pain or pleasure in the slightest form. His mind kept flashing images of the incantations scrolled on the door and walls on the outside of his cell. Losing his patience, he walked up to the door and pounded it with his fist.

"Dammit, Nyctimus!" His voice echoed through the dark hallway. "Get your ass back down here!"

Glaring out the barred window, he waited, listening. It wasn't long before he heard steps echoing through the hall. A warm glow faded into existence along with a stern looking Nyctimus. They stood glaring at one another for several minutes.

Nyctimus sighed, "I'm here."

"Let me out." Demanded Cedric. "Something isn't right."

"We are waiting for Angeline to finish killing the Busse." He leaned against the wall across from the dungeon door. "As we speak, she's currently attempting to bring it down."

Cedric's heart sped up, anger seeping into his voice. "You want to tell me exactly what this prison is capable of doing?"

"It neutralizes demonic and magical powers. I don't think Kronos knows a spell like this can be cast." His hazel eyes scanned over the archaic writing. "But then again, you have to contain defensive magic like Angeline or I."

The muscles tensed in Cedric cheeks, "So you've blocked my ability to feel her."

"Precisely..." He pulled himself off the wall and looked down the hallway, nodding to someone. "Now starts your test."

"My test? I thought this was my test." Nyctimus put the torch in a nearby holder and started to unbutton his shirt. "Exactly what did you and the old mutt plan?"

"It seems she's already been injured, badly in fact..." He was ignoring him, tossing the shirt into the dead end. "Question is, can you handle the flood of emotions that will slam you when I open this door?"

Cedric backed away, every muscle in his body tight. "What makes you think I can't?"

"You being dragged out of your own bedroom the other night." He retorted, shifting into his wolven form.

Swallowing, excitement was rattling through Cedric. It had been a while since he remembered feeling this anxious. Despite it, there was tiny part of him that feared the reaction of being overwhelmed by Angeline's emotions and injuries. He had used the ability without regards to not being able to turn it off. Had it become an instinctual reaction, a reflex even? The lock was sliding, his muscles aching from the tension he was holding. His eyes locked on to the crack where torch light trickled into the room. An inch further and he gasped. Falling to his knees, he panted. It was more than he had expected. Angeline's injuries rattled through him, the amount and severity of them made his stomach twist, making him nauseous. Fear, panic and anger boiled in from her, making him clutch his chest. She was fighting still, pushing forward despite her condition.

Glaring up, he gave a heated stare at Nyctimus. All her injuries were hindering her fight. Clenching his teeth, he took in her injuries, hoping he could improve her ability to survive. His shoulder began to throb, she had dislocated it and managed to correct it at some point. A smirk crawled across his lips, a sense of pride filling him. Cracked ribs, bruised hip, tongue aching, and his back and shoulder blades felt scraped to hell. The grin grew wider across his face, the sensations telling him she was still in motion despite it all. Her injuries wouldn't be an obstacle thanks to the door opening, allowing their bond to reconnect. Sweat poured over him, but his arousal in feeling her tribulations, the way she pushed herself forward was to blame. She didn't need him to take away the pain, not anymore. Standing back up, shuddering off the initial wall of pain and emotions, he approached Nyctimus.

"Did I pass?" He cooed.

Nyctimus snorted, "Her fight isn't done yet..."

***

Angeline leaned forward in the saddle, moaning. Relief washed over her as the pain shifted into the welcoming pleasure from Cedric. She found herself breathing easier, catching her breath, muscles relaxing. Barushka snorted, antsy as he danced in place. Another shout from the Busse brought her attention back to the task at hand. Thumping was coming from the other side of the wooden wall, the stag ramming the tree to get at her. The muscles in Barushka tightened, her heart fluttering in response. Her test was to kill the monstrous golden stag, not watch it destroy the forest.

Silence fell across the forest. Chills trickled over her, gut tightening. Instincts were on high and Barushka started backing up. Her eyes widened, the golden stag appearing in a flash of gold as he leapt on top of the tree. Another round of snorting and ear flicking, he turned with bleeding eyes. He had found her, racing down, charging in their direction. Barushka turned and started galloping to keep their distance. Her fingers fumbled in the quiver, gripping an arrow. She was being jolted every which way in the saddle, but she still took a shot. It stuck in the upper leg, but did nothing to slow him. The bloodied face on the Busse made the beast more frightening. This was like trying to take out a tank with match sticks!

Again, they weaved in and out of the trees. The stag smashed into the trunks, proving to be the only way to damage and slow the raging animal. Flaps of flesh on its flank and shoulders painted the golden fur red. Barushka circled them around, leading the stag through its own debris. More flesh sliced open, the beast bleeding out more and more, but Barushka was taking on injuries in the attempts to push through the mangled splinters.

Leaning forward, she gave Barushka her order, "Gallop by the fallen tree. I'll hop off there and you lead him into my view."

He snorted, turning his direction. Throwing the bow over her chest, she gripped the saddle tight. Nervous, she raised her feet, squatting on the galloping platform under her. Barushka dodged one last tree, lining himself with the fallen wooden titan. Slowing to a trot, he gave her a better chance to leap off. A limb gave her the chance she needed, grabbing it, her feet dangled as Barushka jolted to a full stride, catching the stag's attention. Struggling, her ribs and injuries were still slowing her despite feeling waves of pleasure. Climbing to the top, she coughed up blood, her tongue the least of her concerns. One of her ribs were cracked and another punctured her lung when she leapt off Barushka. Gritting her teeth, she knew Cedric would be coming at this rate. Pulling the bow off, she readied the shot. Barushka galloped pass her and close behind him was the Busse.

He was close, making the kill spot clear. The arrow flew, hard and true, hitting its mark. A squeal came from the beast, rearing up in response to the arrow sinking deep into its chest. To her horror, the Busse turned, barreling in her direction. She stumbled backwards, but any further and she would fall and surely break her legs from this height. Raising her arms, she prepared for the worst. There was always one more wave of life in a deer when you hit the heart, but this was more than she had prepared for. The stag's front legs buckled, its snout sliding through the dirt. Exhaustion, the bleeding, and the punctured heart had all caught up with the monster.

The antlers, driven by the force and dead weight of the deer, they crashed into the tree. It rolled from the impact and inertia of it all. Panicking, she leapt forward too far, trying to accommodate for the roll, trying not to fall. Her stomach sent her into an orgasmic scream, echoing throughout the forest. Looking to the sky, the shadows of birds freckled her face. Hands reached down to the source, groping at a pointed antler. She was barely able to draw a breath. Reluctant, she let her eyes fall down to where her hands had gone.

One single point of the antlers had impaled her. A rush of warmth grab down her legs, blood spilling forth with the tears rolling from her eyes. Shaking, she felt behind herself, hands crawling cautious around her sides and searching her back. Paling, fingers slapped against the point that had punctured through her body with ease. Blood boiled up her throat, gushing from the sides of her mouth. Clenching her teeth, she fought the urge to cough.

I'm so sorry, Cedric. I wasn't strong enough...

Cold and weak, she allowed herself to slump forward. The only thing holding her up was the antler. Her eyes were growing heavier, the forest darkened in the haze of her eyes. Swallowing, she waited for death, yet she lingered on the edge. If she could hold on, she might be able to be here for Cedric still. Chills ran across her, more tears streaming down her face. She didn't want to see his expression at the near death state he would found her in. Feeling angry with herself, she mustered some strength. Digging her heels into the tree, she pulled herself off the antler. Coughing, blood splattered across her feet. Staggering to the edge, maybe she could get down, get Barushka's help. As she neared the edge, her eyes rolled back. Her body tilted forward and she fell to the ground.

***

Cedric's breath was short and quick. Glaring at Nyctimus, he held his abdomen. She was alive, but the pain told him she had been mortally wounded. There was anger flowing from her through their bond. Standing at the crack in the door, he couldn't get pass Nyctimus. His hazel eyes fell to where he held his stomach and flicked an ear. He turned his head, his other ear perked as if listening to someone out of Cedric's range of hearing.

"Am I done with my test, yet?" Every passing second was adding to his ire. "She's been impaled. How near-death do you want me to allow her to get?"

The ears flattened and he side glanced at Cedric, "She's not human anymore. Both of you need to realize that. We need to confirm she's as impenetrable as her counterpart."

Cedric's fingers gripped the edge of the door, his fangs flashing. "You act like I am in denial about this!"

"Are you?" Nyctimus tilted his head. "Neither of you know what she has become. We all know a battle like this will allow her to realize how far this new body can go."

Cedric yanked the door open and Nyctimus didn't offer up any resistance. Still gripping his stomach, he marched up the steps. There were no signs of Romasanta, which further infuriated him. Kicking open the front castle doors, he made the girls in the stables yelp. Seeing Barushka's stall open, he could breathe a little easier.

At least she didn't go into battle alone.

Snorting, he spit at the ground. Standing tall, shaking off the sensations of her injuries, he focused on himself. With a massive roar of frustration, he let himself shift. Wings spread wide, his tail swishing in anger behind him. The half-succubus girls rushed the doorway to see the King Incubus' in his true form. Their faces flushed, a wave of arousal rippling out from his mass release of power. Cedric was annoyed, at them and at the idea of flying. It was exhausting to fly with such a heavy massive body, but this would be even faster than horseback. One massive flap sent him shockingly high, and as he began to fall, another stroke lunged him even higher.

Cedric's skin prickled, the sweat turning icy in the wind. The trees were green and monotonous as he flew, frantic to find where she could have gone. Angeline's injuries were on fire, tingling across his very being. Swallowing, he knew this sensation well. His fears no longer worried over her dying, but what he would find when he got there. The muscles in his body tensed, preparing for the wave of extreme euphoria that always followed the searing heat. A shudder rolled through him as it started.

She's healed... her injuries gone... power gained... but is she really ok? Will I find her mentally intact when I get there?

Anger took over for the both of them. Waving into one another, he hated himself, he hated Nyctimus for exposing the truth, and he hated Romasanta for the damned test that brought everything into fruition. Sensing her below him, he let himself crash through the branches. Blood filled the air, a mixture of Angeline's and the Busse's. Slamming into the ground like a falling comet, he landed near where the stag lay. Unraveling himself he saw antlers laid across a massive tree trunk. Red sparkled in the sunlight, blood painting one point on the rack of the stag. He followed the massive trail across and down the side of the tree. The smell from it was all Angeline's blood, making him tense his abdomen where he had felt the injury. He shifted back to his human form, looking sorrowful at the stag, its fur golden and crimson. Barushka stood close to the beast's shoulder, turning to him, shaking his head. Frowning in reply, he took in a deep breath and approached slow.

Angeline was sitting there in the moss and wreckage, sobbing, filled with rage. As he came closer, she was hugging her legs, face buried in her thighs. He stood there, his heart thudding in his ears with eyes locked onto the horns crowning her head. It reminded him of antelope horns or even a fairy's. Squatting, his worry hit her and her fear swelled. She tightened her hug on her legs, freezing. The body language told him she didn't want to be seen like this, especially by him. He reached out, gliding his fingers across one of her horns, admiring it with a provocative intrigue. Goosebumps rippled across the skin on her arms in response. A smile crossed his face, a wave of pleasure had echoed from her. His own excitement was devouring her fearful emotions. Gripping the horn, he yanked her head back, making her look up.

Her face mottled, a tear still crawling down her cheek. She yelped, flashing her fangs. A shudder of excitement rattled through him at the sight of them. Her brown eyes stared into his, fear rolling into him from her. He drowned her in arousal, making her gasp. On her breath he sensed the Busse's blood. She had hunted the beast, used its blood and soul to heal, becoming no different than himself. His toothy grin stopped her tears. An animalistic hunger waved out of him and she shivered in its wake. His lips locked onto hers, a ferocious kiss as his tongue dove into her mouth. Humming, he could taste the stag's blood there, adding to the rush of arousal. Pulling away, she gasped to catch her breath.

"How did it taste?" He eyed the eyeless Busse, smiling like a drunk.

She laid down on her back, squeezing her eyes closed. "I-I don't... what am I? I don't know what I am anymore..."

"Does it matter?" Noticing the blood-stained hole in her shirt, his hand slid under the fabric, groping her breast. "You're mine, and that's all I care about."

"C-cedric..." Panting, her senses were heightened, everything hitting her heavier, more sensitive.

With each squeeze, her body flooded with pleasure. Her hand gripped his wrist, unsure whether to push him away or encourage him to be more aggressive. She started to moan and he pulled his hand away. His tongue slide across her neck, intoxicating as his hot breath rolled over her. Nibbling at her ear, his neck and shoulder were warm against her lips. He delighted in tasting her sweat, both of them hungry for one another. Deep inside her soul, the animalistic succubus within her blossomed. Her hands griped at his back, his hand slipping into the front of her pants. In her ear, he hummed in response, easing his fingers inside her. She sucked on his shoulder, her fangs grazing his skin making him shudder. Nails popped through his shirt, digging into his skin, urging him to overpower her.

He whispered into her ear, "I've waited too long for this again, my pet. Take what you want so badly... you can't tell me you've dreamt of it since that first taste..."

Her fangs dug deep into him. His scent, his flavor, far more euphoric than the stag she had eaten in desperation. For once, Cedric was the one moaning, his hand leaving her, gripping the back of her head, pushing her to be more aggressive. Her fangs tightened their hold on his flesh and he indulged in the sound of her gulping. Satisfied with her meal, she licked his shoulder, his knuckles knocking into her newfound horns. Breathless and covered in sweat from losing themselves in a sea of exhilaration and erotic desires, he shoved her down, holding her arms. Having him tower over her, overpowering her ebbed her own wants. A wicked grin spread across his face as he felt it.

"Do you feel better?" Panting, he refused to take her or allow her to go any further. "Are you recovered enough to make it back to the castle?"

Winded, she swallowed back the sensations, "I-I do. Is, is this what it's like to be you?"

He leaned down, whispering in her ear, "It is."

Clouded by want, she pushed past it all as he forced them to ride out their desires aching in their bodies. "It's terrifying... I understand now, on that day..."

"You have no idea how many seconds in a day I fought the sensation back." Satisfied she had come down far enough, he let go of her and stood. "But at least your lust is directed at me, someone who not only can survive it, but desires to feel it flow out of you."

Panting, she was afraid to move. "Can we go back after my horns go away?"

Laughing, he patted Barushka's neck, "In that case, I need to leave you alone. My very presence is only going to keep your arousal on the edge. Why do you think I disappeared so often back in those days?"

She frowned, "And what if..."

"Don't worry about that. We'll find out another time." He started walking away. "Plus, Romasanta's watching."

Her face reddened, her sense of smell moving off of Cedric and catching the wolven musk. "He is... I, I can smell him..."

"You and Barushka head back when you're ready." He chortled, "Unless you want to finish what we started?"

Shaking her head, she pleaded, "No, not with watching eyes..."

Content she was calming down, he turned, heading into the forest. Romasanta would have intervened if he thought she would be killed, but to let her go that far. *Was it necessary to force that side of her out to the open? Doesn't he get that the moment she crosses that line, there's no turning back? It only took that one time in Williamsburg and all my humanity was gone. The slightest thoughts of desire, the faintest memory even, would send my body boiling. I discovered the struggle was overwhelming when I came near others, and especially after feeding. How long will I be able to be the shield between her and the world? She's not half moroi, she's technically succubus and something magical. Will there even be a time she will no longer have to struggle with the curse I placed within her veins?*

"Did we pass?" Cedric looked over his shoulder, Angeline and the Busse were far out of sight. Romasanta had been leaning out of site against a far off tree during the commotion of Angeline's battle. "Or did we fail horribly?"

Romasanta flicked an ear, opening one amber-colored eye in his direction. "You will both be useful. It's quite the relief you both can heal one another with such... vigor."

Cedric leaned his back against the same tree as Romasanta. Huffing, he slid down to the ground, sitting with his shoulders slumped. Weathered from the events, he took this instance of peace to gather his thoughts. Cedric covered his mouth, knotting his brow. His regrets were swallowing his soul. Angeline could never go back, her humanity swallowed down with the blood of the stag along with his own blood alive within her veins.

"You look older than me, pup." Romasanta snorted. "Does this part of her worry you so deeply? Should I be concerned?"

Cedric's voice deepened, lowering to a whisper, "Did you ever regret taking someone's humanity?"

"Even Fenrir would have to answer yes to a question like that." Romasanta's voice lowered, the sorrow echoed between them. "If there was a chance Rhea could have stayed human, we both would have taken it..."

Cedric punched the ground, "It can never stay simple."

"But..." Romasanta was walking past him, pausing to look over his shoulder. "If you asked Rhea, she never regretted a second of the curse or her time with us."

CHAPTER 12

BLOOD TIES

"Tony!" It was the red headed bartender Becca snapping him out of his thoughts. "Are we closing the bar on time or not? You feeling ok?"

Blinking, he had been standing at the register struggling to focus on the task in front of him. Looking at the watch on his left wrist, they were pushing ten minutes before official closing time and he had failed to do last call or even flip the lights on to signal they were closing soon. Rubbing his forehead, he was feverish, sweaty even. Tony handed Becca the receipt he had held hostage for the last fifteen minutes and shuffled to the office. Flipping on the lights, he rolled to lean his back on the wall, feeling breathless under the weight of the sudden illness. Nothing felt the same, physically or even emotionally.

The back of his neck held an addictive sensation where Lillith had touched him. A shudder rocked Tony's shoulders, the tingling as if she were still standing over him, gripping him like you would scruff a dog. Heat surged through his veins, his blood boiling with excitement at the thought. His heartbeat skipped, an obscure sense of excitement washing away the heaviness in his body that had distracted him only a minute before. Smells, sounds, taste, and touch had all grown into something more sensitive, more arousing. Chills scurried across his skin, his shirt soaked from the marathon of sensual uproars. Flustered, he locked the office door, pulling a spare shirt from the desk drawer. Pulling off the wet shirt, he froze. The brisk sensation of naked skin-to-air waved a thrilling vexation through his core. He was panting, terrified moving would add to the sexual enticement. Closing his eyes, he pushed the sensation

98

back and focused on Lillith's handprint on the back of his neck. Dropping the shirt into the drawer, he slid on the dry one, praying it would bring relief.

Unlocking the door, Tony sighed. Before anyone noticed, he had managed to change clothes thanks to the spares he kept on hand. Working a bar left the potential to have some drunk spilling beer on you, a daily job hazard. Taking in a deep inhale, he held it in, walking back out to the fray of closing rituals. Regardless of his attempts to carry on like normal, Becca had asked if he was feeling well multiple times during the remainder of the night. Closing his eyes, sweat was trickling down Tony's spine, sending chills across his body. He shook his head and waved off Becca's concerned looks and questions. Arousing waves from every motion, interaction, and thought added to his panic with the tingling on his neck starting to burn. He kept glancing at the door, at the stools at the bar, wondering when Lillith would be coming back for him. Despite seeing Romasanta's true form, Tony was wishing the old man was there, or even Cedric.

Why did this have to start the moment they left? Was their presence preventing it this whole time? How sure can I be Lillith isn't causing this... she can do this to someone, can't she?

"T-tony?" His condition was not improving, startling the vampress Becca. "Why don't you sit down and I'll finish closing up. You're not looking good at all... the last ones tabbed out, I'll kick them out."

"Thanks..." He huffed.

Flopping on the stool by the office door, Tony leaned back, knocking his head against the wall. Becca started tabbing out everyone, pushing them out the door, insisting they were closing due to an emergency. His jaw muscles tensed overhearing the commotion, but perhaps she was right to tell them that. This wasn't like the flu, he was fighting the unknown. Internally, he was conflicted as to whether or not Lillith helped pull it out or was the only thing keeping it barely under skin surface. Dragging himself off the wall, stumbling into the office, Tony flopped in the chair. Elbows on his desk, he held his head, staring into the empty space between him and the papers scattered there. Again, a wave of heat rushed through him, gripping his soul in a manner he never thought possible.

Tony whispered to himself, "1 and, 2 and, 3 and, 4 and..."

Lillith's mark came to life. The way it both absorbed the boiling sensation yet sent his heart racing was frightening and exhilarating. Each time it hit him, that five second pause before her mark intervened, it became clear she was the shield between him and the darkness drowning him. Closing his eyes, Tony could hear the *cha-ching* of the registers. The last of the patrons paid up and out the door. He could follow Becca's footsteps across the floor, even hear the sticky velcro sound it made in a few spots with the sole of her shoes. The sliding of the lock rang metallic and he felt her sigh from across the building.

Is this what the world is like for them? When Cedric resorted to stabbing himself to relieve himself of his incubine tendencies, was it to overcome this sensation I am drowning in? It's like my soul is being choked by my physical desires, it's painful in that way. As for how it feels, I don't think I've ever has sex that felt this amazing...

"Tony, what's going on with you?" He didn't even flinch at the sudden sound of Becca's voice.

He had sensed her using her unnatural speed to make it back to the office door. The scent of her breath was minty iron, screaming she had snuck a bite of someone's blood at some point tonight and masked it with cheap bubble gum. Her perfume was loud in his nostrils, musky vanilla and sugary. Not exactly his type of scent, but his observations did not stop there. Without even a glance at her, he could tell she was sweating. Grimacing, the taste of it reached his tongue, daring him to grab her up and lick the honey of it off her skin. It was a mixture of a cold fearful sweat and one induced by sexual wants. With each inhale, his body shook with excitement and it took every ounce of his soul to tie him down, to keep him staring into the empty space wtih muscles locked.

Christ, this is insane. Overwhelming and addictive... never in my life could I fathom the sort of struggles Cedric and Lillith...

"Answer me." Becca's breath was hot, even from the doorway.

"Something's wrong. I, I think I'm losing my humanity somehow." The words came out as a disconnected mumble. "If Lillith hadn't been there earlier, I, I don't know who or what would have been here waiting for you..."

After a long pause, Becca's voice was soft as she asked, "Does Cedric know?"

"No. It hit me the moment they left through the portal yesterday." Jerking his head up, Tony locked eyes with her. "C-can you sense things in blood? You're a vampire right? That's something you can do, tell if someone is, isn't human."

Blinking at the question, she smiled. "You are catching on. I can't, but Lisa can. All I can do is tell you the flavor of your blood. It has a sweet flavor because there is some incubus in your lineage, but that's how your kind is, attracts all beings in some shape or form. It's a talent we vampires never seem to master, or at least not to the levels Cedric is capable of performing."

Pondering a moment, Tony asked the next question with no fear. "Does it become sweeter the closer to pure blooded you are? Would Cedric taste better than me on some level?"

The question made Becca stumble on her thoughts for a few seconds. "Why would that matter? This isn't some sort of tasting contest... and I would be scared to even dare sneak a drop of the Vampire Lord's blood... even if he is the Incubus King."

Looking to the desk, Tony scrambled through the two cups of pens. Flustered, he poured their contents across the desk. Finding the letter opener, he started to dig the sharp end into his pointer finger. Wincing, the shocking wave of delight when it sliced through his skin was unnerving.

Will I ever be capable of feeling pain ever again? Is this the sensation Cedric used to satisfy the lustful desires strangling him?

"What are you doing?" She barked.

"Taste this..." Becca's face mottled at the request. "I think, I think I'm changing..."

"C-changing. That's ridiculous. You don't become pure blooded all of a sudden, you have to be that way to begin with." Blood was rolling off the tip of Tony's finger, dripping across the linoleum at their feet. He could feel her excitement as the scent of his blood filled her nose. "But, if you're offering..."

Becca's eyes looked into Tony's as she grabbed his finger. Skin against skin sent his blood racing. Licking her lips, she slid her tongue slow across the puncture mark. A wave of arousal came from her and his body was sent into a raging heat. The sexual undertone of her actions had shoved him off the ledge he had been clinging onto. Lillith's mark struggled to tame it as Becca suckled on his finger, her fangs starting to show, her excitement from the flavor and sensations enticing her to play further.

Sweat covered his body, panting, he jerked his finger from her mouth. One of Becca's fangs caught the side of Tony's finger, slicing it further and he moaned in reaction of the ragged slice. Fear engulfed him. Pain no longer existed, but was overtaken by a sexual sensation spurring his lustful desires further. Breathless, he stared at her, sweat dripping off his chin. She backed herself against the wall, covering her mouth. Fear and confusion written across her face.

"It can't be..." Her voice was hushed by her hands.

Another wave of arousal hit him, Lillith's mark burning the back of his neck turned from pleasure to pain. The bitter sting and bite of it was a warm welcome and he took in the excruciating sensation which poured water on the flames of uncontrollable desire. Gripping the arms of the office chair, he was afraid to let go, afraid to allow himself to move from his anchored prison of choice. The fact Becca had gotten aroused by the taste of his blood had created a drowning wave of want in him. Closing his eyes, he felt himself spiraling out of control, praying secretly Lillith had been close.

Shit, I don't know what will happen. If Becca would leave, just maybe I can get a grip on this. Even with the pain rattling every nerve in my body from Lillith's mark, I am still struggling not to fold under the weight of this want... like I want to fucking tear her to pieces while she moans in delight... I wish Lillith was here... she, she could stop me... she understands what's happening...

"Where are you, Lillith?" Tony breathed.

Claws dug into the back of Tony's neck, his eyes snapping open. He took delight in claws popping into his flesh, the sensation breaking his fascination towards the terrified vampress. In the reflection of Becca's frightened eyes he saw Lillith towering behind him. The very thought and wish of her to be there had brought her to him. He found himself grinning, drunk with the longing to have Lillith overpower him so easily. Becca had become his prey in an instant, he had failed to take in what she had implied when she said, *how your kind is, attracts all beings.* In short, she was telling him he was the top of the food chain in the world of darkness.

"On your knees." Lillith growled, claws digging deeper making him moan, eyes rolling back. "What the fuck did you think would happen, Tony?"

Lillith shoved him out of the chair, his cheek slamming onto the floor with a slap. Becca yelped, shaking and unable to flee. The overall sensation coming from Lillith melted away the uncontrollable want he had been swallowed by. Instead, he was being invaded by her desires with one aggressive touch. Burning, tingling, he felt her power quelling his own, putting everything back in its place as it worked him over. Breathless on the floor, he had no fear from her actions. The smile on his face fell away into a look of relief. His blood no longer boiling through his body, something he had unknowingly started. With every intoxicating wave she pulsed through him, his eyes fell further out of focus. Minutes, maybe an hour, went by and no one dare stir from where they stood, waiting on Tony to come back from his heated moment. Lillith's grip released, but her mark continued to eat away at the last of the incubine sensations inside Tony. Squinting his eyes, he took deep slow breaths, trying to will his beating heart to slow.

"What happened here?" Lillith's heated glare was aimed at Becca.

"H-he asked me to taste his blood, b-but..." Tears were falling from her eyes, her fingers still over her mouth. "I didn't know... I didn't realize something like this could..."

"I see..." Lillith grinned, a dual set of fangs flashing. "Do me a favor, you and Lisa are going to have to help me keep Tony in check. Until I get a chance to figure out whose pulling his strings, I need to make sure he doesn't do stupid shit like this." Lillith dug a heel into his shoulder and he shuddered. "He's far enough into this that pain doesn't exist. Getting hurt, cut, anything can send him spiraling back into a wave of desire..."

"Y-yes ma'am." She chirped. "Exactly why is he less human than before?"

Tony's heart fluttered. He kept silent as he listened to the information, fear quelling the last of the desire in his blood. *This is like Cedric, but it isn't Lillith pulling it out...then who?*

"Someone on my level, maybe even higher, is pulling his demon blood into fruition." She flopped into the office chair, propping her feet onto Tony's back. "Congratulations, Tony, you're not going anywhere unsupervised. I don't care if these two have to drop their panties to get you redirected, we can't let the mystery powerhouse play this out to its full Monty. Once Cedric passes into the spirit realm, I'll have a chance to break this spell. So, the real question is, who is messing with us?"

"Should we tell Cedric?" Becca looked down at Tony with sorrowful eyes. "I never wanted something like this to happen to him."

Scoffing, Lillith glared down at him, her anger unmoving. "No. I stayed behind because I knew about it, smelled the spell a few days ago. Keep this matter silent, those blind buffoons have their own mission to worry about. We're going to be lucky if they make it pass Delphyne in one piece."

"Y-yes ma'am." Becca's hands were trembling as she bowed and left the two of them alone in the office.

Lillith's nails tapped across the desk, her legs a welcomed weight across his back. The linoleum floor was a cool welcome on his face, his body shivering from the air conditioning hitting him. He started to sit up, but she dug a heel in his shoulder and he froze again. Determined to shift, he pulled his arms closer to his head, a hand feeling the back of his neck where she had torn into him. Gulping, his finger found blood, but the wounds were nowhere to be found. Fear exploded from him and she removed her legs. Sitting up on his knees, he glared at her wide-eyed, questioning whether the aggressive claws had ever broken his skin at all.

"You're lucky I didn't snap your neck." She hissed, displeased with him. "This is another perk from what you are becoming."

"What is?" His hand was covered in blood, the scent in his nose declaring it as his own. "Where are the cuts? Am I still bleeding?"

Leaning back in the office chair, she flustered. "Yes, that is your blood. No, the wounds closed in an instant."

"How... how did you get here so fast?" He leaned forward, palms on the floor as he knelt in his reprieve.

"Did you not wish for me to be here?" Tilting her head forward, she lifted an eyebrow. "Did I not hear you demand to know where I was?"

His eyes grew wide, blood smudged on the floor from the event. "But, I only thought those things..."

"Using my name in thought is more than enough to shout for my attention." The office chair squeaked, she stood in front of him, but he dare not look up at his impromptu savior. "Feeling guilty, are we?"

Biting his bottom lip, the muscles in his back tensed. Anger was rising, she was toying with him despite the situation. His fingers curled into his palms, forming fists as the his arms and shoulders twitched with each sour thought burning through him.

Leaning down, her breath fell across his ear and neck like boiling water. "Be careful what thoughts you have of me, I just might hear them."

Clenching his teeth, he let the thought roll across. *Fuck you, Lillith.*

Her lips curled in a devilish manner, her mark tingling at his neck. "Wash up first, we'll discuss the matter back at my place."

CHAPTER 13

THE STONE OF THE ORACLES

The sky was a brilliant gold with brush strokes of dark peach floating above the purple mountain range. Angeline was gripping the wooden rail of the wrought iron balcony taking it all in. They had been there for a few hours, but she was stunned by the view from their room at the *Fedriades Delphi Hotel*. Flying here had been thrilling and frightening. There were so many new things, all made by human hands to learn about and discover. Her heart was racing taking in this new and exotic place called *Greece*. The beauty of the landscape was romantic with the setting sun deepening to match the terracotta tiles of the buildings. Behind her, Cedric was coming through the door. Their eyes met and her face flushed. Since the Busse, those sharp green eyes had softened their edge and it frightened her.

His eyes fell away from her, a look of guilt written across his face. "We leave at midnight for the *Temple of Athena Pronoia*."

Turning away, she swallowed her thoughts back down, "I-it's so beautiful here."

Cedric wrapped his arms around her tight, pulling her into him. "Then I'll bring you back here after this is done..."

They leaned into one another's warmth watching the last slither of sunlight fade. The stars twinkled into existence in the deep purple that hideaway the mountains. One by one, the windows on the buildings came to life, their golden color competing with the luminosity of the stars. A breeze caressed them both as they enjoyed a chance for a peaceful embrace. Angeline leaned her head against his chest, enjoying the subtle rise and fall of each breath he took. Her hair flipped up, tickling his nose. His arms tightened around her. Smiling to himself, he took in her scent. Despite everything, including the passing of time, it still reminded him of their first time meeting. A weight hit him, his smile fading as his thoughts wandered back in time, *If only it had been a memory more like this moment here and now.*

Knock-knock-knock!

"We're ready." Romasanta's voice grumbled through the door. "We'll be outside."

Sighing, Cedric let go of her, grabbing up his sheath from the bed. "Are you sure you want to come?"

"Absolutely." She turned and followed him back into the room, her brown eyes fierce.

A smile crept back across his face, watching her pull on the black turtleneck over her white tank top. She was sliding the leather tunic on top, but it was catching her shirt and she was having a hard time pulling it down. Pausing, he walked over and yanked it down and on, making her yelp. He managed another squeak from her as he pulled the lacing tight and she sighed in defeat. Finishing sliding on his own leather tunic, he buckled on his sheath that held the silver sword of Boreas. She had finished strapping on her quiver and was securing the thigh-high knife holder over her jeans. The intense look on her face was exciting, reminiscent of his last hours with her. Once again, side-by-side, they would be facing the dangers of a world, going to war against beasts. Her cheeks reddened at the wave of arousal that slipped through, but willed herself to stay focused. They grabbed up the packs of supplies, nodding to one other.

Romasanta and Nyctimus were outside as promised, waiting in the shadows of the nearby buildings. The walk to the tourist site was silent and long. It was pivotal they waited to speak until they got through the barrier or at least far enough from the security guards who patrolled the archaeological site. Cedric was using the ability he absorbed from his grandfather Vladimir. As long as they moved in a tight unit, he was able to mask them in the shadows and limit confrontation with anyone unnecessary. In fact, the skill was handy enough it would even allow them to slide pass most inferior demons and beasts, but he was limited to the length of time he could hold that state. They were flawless traversing the site, the maps readily available for tourists had served their purpose well in their favor.

Snaking past several security guards wielding large auto rifles, they went unnoticed despite the lights setup across the pathways and buildings. They were drawing closer to the location where the Sibyl Stone sat, and thankfully, the amount of guards dwindling. Next to the ivy covered rock was what little stood of the *Athenian Treasury*, three walls with no roof and a two columned entrance. It was all they needed to duck out of view of the guards and prep themselves for entering the barrier. They huddled together, squatting against the wall closest to the Sibyl stone. Romasanta and Nyctimus started setting down their packs. Rummaging through his, Romasanta found the wooden and silver box Daphne had created to keep the Eye of Gaea from being detected. Gripping Cedric's wrist he forced the box into his hand.

"What are you doing?" Cedric looked at him baffled. "Why are you handing this cursed thing to me? Especially since you didn't want me here to start with."

"But I trust you. You are as strong as I am, but I plan on going through that barrier first with Nyctimus." He glanced at Angeline and back to Cedric. "And it's already your job to protect what is mine, pup."

Gripping the box tight, he yanked his wrist free of Romasanta's grasp, scoffing. "What's yours... consider this a favor out of mutual respect. As for the other, I do that regardless of your involvement, old mutt."

"Stop your bickering." Nyctimus sighed. "Angeline, stand guard for us."

She nodded, trading spots with him, she squatted between the wall and column scanning for any signs of movement nearby. "Where is the entrance?"

"It's the Sibyl stone." Romasanta gave a hard glare at Cedric. "Don't make me regret…"

"Isn't this the *Sanctuary of Apollo*?" Cedric smirked, changing the subject. "I am pretty sure the tourists were jabbering they paid tribute to you here in this building back in the day."

Romasanta frowned. Annoyed with him for acknowledging a name he failed to keep secret in their latest meeting, he turned his back to Cedric. Nyctimus was smirking over the fact Cedric, for once, bested Romasanta in conversation. Nyctimus and Romasanta unbuttoned and dropped their shirts to the ground. They had no intentions of being in human form for the trip, both thrilled to run as a pack again in centuries. Winking at his hazel-eyed friend, Romasanta unbuckled his pants and let them fall to his ankles, leaving him nude. He heard Cedric groan and scoot closer to Angeline to watch for guards, earning chuckle from Nyctimus. Shivers sent Romasanta's shoulders shuddering, the night air cooling so quick that even their breaths were visible just beyond their lips. Inhaling deep, he recalled Badbh's instructions within his mind.

She had helped him with the research of at least how to get there and where they were going. There was no telling what monsters they would face before reaching the summit where the mother of dragons, Delphyne , guarded the Oracle. They did know Mt. Parnassus would appear far larger, wilder with a forest taller and thicker than what they saw here. The odds of humans living within the barrier was slim, but running into Wyverns and dragon-like beasts would be inevitable. After much digging, it was decided they should be able to place a hand on the Sibyl Stone and state *We have Gaea's Blessing to see the Oracle*. With being tasked with returning her eye, the oracle the only gateway in, it should invoke a response. If it failed, he would have to attempt to use his gate opening for the

Black Forest to force the Sibyl stone to let them into Delphyne's own barrier.

"Are you two ready?" Romasanta turned to look at the stone within view just above Cedric and Angeline's head. "You remember the phrase in case I get through, correct?"

"Yes. Badbh made it cl..." Angeline's face paled and she shift back to the stone. "Why are you two always naked at such bizarre moments?"

Laughing, Nyctimus answered, "When you've spent more time as an animal than as a man, clothes are no longer a necessity in life."

Still grinning, Nyctimus' face distorted into a large golden brown wolf head. The way his exposed toothy grin shift from human into fangs inside long jaws was nightmarish. Despite it all, she had to accept these two men had lived like this long before her time, long before even Cedric's time. Two wolven forms flew out from between the columns to her right, approaching the Sibyl stone. Amber and hazel glowing eyes gave them one more look before they placed their claws on the ivy covered boulder. At first it seemed like nothing was happening. Romasanta's ears flattened, he went to pull his hand away, but the sudden jerk in his shoulders said he was stuck. Pricking his ear's forward, his golden eyes wide, tugging again, he couldn't break his palm from the stone. Nyctimus was also caught, with added leverage of a back foot on the stone, still he couldn't break the hold.

A humming and rattling sound was coming from Cedric's bag. Reaching in, the box holding the Eye of Gaea was hot and glowing red. The color was bright despite the box still being sealed. Romasanta's eyes locked onto the box in Cedric's hands. The last time the stone glowed in that manner, Fenrir's soul had been burnt into his chest. Flashes of Fenrir being sucked into the stone, Daphne transforming, all sent his nerves on end; nothing good happened when the stone came to life. Freezing, his mind raced as to what it all meant, what curse would befall him yet again. His heart pounded in his ears, his chest aching where Merlin had scorched his very soul. Growling, he struggled to clear his head, shaking it free of his fears.

"Cedric!" He barked, the urgency in his roar sent chills across Cedric. "Grab Angeline! Both stones are the key!"

Swallowing, he snatched Angeline's wrist, dragging her behind him. Slamming her hand against the Sibyl Stone, it began to match the hum and vibration of the box in Cedric's other hand. Looking to Romasanta, he gave a nod.

"I guess we're all going through at the same time, then." Smacking his palm beside Angeline's, the boulder began to glow red, the vibration rising.

The light intensified, blinding them to the ruins they were standing in. Shouts from security guards and an alarm were sounding off, but they were now tied to the stone of the Oracles, the Sibyl stone. Tensing, they awaited the barrage of bullets in the depths of the light that kept their eyes tight. The humming from the boulder drowned out everything, the wooden box hot in Cedric's hand. Grinding his teeth, he refused to let go as it began to burn his flesh. Cedric's stomach knotted, the sensation reminiscent to the time Merlin's magic melted through his finger was resurfacing. He tightened his hold, feeling the sizzling and bubbling of his skin against the wood like sausage on a frying pan. Sweat dripped from his chin, but this was their key, the whole reason why they were taking on such a dangerous mission. The pressure in the air around them shifted, eardrums popping as the light dispersed. Cedric was panting, opening his eyes in an instant to make sure Angeline's own hand was still there next to his on the Sibyl stone. It was still night time, but there was no mistake her hand was there.

"C-cedric..." Tears were in her eyes and he looked to his hand holding the Eye of Gaea.

Stunned, he paled to see she had reached out at some point and gripped the box to keep him from dropping it. "W-why..."

His fingers had been charred and worse, if she hadn't taken on the task with him, he would have lost the stone while traversing the barrier. They slid to the ground, the flesh on their hands glued to the wooden box and to each other. Each breeze, each movement made the both of them wince, sweat trickling down their faces. Romasanta and Nyctimus had turned their focus to their surroundings first, not realizing the severity of their state. This was not the place they had left. The Sibyl Stone was no different, but the temple devoted to Apollo looked as if it were well kept with offerings laid across its steps. Flicking an ear, he nodded for Nyctimus to go check the inside. Looking up to Mt. Parnassus, it was hard to make out through the large dense forest, the trees towering high like redwoods. What his eyes could see was the orange glow of a fire and a larger temple at the summit. It was a match to the images sketched in the books Badbh had shared with him.

"It's clear." Nyctimus' voice was low and soft on his return from the building. "Can you two move?"

"Yes." Cedric answered for them both, eyeing Angeline who panted with dull eyes.

With the burning heat of the stone no longer present, the pain they had encountered was gone. Instead, orgasmic waves pulsed through them, intensified by the gruesome melted grip on the box. Cedric was having a hard time pulling away the intoxication of the lusting starting to build within her. Angeline's eyes starting to roll back as she moaned with each pull. Breathless from the weight of the incubine bond, he managed to give a startled expression to Romasanta. Muscles in the old wolf visibly tightened in response. Wrapping an arm around her waist, he and Cedric rushed into the temple. Dropping her by the light of the brazier burning inside, Romasanta stumbled back from the two figures towering over him.

These were not the statues of Apollo found on the outside of the barrier. At the back wall of the temple, surrounded by another assortment of offerings, howled two large statues. Black marble reflected the flames reaching up and out of the brazier, hitting the eyes of both statues making their eyes glow as golden as Romasanta's own. One was a monstrous wolf and the other an exact replica of himself in human form. Looking across their base, wine, flowers, sacrificed game, fruit and more laid across the floor in dedication to the black figures. His fur ruffled, his eyes wide as his chest rose and fell ever quicker. Cedric realized this was the first time he had ever seen panic strike the old werewolf. Angeline moaned again, panting as her freehand gripped his shoulder.

Cedric was losing her. "Dammit, I hate to do something this drastic, but we don't have much time."

"Romasanta... Romasanta?" Nyctimus' voice couldn't reach him at first. "What's wrong, Romasanta?"

"This, this place..." Shaking his head and shoulders, Romasanta peered around the room. "Is there anything written here..."

Nyctimus' eyes widened, "Not inside, but in the ruins in *Delphi*, something had been written on the outside. It could be the same for here."

"Romasanta, wait!" Cedric's horns were pulled out, his voice desperate. "You're going to have to cut the box out."

"W-what?" Nyctimus' ears flattened.

Cedric pulled out Boreas' sword, offering the hilt to Romasanta with a dangerous look in his eyes. "Doesn't matter how much you take off of our arms, just take this fucking box back and whatever you do, don't come in here. I told you there were consequences to pushing her over the edge..."

Romasanta's lip curled, snarling as he took the sword. "Nyctimus, grab the box. Once we do this we're going to be targeted if we don't leave immediately. You want the sword to stay?"

A bone chilling grin crawled across Cedric's face, wild and animalistic. "Fuck your sword. This is why she's mine, and mine alone."

Snorting, Romasanta held the sword high, a stonewalled look on his wolven face. Looking to Nyctimus, he grabbed the box, ready to dash away. With elegant skill, the sword slid through their forearms. Angeline's back arched, a blood curdling scream erupting out of her, but Cedric was pushing her to the ground, crushing her under his weight. Nyctimus had beaten Romasanta out of the temple, box and dangling arms in hand. Stifling to a stop between the columns, Romasanta turned, the sword still in hand wet and dripping with their blood. Angeline was still screaming as Cedric held his remaining forearm across her chest. Her fingers dug into his shoulder, blood snaking down her arm from the depth her claws were digging into his flesh.

Cedric had let himself transform, using his wings to hold himself in place where he sat across her thighs. The leather tunic and shirt ripping apart, unable to adapt to the increased muscle mass and new appendages. His tail was wrapping around her shins, he had successfully detained her. Romasanta's ears flattened, a sense of pity for both of them stirring at his core. Angeline's horns had returned, but the savage aura coming from her was far from what he had seen in the forest. Cedric's expression hid behind the hair covering most of his face, besides the clenched fangs. Stunned by the events unfolding in the temple, a smell of salt interrupted the blood his canine nose had observed. Tears fell from Cedric's hidden eyes, tearing apart Romasanta's own soul as he dare not watch any longer.

Joining Nyctimus on the south side of the temple, he gave him a grave expression. "There are far worse fates than our own..."

Swallowing, Nyctimus nodded at the temple wall, handing the box back to Romasanta. "You were right, something is written here. I can't help but think it's a message for you."

Romasanta ripped the box free of the burnt fresh still clinging to it. "What does it say?"

"*Dýo psychés , éna sóma...* it's Greek." Turning from the inscription, he locked eyes with Romasanta. "*Two souls, one body.* What do you think it means?"

"It means they know who I am, and worse, knew I would be coming." Angeline's screams had stopped, but he dare not see for himself what travesty Cedric had to commit to quell the savagery that took hold of her. "Let's scout the parameter. I have a feeling we've been in this forest before, Nyctimus."

Sighing, he nodded. "I was wondering if you were smelling that sense of nostalgia, from that time when we first became comrades."

***

She had stopped screaming, but the succubine blood inside her was pulling him into her lustful rage. Euphoria like no other had resonated through both of them, an endless sea of ripples causing more within each other. The last time he came this close to the edge was his fight with Lillith. He was pushing back his sexual desires, afraid in this state one of them would regret the demonic tendencies it brought to the surface. Swallowing, the arousal between them was powerful enough that they had both recovered their arms up to their wrists. The efficiency of sexual desire that fueled the healing of a succubus and incubus was frightening, yet sufficient. Her fingers pulled free of his shoulder, her eyes wild and scared. She smudged his own blood across his face, taking a tear into her fingers. A savage grin crept across her face as she licked it, her eyes diving deep into the terrified green ones staring down upon his own curse. His tail was still wrapped firmly around her shins, but he let himself sit up, relieving his arm off her chest. He sat on top of her, straddling her thighs, his mind lost seeing a reflection of his own inner demons.

Her hair clung to her flushed face drenched in sweat, the fever burning through her veins. The desire from her hadn't lightened. He knew there was nothing he could do, but to accept each wave and attempt to not let his own excitement respond. She leaned into his chest, her tongue sliding from the top of his abdomen up between his pectoral muscles, sending his heart racing. Every part of him ached to return the erotic delight, to join in the exchange of euphoric behavior, but he had to make her come back. Her lips were like hot silk as they crawled to his neck, making his eyes roll back against his will. The weight of her lust flowing into him was drowning his soul. This was his curse swallowing up the woman he loved, nothing enjoyable would come from reciprocating her playful suckling. Her fangs pressed against his skin. Alarmed, he gripped her hair, yanking her head away before she could finish the action she started.

"I thought you couldn't wait..." His ire hit her eyes and she faltered.

"You know nothing about what happens when you feed in this state." He hissed. "If you knew how this wretched curse worked, you'd have your hand back as well..."

He let go and she realized he had used the missing hand to rip her away. Looking to her own hand, all she had recovered was her palm. Fingerless, the site of it brought her lust down further. A sigh of relief left his lips as a ripple of fear broke the resonance, ending the escalation. Tears were streaming down her face, her body trembling under him. The realization of her new inner demons had reached the woman he loved. His tail let her go and he wrapped her in his arms. Choking sobs and screams of frustration flooded out of her. Her face pressed ever harder against his aching chest, tears like hot oil against his skin. He could feel her fingers grasping as his back, and he smiled.

Perhaps her lust was only one part of the way her magic and my curse heals her body. If we can just get through this...

"I'm so sorry!" She shook her head, gasping to catch her breath. "I don't know... I just felt..."

He shushed her, "I am very aware of how you felt." Pulling her away, he looked into the softer, gentler eyes he knew well. "I thought you said you wouldn't cry anymore, my pet."

She opened her lips to plead with him, but his lips met hers.

Pulling away, feeling her shivering had stopped, he whispered, "Sorry Romasanta cut off your sleeve and ruined your shirt."

Flopping her forehead on his shoulder, she managed to laugh a little. He sighed, her horns had vanished, the struggle to keep her in control ending at last. Standing to their feet, he yanked away what was left of the leather tunic and shirt clinging on his hip. It was a shame he had lost it so soon after coming through the barrier. Stepping outside of the temple, fog was creeping across the forest floor. Morning was approaching and they found no signs of Nyctimus or Romasanta. Huffing, they walked back inside grabbing up their supplies once more. Angeline was tight lipped, pale from her encounter with the lusting she had witnessed from Cedric when they first travelled together.

Gripping her arm, he swung her around, placing a familiar hilt in her hands. "Here. I think you know how to use this."

Blinking, she looked down at the chimeran horn hilt and black blade of the dagger he had given her. "I, I thought I lost this..."

Smiling, he gave her a wink. They walked back out, ready to make their way to the summit. Romasanta and Nyctimus were back, the fog thicker than before. The sky began to fade from blue to lavender through the canopy of the trees. They seemed tense, both having their fur standing up, razor-backed from the top of their wolven heads all the way down between their shoulders.

Turning to face them, Romasanta shuddered. "This barrier apparently opens and closes at various locations in the world throughout time. Besides the temple, there's a rusted car smashed into a tree to the west and worse, parts of this forest are from a time when Nyctimus and I ran together as a pack."

"Should I take this as bad or good news?" scoffed Cedric.

"Bad. It means they knew we were coming." Nyctimus snorted, looking to the summit. "I think they set that trap to take the stone when we crossed over. It worked out you two were able to hang on to it."

Both Cedric and Angeline dropped their eyes to the ground, not feeling comforted by the fact.

"H-HELP!" A man's shout echoed out from the fog in the shadows of the tree.

They froze, all looking to one another unsure.

"Please! HELP!" It echoed out to them.

"You guys checked the parameter already, right?" Cedric flicked his fingers and Romasanta tossed the sword back to him. "So there was no chance a security guard got sucked in."

"Exactly." Nyctimus dropped to all fours, his nose twitching. "We had no scent trail for humans... so it must be a mimick dog."

"Mimick dog?" Angeline started to pull her bow off as she stared into the fog looking for any signs of movement.

"It has a lot of names; black dog, devil dog, mauthe dhoog." answered Cedric. "It's a lot tamer, easier to kill than the hellhound."

Taking in a deep breath, Angeline drew back her bow, prepared. Laughter started echoing through the fog from several directions. A pack of mimick dogs had located them and taunted them in the safety of the shadows. Without another word, Romasanta and Nyctimus broke into a full stride, disappearing into the rolling white clouds between the trees. Yelps rang out, smashing and crackling sounding out. A peach color was trickling through the trees, making the fog look more elusive. A shadow shifted in Angeline's peripheral. She turned, smooth and graceful, without a second to waste, she let her arrow fly. A squeal erupted and a black shaggy beast of a dog fell to its side, dead with an arrow through its neck. Growling burst from behind her, but Cedric had countered the lunge.

Teeth gnashed on the silver blade. Scruffing the canine, he threw it back into the fog where the sounds of the werewolves' carnage still continued. Another mimick dog came around the corner of the temple, and again, Angeline took it down in one hit. Growling from behind made Cedric spin on his heel. Leaping off the top of the Sibyl stone, another was attacking and Cedric lunged forward. The sword impaling the dog's chest, sizzling at the flesh. He twisted his arms, the point of the blade falling downward to allow the dead beast to slide off. Turning back around, his newly made forearm landed in the jaws of another dog. Cursing under his breath, he drove the sword through its neck, wrenching the annoyance off.

Angeline squeaked in surprise. A mimick dog flew out of the fog before she could pull another arrow. Her hand yanked the chimeran dagger, she braced herself. Foam dripped from its jowls as it stopped short. The black shaggy fur damp from the morning dew still did nothing to shrink the size and power it held. Nyctimus' brown head exploded out of the fog, jaws clamping down on its back and midsection. Violent shaking ensued, the mimick dog shrieking as it's body began to rip apart. A gasp escaped Angeline, catching the sense of pleasure Nyctimus took in shaking his prey before dragging the broken corpse back into the fog. Sweat trickled down the side of her face, she could feel the immense joy radiating from both Romasanta and Nyctimus.

Her thoughts wheeled, *all this time, Cedric could feel moments from others like this?*

Cedric grabbed her shoulder, "I think that's the last of them."

"Did I just feel..." Her heart was fluttering.

"Another odd thing about being like this. If anyone around us takes extreme pleasure in anything, we feel it." Sighing, he flopped to the ground, huffing over his arm. "They'll be out of the fog as soon as their done eating."

"E-eating?" Stammering, she was too afraid to let go of the hilt of the dagger.

Cedric's green eyes cut through the fog with ease. "You can't tell me you don't feel how thrilled they feel eating raw flesh?"

Swallowing, she looked to the unknown where the waves of joy filtered from. "When you faced Lillith, even Boto... was this weight far worse to bare?"

"What does it feel like when I slam you with my own arousal?"

"Like my soul is drowning..." she whispered.

"In battle against another incubus or succubus, it's a hundred times heavier than that."

Silence fell between them as they patiently waited for the wolves to finish their meal.

CHAPTER 14

GYPSY'S CURSE

With each passing week, Tony was growing more irritated with his situation. He was struggling with a terminal illness, or at least that's how it was starting to feel. The feverish waves were sending his body into a heat so strong that sweat dripped from his chin. Worse, it was becoming more frequent despite avoiding contact and isolating himself as much as possible. He was leaning over his desk, hiding in the back office of *The Lion's Den*. Lillith had forced Lisa and Becca to be his personal guards, humiliating to acknowledge. Every night, one or both of them would walk him home. He would pace his bedroom floor as they sat in his living room, the entire situation awkward. The unease he saw in their eyes and body language told him this was something even demons found unsettling. Another arousing wave hit him, and he counted. Those five seconds before Lillith's mark reacted were agonizing.

A knock on the office door made him flinch. "Yea?"

"It's Lisa, I just wanted to make sure you're ok?" He huffed as she spoke through the safety of the door. "We haven't opened yet and you're still having trouble. Why don't you go home, Tony?"

He pounded a frustrated fist on the desk. Thoughts whirled in his mind, decisions and questions warring one another. Another punch against the desk sent shivers of delight as the wood cracked and his knuckles began to bleed.

Anger gripped him and he demanded, "One of you take me to Lillith's."

The door jerked open, "You what?"

Glaring at Lisa, he commanded, "Take me to Lillith."

Looking her in the eye, she nodded in agreement. She motioned for him to sit there and wait a minute while she gathered her things. Opening the desk drawer, he grabbed his keys up and headed out of the office. Becca winced at the sight of him, her eyes dodging away. All this week she had avoided being alone with him, which told him the curse was getting more aggressive. Worse, he had managed to frighten her from the small incident at the start of his struggles. Lisa was gathering her purse, her face taut with worry.

"Here." He handed Lisa the clump of keys.

"What are these for?" She gave him a befuddled expression. "You can't be serious?"

"Someone has to keep this place running." He started for the door, his frown deepening. "It's clear I can't be near this many people at this rate."

Lisa chased after him as he slid out the door. Her high heels clicking on the sidewalk were racing to keep up with his urgent pace. He knew the way, but he was too afraid to know what would happen if he lost control like he did with Becca. If anyone could keep him in line, it was Lillith. He stopped in front of her apartment building. Looking up at the dizzying height of the building, swallowing back his hesitation once more. He tightened his fists, trying to will his heart to slow down as chills rippled across his skin. A bead of sweat trickled down the divot of his spine, doubt creeping forward in his mind, mocking his efforts and resolve.

"Do you know which floor it is?" Lisa's voice was soft and tender. "Come on, I'll get you there."

She opened the door and he marched in, struggling with his thoughts. The elevator doors slid closed and it began its ascension. Lisa had put herself in the opposite corner. Not too long ago they had toyed with him, breaking glasses on a whim so that he would cut his hand. Granted, Romasanta and Cedric showed up and it came to a screeching stop. Her eyes shifted, looking at him from the corners as if a mouse eyeing the cat in the room. He dodged his eyes away, unsure how he should be translating her behavior, the new tense body language and desperation to keep out of his reach.

"Are incubus really that frightening?" Tony refused to look at her expression, fearful he would not be able to shake it from his memory. "I would think a vampire would see them as inferior..."

"If I were to answer this in honest..." She paused, choosing her words carefully. "Incubus tend to lose who they are to the whims of their thirst for pleasure on a physical level. They are strong, their powers animalistic and they are able to persuade demons in higher ranks."

"R-ranks?" It was the first time any of them had revealed there was more to this world full of demons and mythical beings. "There's some sort of order?"

A smile came across her lips and she giggled, "Let's just say I am on the lower side of this pyramid. Consider yourself lucky, Tony. You've managed to befriend the top ranks we all are afraid to even approach."

"Then who is at the top?" The elevator slowed to a stop, a soft bell ringing as it opened.

Lisa motioned for him to get off, waiting for him to step pass the elevator door threshold. "And I'll leave you in the care of the top of that pyramid."

He turned, the doors shutting with her waving farewell.

Rushing for the closed doors, his heart was pounding in his ears. He was officially in over his head. Turning around, he leaned his back against the cold metal, staring down the hall and into the apartment. The sun beamed into the far wall of windows that looked out over the city. Taking in a deep inhale, he willed himself to walk into the apartment. He made it to the room at the far end of the hallway from the elevator. Blinking, he admired the contemporary styled living room which had the square footage of his entire apartment. Wandering deeper into the room, no one seemed to be there, let alone recently. Sighing, he walked to the windowed wall, marveling over the city from so high up. The sun's heat radiated through the glass, warming his face.

"Well, I see we've decided to move in with the rest of the lot..." Lillith's voice made his body jolt.

"That wasn't my intentions." He turned, blushing to see her in nothing more than a towel wrapped around her. "I-I didn't mean to intrude..."

She laughed as he turned back to stare out the window. "Come now, you can't be that shy?"

"It's not like you invited me over." He flustered. "But, I am having a hard time being anywhere else. I, I think I'm losing control."

"Is that so?" He caught her reflection in the glass and she smiled. "So your babysitters brought you here then?"

"No. I demanded to be brought here." She let the towel go and he darted his eyes elsewhere out the window. "You seem to be the only one not terrified of me."

"Well, give me a moment to dress and we'll discuss uncovering who did this." Looking over his shoulder, he watched her naked backside slip down the side hallway.

He sighed, breathing again. Pacing the floor, his mind wondered who had placed the curse on him. There had to be a hint, something he failed to notice. *Was it before I met them? Was it after?*

"So..." Again, her voice startled him as she stood there wearing a man's white button up blouse and not much else. "Let's run through the details, shall we?"

"I suppose asking you to put on more clothes would be pointless..." Huffing, he allowed himself to sit on the couch. "So, you were saying, details?"

"Thinking things over, whoever cast this spell came before we did." She walked to the window, drying her hair in the towel as droplets fell across the tile. "So I need you to really think about a time before we came here, when someone said something so bizarre then, but makes sense now. You have to understand, you have to touch a person, or look them in the eyes and say the curse with the weight of magic and desire behind you. If they had approached after we found you, we would've noticed... maybe they knew we would be coming for you even..."

"Huh?" He leaned forward, his elbows on his knees. "Is there a special phrasing or some clue to what I am trying to recall?"

Lillith paused, looking over her shoulder she replied, "They would have needed to know your name and invoke a curse that regarded your bloodline. Perhaps even heritage... something along the lines of bringing your demon blood into focus."

Leaning back on the couch, he flopped his head back and searched his mind. "That's a little more detailed than I was hoping for..."

"Curses are no light matter." He heard her bare feet slapping against the tile, heading back to the bedroom as she spoke, "Whoever it was, was very aware they would be receiving a recoil causing a duplicate curse of sorts."

"Recoil?" Covering his face, he thought long and hard. "Why would someone risk a recoil over someone insignificant as me? I'm just a small fry, no different than the humans around me. Or used to be..."

"Oh?" She giggled, staring at him from the hallway, brushing her hair. "Did we finally decide which we were?"

He raised his hand and flicked her the middle finger.

Scoffing, she turned on her heels, "I'm going to go brush my hair."

With her gone, no more distractions were left to pull him away from his thoughts. This person had to touch him, say something off the wall in regards to what he was before he had even known. He had no clue of the blood ties he held, so when did someone bring it up before. Up until recently, he had no clue he was different from all the people he walked passed, served drinks to, and even shared the crowded subway rides with. He had run into plenty of weirdos in his life before Romasanta, before Cedric. Religious fanatics, desperate homeless, and even the few nights where he had to deal with people high on some illegal drug. How many did he walk out of the bars he worked in? Could it have been one of those?

Shaking his head, he walked himself backwards, his head pounding from the effort. From one blurry memory to the next, all people who said something, things he had forgotten and no longer visible. His heart fluttered as his mind raced further back. It was the first day on shift at *Rusty's* when he met someone mysterious, someone there for a few drinks. She had sat in silence, face hidden under her hoodie. Squeezing his eyes tighter, he clung to it, his stomach knotting. This had to be the moment it happened. She asked for her tab, he went to hand her change when she gripped his wrist tight. He could never forget those fierce eyes, one green and one brown. Her lips cold as she hissed, '*I hope your bloodline turns on you when you are at your most vulnerable moment!*' It was unwarranted, she let go, walked out and he never saw her again. She had left him there, shocked and confused, still holding her change.

"LILLITH!" He flew off the couch, racing down the hallway where she waited, leaning on the bathroom door frame brushing her hair. "It was a woman! She, she had one green and one brown eye and she made a comment about, about my bloodline turning on me. I think it was her."

"One brown and one green eye?" She blinked, and then she frowned. "Why on earth would she show up and pull a stunt like that?"

"Y-you know her?" The look she shot him quelled any chance he had at redemption. What hope had surged up was shattered.

"She's a phantom if you ask me. One that meddles in the lives of demons and is clearly a witch serving Gaea's whim." She slammed the hair brush down on the marble vanity. "The bigger questions is what need does she have for her own bloodline to turn on her. Exactly *who* is she referring to..."

"So, that means there's no way to undo this..." Tony turned away, holding the back of his neck where the mark she left tingled.

"No, but we will have a small window of opportunity to cast a far more powerful spell. The question is, do you want to become a demon under your own terms or until you eventually lose to this curse." His hand tightened on his neck as he remained silent. "Tony, you don't have to decide now, but I'll ask only once when that time comes."

Unable to respond, he sighed in frustration.

"Until then, you are right to have come here." She brushed pass him, making him shudder. "At least here I can use my ability to keep you tamer than what you were feeling in the office or at home. The room at the end of the other hallway is taken by Cedric. If you follow the hall back to the elevator and around it is a mirrored side of this apartment. There should be two rooms to choose from there. For now, I'll be doing a search for the phantom gypsy."

"Gypsy?" He blinked.

"Yes." She was digging through her purse on the couch, the shirt barely covering the top of her thighs. "She's the bitch that sent Romasanta on a wild rampage once."

"Romasanta?" Images of the infamous stone-faced behemoth shaped man flashed in Tony's mind. "I imagine that's a rather hard thing to do..."

"I can't tell you how many people he ate..." She was dumping the contents out across the couch, frantic. "Where is my cell phone... shit."

"A-ate?" A shuddered rattled through him. "He ate people?"

Standing tall, she placed her hands on her hips. "We've all eaten people at some point, I suppose."

"Wait, what?" She turned, brushing against him again, but he gripped her arm. "You're joking, right?"

Looking down at where he gripped her hand, she frowned. "Either you're an idiot or brave as hell. No one ever grips me like the way you do."

His eyes fell to his own hand and he released her. "S-sorry... Your phone, I think it's on the vanity."

Lifting an eyebrow, she smirked. "I'll make a call... see if we can get more information."

"Thank you..." He mumbled, watching her march down the hall once more.

CHAPTER 15

WYVERNS

"I didn't think the summit was this far off." Cedric wiped the sweat from his forehead. "Are we at least getting closer?"

"We are, but inside Delphyne's barrier, time and distance is skewed." Nyctimus shook the heat from his fur. "But having you two on foot is slowing us down."

"I'm so sorry." Angeline was leaning on her knees, trying to catch her breath from hiking up such a steep hillside for the last three miles. "If only Barushka was here..."

Cedric looked over his shoulder at her then back to Nyctimus. "You think a shag foal has the power to get through?"

His ears perked, "Call him and see. He's proven to be able to sneak into the Black Forest, then again, we don't consider him hostile."

Taking in a deep breath, Cedric let out one long ear-shattering whistle. It echoed through the trees, a pack of mimick dogs howling in response someplace else on the mountain side. They waited, listening for any signs of Barushka and his flames. Galloping came from the brush beside them, all of them turning in its direction. Cedric gripped his sword, not sure what would be bursting through. Romasanta's bulk busted through the underbrush, sliding to a stop, he gave the group an annoyed glare. He had been making his rounds, scouting ahead as well as trying to identify something that had been following them since they left the temple.

"Was it necessary to reveal our location to the entire forest?" Everyone bowed their heads, avoiding eye contact with the enraged Romasanta. "Don't just stand there, RUN!"

Confusion crossed Cedric's face as he gripped Angeline's wrist and bolted further up the hill side. There was no time to question why the old man had made it so urgent, but something would be coming to see what had screeched so loud across the serene landscape. Cedric eyed Nyctimus, as if blaming him for being incorrigible to his own mistakes in judgment. Angeline was whimpering barely keeping up. Her foot slipped. Yelping, her shin bashed against the rocks. Inside his own leg, he could tell it hit hard enough to fracture the bone. Clenching her jaw, she kept quiet rolling so she could see the damage. Romasanta and Nyctimus had paused just ahead, her blood making their noses twitch.

"Pick her up and get moving." Growled Romasanta, fur prickling outward. "A wyvern's nose can be just as good as mine."

Down below, trees where cracking and a grumbling groan made the air shake. Without further hesitation, Cedric lunged her over his shoulder and bounded after Romasanta and Nyctimus. Wyverns weren't small, and like their dragon cousins, just as difficult to kill. As they reached the next plateau, turning sharply to run parallel to the summit above them, they saw the trees falling in the small field where they stood minutes before. Exposing the wyvern, it was crawling about like a winged snake. The tongue flickered, frantic to catch their scent. Cedric swallowed as it snapped its head toward where she had fallen. With one flap of its winged arms, it landed on top of where her blood still shimmered on the rocks. Snorting and licking at the blood, it rattled its entire body, scales clattering. Like a wolf howling at the moon, it screamed out into the air. Goosebumps ran across Cedric's skin. There wasn't just one, but several replies in every direction. This was a hunting pack of wyverns and they were on the menu.

"Shit, there's more than one in the area." Cedric looked to Romasanta, hoping for a plan.

"I was planning to avoid fighting any of them, but then some buffoon whistled for a horse that may never show!" He barked over his shoulder, his amber eyes burning with rage. "Nyctimus and I will split off, you keep straight. Let's hope we can split the pack."

Romasanta shot up and between the trees while Nyctimus dove down the hillside into the underbrush. Angeline's hands were clinging to his belt afraid she would slip off his shoulder. Biting her lip, blood from her shin splattered hot against his belly, leaving a trail across the ground. With those two gone, they could try to heal her, but he was gaining more speed with her on his shoulder than when she was on foot solo. Hugging her thighs tighter, he pushed himself to run faster. He could fly them away, but a Wyvern would spot him in an instant. They were keen in both sight and smell, making them the lions of the beast world. Unlike dragons, they could not speak nor were they as clever. If they had faced just one with all four of them, they could win, but a pack this large would set them back with injuries for a while.

Looking back to where they started from, the wyvern was gone. Frantic, he eyed around him, praying it had gone after the others. Turning his focus to in front of him, the path was going to force him to travel high or low. The wyvern had come from below, and Romasanta was on higher ground, so he dashed through the trees. A tree limb smacked Angeline across the butt, making her tense. He grinned, relieved she was staying calm though a wave of panic still resonated from her. As he twisted and turned through the trees and brush, he was met by an even steeper ledge. Stopping, he swallowed, catching his breath. He let her back on her feet, rolling his aching shoulder. Staring up, he was gauging if they would be able to even climb the wall. She had kneeled, assessing the rip in her jeans. The wound had stopped bleeding, shrunk some, but it still ached.

"W-what should I do?" She looked up, her brown eyes knowing she couldn't continue in this state.

Leaning down, he grabbed the hilt of the Chimeran blade and cut deep across the under part of his forearm. Her eyes widened, gripping her own arm that had once had a scar across it in that very spot. She grimaced at the bleeding wound, but his eyes urged her to drink. Trembling, her eyes shut tight, she ran her tongue across it. He shuddered in delight, his eyes watching her shin as it closed and the aching reflected in his own stopped. Her fangs scraped his skin and he pulled away. She wiped the blood from her mouth, unable to meet his eyes. Placing the knife back in her sheath, he motioned for her to start climbing. Rocks crumbled underfoot, finding a solid footing was proving difficult. His aim was to get them one more level higher than the wyvern who had her scent. The sun was still high in the sky, its heat draining their energy with each passing minute.

Relief sighed out of his lips seeing Angeline hit the ledge just above him. She pulled herself over and leaned over to see if he was safe. With her out of the way, he could start climbing in his own way. Claws out, he smashed them into the weak rocks and clay that made up the cliff side. He was beating her pace by threefold. Two thirds up, the ground shook and he slid down about halfway. Staring down, a wyvern came crashing out of the trees, smashing into the cliff wall. The rocks he had been gripping onto broke loose. As he fell backwards, Angeline screamed, her fear waving through him adding to his ire. Pulling the sword from its sheath, he barely made the swing in time. It glanced the side of the wyvern's snout, saving him from its fangs. Slamming into the ground at its feet, the wind was knocked from him. Wheezing, he had landed on his back, rocks raining down on him and the beast.

The wyvern's black eyes pulled away from him and to the top of the cliff. It's tongue flickered wildly, the nostrils inhaling deep. Wings opening, rearing up on its two legs, he realized it was after Angeline, her blood had enticed. Kneeling, he swung with all his strength, the blade ripping deep into the backside of an ankle. The weight of the monster was too much for the injury and it fell onto its side, landing on top of him. Scales dug hard into his shoulder, his forearm against the rocky ground trying to keep his head from being crushed. The beast's screeches, sent his heart racing. At this rate, another one would show up.

Rage consumed him, the sword lost under the massive body of the wyvern, he would have to default to using his powers. Roaring in frustration, he felt a wave of arousal come from Angeline and he faltered in fully letting out his incubine blood. Ever since the night in the temple, her own blood didn't take much to be stirred into a lusting. Instead, he had agreed to no longer take her pain away. Worse, he had forgotten the weight another incubus or succubus could have on one who was on the verge of being overwhelmed. He wasn't Lillith and he had no such ability to pull away those sensations.

The wyvern shifted, a snout wiggling under. It was counting on weighing him down so it could confirm he was dead. Teeth snapped closer, the heat of the wyvern's breath added to the stench of the animals it had eaten. Cornered, he had to think fast. Blood dripped across his face from his arm. Eyes widening, the wyvern was seeking him out by smell. A malicious grin came to him, smudging his blood across the scales above his head, urging his wound to bleed. The tongue flickered out at him, tickling across his arm. The snout pulled away, the body crushing him intensifying. With all his strength he shoved himself further under the beast as the snout lunged forward once more. He let the body drop, the spot painted red in front of the snarling fangs latched on. The weight on him pushed the wind from him, but he grinned knowing the screeching meant he had managed to trick the wyvern into biting itself. Screaming, the wyvern rolled off of him, a gouge in its snakelike belly.

The silver sword flashed in the sunlight and he ran for it. Gripping it up, he took a high leap, digging it into one wing, ripping it open, rendering it useless. If Angeline made it out alive, that's all that mattered. The wyvern's tail swung around, slamming him across his midsection. He thudded hard against the cliff, rocks trickling down on him. Blood was crawling down across one eye, his chest and back scratched and bruised from the rocks and impacts. Opening one eye, the wyvern licked its wound, hissing at him once it realized he was still alive. It slithered closer, but flinched as an arrow ripped through its other wing. Looking above, Angeline stood at the cliff's edge, aiming to take advantage.

Angeline readied another arrow. Cedric wasn't moving, though he at least had his sword in hand again. Letting the arrow fly, it missed. The Wyvern snapped its jaws, snatching the arrow from the air before it hit its mark. Cursing under her breath, she didn't let it discourage her and reached for another arrow. She was drawing its attention, hoping to buy Cedric time to think of a counter attack. Again, the Wyvern blocked, screeching and hissing at her. Raising one wing between them, the wyvern cut off her ability to aim for its face. She paced the ledge, looking for any opening she could. Her arrows bounced off the scales, rendering any direct attacks useless. The wyvern was turning its attention back to Cedric, ignoring her arrows.

Everyone froze as screeching vibrated through the air from all around. More wyverns were coming to join the fight. Angeline turned to face the trees behind her, trees splitting open as two black eyes rushed out at her. A forked tongue and snapping fangs sent her racing backwards, her last step finding no ground. Her arms wobbled out, a last effort to regain her balance. Sour and bitter air slammed her, sending her over, falling backwards.

"ANGELINE!" Without a second to lose, his wings burst to life.

Another Wyvern came around the injured one, aiming where he was backed against the rocky wall. Slamming his sword between its nostrils, it was enough to clamp its jaws shut. With a well-placed foot between its eyes, he launched himself up. Angeline slammed into his arms. Wings flapping, he redirected himself with a kick off the cliff wall, missing the wyvern's lunge from the top of the ledge. He aimed to get above the cliff and wyverns, howls from Romasanta and Nyctimus from below let him know they had worked their way up the summit. A shimmer of blue caught his eye and he nosedived for the trees. Two of the wyverns still had the ability to fly and they were screeching, enraged, not willing to crash through the branches as Cedric had done.

They slammed to the ground, beaten and torn from the feat, he was struggling to stand up. Angeline had been flung from his arms, rolling until she slammed into a tree. She was scrambling to her feet, ignoring her injuries. Running, she slapped against him, hugging onto him.

"It took you.. long enough." Cedric panted, pulling her off and spinning her around. "Where were you, Barushka?"

Steam billowed out of Barushka's nostrils, blue flames growing bright even under the light of the sun. Wyverns were clawing and digging through the tree tops above them. Cedric stumbled towards Barushka, but he reared, pawing at the air. Stunned, Cedric and Angeline stumbled back as the flames exploded wider. The trees all around them were set aflame and he continued neighing and snorting. Clinging to one another, they marveled over the blaze he set, catching trees and anything else it touched in its heat. Screams rang out from the wyverns from above, the flames sending the wyverns into a retreat. Trotting in a circle around them, he looked like a mama bear protecting its cubs. Content there was no longer any danger, the flames vanished in an instant. Charred trees and scorched ground was all that remained of the wildfire that had been there. Bobbing his head, Barushka praised himself in being a valuable warrior. After his mini march, he nuzzled Angeline as if apologizing for being so late.

"What the hell sort of magic was that?" Nyctimus came bursting through the brush, Romasanta not far behind. "B-Barushka!"

"I guess we forgot the best weapon we had against wyverns." Cedric managed to smile, eyes rolling back, collapsing at the feet of the werewolves.

"Shit, we'll have to camp." Romasanta's nose twitched. "Come, there's a cave not far. We'll have Barushka carry him."

"H-how are we going to take down a dragon..." Angeline whispered, not expecting an answer.

"By the grace of Gaea, I hope." Muttered Romasanta as he slumped Cedric over Barushka. "But to hold up solo against one wyvern was impressive."

"There were three." She corrected, watching Romasanta secure Cedric to the saddle.

Nyctimus' ears flicked. "Yes, but he only fought one. Imagine if he had attempted to fight all three..."

Angeline fell silent, following obediently behind Barushka.

***

Cedric was healing slow from the severity of his injuries caused by being bashed against scaly muscles and rock-laden earth. It didn't help neither he nor Angeline were willing to tempt fate to speed up his recovery by other means. Internal bleeding, broken bones, muscles and tendons torn asunder. If he had been a mortal man, he would have been dead. Wheezing on the cave floor, Angeline curled herself in the nook of his chest and arm. Both had been asleep for hours, the sun long gone from the sky.

Barushka paced outside the cave entrance where Romasanta and Nyctimus sat pondering. Wyverns had proven how ill prepared they were for the fight against Delphyne, an actual dragon. They had double backed to the scene of Cedric's battle, picking up dropped gear and supplies, including Angeline's bow. There was no room to leave any of it behind, every piece of weaponry they had needed to be accounted for and on hand. Nerves were rattled at the ease in which everything went to hell.

"Do you think he was too distracted by the girl?" Nyctimus broke the silence.

A heavy sigh left Romasanta's chest before he answered in defeat, "Yes."

Huffing out his large nostrils, Nyctimus flattened his ears. "You think the Wyverns was enough to correct it?"

"I hope..." Romasanta flicked an ear. "At least with the shag foal here with us, we can deter the wyverns from getting close again. We can't afford for any of us being caught in a fight with even one of them. If it had been you or I, healing would have set us back a week rather than a day like those two. Incubus blood is indeed tenacious."

Barushka stopped, snorting and bobbing his head.

A toothy grin came across Romasanta's wolven face. "I know, I should have taken you with me back in those days in my sister's village. Forgive me for not seeing you as a fellow warrior."

Chuckling, Romasanta watched as another bob of Barushka's head replied to his remarks. Satisfied with the recognition, he continued his restless pacing.

"Do you miss him?" Nyctimus fell to the ground on his back, staring through the canopy of the forest at the few stars peeking through the leaves.

"Fenrir?" His ears flattened as Nyctimus' side glance confirmed who he had meant. "We shared this body for so long, I still feel like part of me went missing..."

Nyctimus watched Romasanta rub his chest where the stone had merged them so long ago. "Honestly, I miss him too."

Ears pricking forward, he gave him a skeptical look. "It's not like he directly communed with you. He was funny like that. Only growing attached to me, and Rhea, of course."

"Still," sighed Nyctimus, "Hearing you talk to him, it was clear to me that I could never achieve the friendship that a man and wolven god had achieved. And, oddly enough, I was ok with that."

Romasanta snorted, "Did I really talk that much with him out loud?"

Nyctimus laughed, raising to his feet. "From my perspective, the two of you never seemed to shut up, the Farmer and the Wolf."

They laughed, memories of all the times he was caught talking out loud to Fenrir flashing across both their minds. Satisfied Barushka would be able to stand guard, the two of them went racing through the trees, determined to check the parameter yet again. Blood rushing through their veins, excitement vibrating through them. It was freeing to run as a pack, allowing their wolven nature to have its way for a change. Running the outskirts of where they camped had proven effective for pushing back the mimick dogs.

After their initial feast on the first pack when they arrived, the mimick dogs had become terrified of being eaten by the two massive werewolves. Wyverns were keeping their distance, fearful of the strange fire that could lash out at them without warning. Unlike the fire drakes that lived in swampy areas, wyverns were vulnerable to fire and other elements. If Angeline had managed to master any magical abilities, much like the Lykoan clan from Romasanta's human days, she could have easily subdued all three or pushed them back.

They were racing through the area behind the cave, Romasanta's nose twitching as a scent revealed itself. Sliding to a stop, he stood, drawing in the air slow and deep through his nose. Nyctimus caught up to him, panting on all fours with his own nose twitching. There was something following them still, but no signs other than a faint smell on the breeze flowing down the mountain. It was some sort of dragon, not wyvern and much smaller. There were no signs of what it could have been. Nothing revealed itself under the glare of their wolven eyes. Whatever this thing was, it was keeping a safe distance from them and hadn't made any aggressive moves toward them. Perhaps they were avoiding an unnecessary fight. Snorting, Romasanta was satisfied there was no danger just yet and headed for a small clearing. He needed to gauge the distance left before they reached the temple on the summit.

The temple was more visible from where they stood. From where he stood, he could count the columns lining the one side. A massive fire burned within, an eerie orange glow wavering from within its open air walls. It was a beacon in the night, as if luring them ever closer to their inevitable end. Still, there were no signs of the massive dragon the tomes had adorned across their pages. Romasanta shuddered. According to all the sketches, Delphyne was so large she would roost on top of the temple, overseeing all who travelled through her land. Everything here was accurate with the information Badbh had gathered for them, except that one element. His fur began to prickle and he shook it down again, his anxiety trying to take its hold. The barrier was still up, stronger than his own, which meant she was here hidden from view.

"If Aitvaras could pose as a cat, what do you think Delphyne can disguise herself as?" Romasanta rolled his shoulder, his unease making him tense as he looked over to Nyctimus. "You think she could pass for human?"

Nyctimus scratched his cheek a moment, "I think you have a point. Honestly, all top tier demons have a means to be seen as human, don't they? Hell, we're cursed humans. Lillith has to be roughly the same age as Delphyne... it's a definite yes if you ask me."

Romasanta glared back to the orange glow on the summit. "We don't know what or who the Oracle is, besides the assumption of being a human girl. I assume it's someone like Daphne or my sister Artemis, gifted in foretelling the future. We will have to be cautious we don't mix up the two once we approach."

"The last person I knew who could do that was... Rhea." Nyctimus' canine face frowned as his brow knotted. "You don't think..."

Turning his back to Nyctimus, his fur ruffled at the thought. "There will be hell to pay if it is, but I know of one other, a gypsy girl with one green and one brown eye. Out of all of them, she truly sees the future in such detail that it's unnatural."

"Is she the one..." The golden glare shot over his shoulder stopped Nyctimus' tongue in its tracks. "I see."

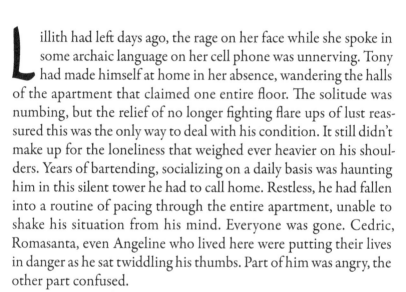

Chapter 16

Resolve

L illith had left days ago, the rage on her face while she spoke in some archaic language on her cell phone was unnerving. Tony had made himself at home in her absence, wandering the halls of the apartment that claimed one entire floor. The solitude was numbing, but the relief of no longer fighting flare ups of lust reassured this was the only way to deal with his condition. It still didn't make up for the loneliness that weighed ever heavier on his shoulders. Years of bartending, socializing on a daily basis was haunting him in this silent tower he had to call home. Restless, he had fallen into a routine of pacing through the entire apartment, unable to shake his situation from his mind. Everyone was gone. Cedric, Romasanta, even Angeline who lived here were putting their lives in danger as he sat twiddling his thumbs. Part of him was angry, the other part confused.

On occasion his cell phone would ring and he would trip over himself to answer it. Every time he found himself disappointed. It was only Lisa calling to update him on the bar or ask what to do about something dealing with inventory or the registers. Time flowed forward, agonizing as the wall clock tick-tocked through hours, minutes and seconds, day after day, with no word from Lillith.

His footsteps echoed off the walls and ceiling, the slapping of bare feet on tile, but all he heard was that one soul gripping question, *do you want to become a demon under your own terms?* Anxiety tightened its grip in his chest. Marching down one hall then the next, winding himself around until he found himself in the kitchen, yet again. He had made this merry-go-round trip at least five times this morning. Feeling defeated, he leaned on the kitchen island, palms flat on the cool counter. Staring down at the glossy black marble, he glared at himself. His throat tightened with the weight of his nightmare, his heart racing. Thoughts were trying to grasp at everything, entangling panic with anger deep down in his soul. Compared to those in his life, he felt powerless. They were off fighting dragons and he was failing to win the fight against his inner demon.

Even if I become a demon on my own terms, exactly what happens to me? This person staring at his reflection, this person who used to be a man, where does he go? How much will I be sacrificing if I say yes...

His chest ached and he pulled away from the counter. Fears devoured by his frustrating rage. Peering up at the shelves, he spotted the large bottles of vodka. Pulling one down, he popped the top as he marched to the living room. He was desperate to relieve himself of the thoughts still haunting him since Lillith left. Flopping onto the couch he took down a hard swig, squinting as he urged himself to keep going, drowning out his nerves.

The sun had been up for a few hours, but he had given up on tracking the hours, and soon, the days. He was depressed, and worse, a prisoner to a curse no one understood the purpose in which it was intended for. They all knew there was a recoil, so why risk one involving one's bloodline? Huffing, his throat and belly burned with the liquor as he stared out at the skyline before him, a shade of peach and soft yellow the morning often brought.

How is Lillith planning to turn me into a full blown incubus? And why does she have to wait? There has to be something in this for her. Then again, who cares? If this thing is going to eat my soul, I'd rather for someone I know to have it... and out of all the non-humans I know, deep down, part of me would rather have Lillith be the one responsible for my leash.

Another hard long gulp of the vodka seared the sour resolve in his mind and heart. If he ended up as someone else, at least leaving it in Lillith's hands seemed more promising than the mysterious woman whose pissed off everyone he knew and trusted. Capping the vodka off, he pulled himself off the couch, leaving it there. Dragging his feet, shoulders slumped, he made his way to the bathroom. Taking a deep breath, he glared at his reflection with disdain. He hadn't showered once since he came there, his chin scruffy and his green eyes tired. Sleep had eluded him, but perhaps he could drink himself to a peaceful round of slumber after a fresh shower. Flustered, he pulled his shirt off, making a face as he caught a whiff of himself. Cranking the shower knob, he was eager to get the water warmed up and to rinse his sulking filth away.

Steam rolled away from the stream of water and he let his pants fall to the ground, diving under the showerhead. Slamming the glass door shut, the water beat between his shoulder blades. Leaning against the tiles, the water melted away his tension as he took in slow steady breaths. Looking upward, the water slammed across his face, washing away the smell of vodka and grime. Spinning around, he leaned against the wall of the showerhead, watching the water swirl down the drain between his feet. Mesmerized, lost in his own mind, he sighed.

Life as I know it will never be the same. And here I thought owning a bar for demons was a drastic change. Maybe I will feel like I have a purpose in all this, other than a backdoor key to an island I thought was a fairy tale.

The tiles were icy against his forehead. Tingling pulsed at the back of his neck and he grunted, annoyed. It was as if Lillith was checking in on him. He hadn't felt any overwhelming waves of desire, but several times during the day he would feel her touch and it would send shivers across his spine. He slammed the shower off, feeling drained. Grabbing up the towel, he wrapped it around his waist and marched for the living room, aiming to drink more in hopes of passing out. Water dripped across the floor as he came out of the hallway where he stumbled to a stop. Lillith was sitting on the couch, drinking from the bottle of vodka staring out the window as if lost. Her face was stern and he realized this situation was weighing heavy on her mind too. Part of him felt relieved seeing it written there. Continuing into the living room, he flopped next to her on the couch and she promptly handed over the vodka so he could join in the drinking.

"I decided I wanted to do this on my terms." Taking a swig, he handed her the bottle back. "If you can do it, I rather it happen with you in control."

"Good." She took another gulp before continuing. "Because it was either you let me, or I forced it myself. Either way, I wasn't going to hand you over to the Gypsy's curse. Something about it doesn't sit well with me..."

"Thanks, I think." Grabbing the bottle back, he finished the last of the vodka. "So, do we do this thing now? This whole turning me?"

Lillith pulled herself off the couch, walking to the window, her back to him. "We wait until Cedric and Romasanta start the next stage of their journey. Until then, we have to keep you under control. If you are going to become full blooded, I might as well give you the best circumstances any of us would take..."

"R-right." He looked longingly at the empty bottle. "Exactly what will you do to me? How does this work?"

"Don't worry about it. It's something you've done before, if your that worried about it." Turning around, she gave him a grave look. "I have a feeling you'll know when the opportunity is primed. The key is for you to make sure your heart and soul are without a doubt devoted to this. Not everyone gets an opportunity like this one..."

He groaned, "Why is everything so cryptic with you?"

"Because not telling you greenhorns everything is far easier to deal with than watching you all act like scurrying ants over the small details." Her voice brought his eyes to hers and she smiled. "If you want to know, then I'll give you a hint."

He lifted an eyebrow. "A hint?"

She laughed, marching across the room, her heels clacking in his ears to the rhythm of his heartbeat. Before he could flinch, she had leaned in, her lips locking onto his own. A thrilling arousal filled him and he began to kiss her back. Her tongue teased his own and pulled away before he could give chase. He found himself breathless as he watched her walk away and disappear down the hall. Never had he felt so exhilarated from a kiss and it made his heart ache that he couldn't see her face.

How much of that moment was truly heartfelt or was she toying with me?

Looking down at the empty bottle, he huffed. Standing, he decided to hunt out another bottle and take it to bed with him. Nothing more would happen, not with her mark tingling at his neck and him struggling to swallow down the wave of desire that had been spurred to life.

Am I going to be able to govern myself against this drowning desire when the day comes to embrace this demon I will become...

CHAPTER 17

THE JAVELIN

Aching injuries woke Cedric and he found his arm caught under a still sleeping Angeline. His lungs stung as he failed to take in a deep breath. Coughing for a moment, he was healing slow. He was annoyed, passing out before having a chance to heal himself proper was a setback. Still, Barushka had saved them. Looking around, he realized they were lying in a cave. The smell of ashes made him turn his head in time to watch the last of the glowing ambers of the fire crumble. It had done its job and kept them warm. Bright sunlight was pouring into the cave's opening, but they were left alone to recover. If he knew Romasanta, he would be scouting ahead and they wouldn't be going anywhere without him fully recovered.

Squeezing his eyes closed, Cedric mumbled curses under his breath. He had let Angeline distract him more than once in the fight against the wyvern and his injuries were proof of that fact. Pounding an angry fist on the cave floor did nothing to relieve the tension building across his entire body. He had made several mistakes. Too much time had passed since he had fought any sort of beast. His last several hunts had happened centuries ago against feral vampires and eventually earning his position in their hierarchy as final judge and jury. Compared to Vladimir and Elisabeth Bathory, all the new issues had been easy to defeat. But, this was a dragon. Most were gone by the time he came into existence.

Delphyne would be a hundred times stronger than a pack of wyverns. And even with four against one, chances are it'll end with one of us not breathing.

Flinching at the movement against his arm, Angeline nuzzled tighter against his ribs and he sighed. Regrets were eating away at him. He should have been strong enough to take one wyvern down by himself. Chances were when they face Delphyne, Angeline would have to endure being mortally wounded and he wouldn't be able to acknowledge it until the dragon fell dead. Rolling onto his side, he slid his arm out from under her head, letting her cheek fall softly to the ground. Sliding his fingers across her other cheek, he pulled short strands of her hair back exposing her face. His heart swelled taking in the peaceful look on her face, his jaw tensing from his thoughts. During this whole mission she hadn't been plagued with the nightmares that haunted her in the safety of the apartment.

Here inside Delphyne's barrier, it feels like we are picking up where we left off. She has new confidence in her fighting, but as for me, this unknown element inside her has changed how I have been treating her. I'm tired of tiptoeing, I'm tired of seeing her as someone new. I want our life together to be where we left off too, my Angel. But can I really afford to let your emotions drown me?

His hand slid across her jawline and neck, pushing her hair up and away. Her neck reflected in his eyes, delicate and bare. A wicked smile came across his face, nostalgia and ancient wants rushing back to him. She was his Lady, his elixir that made him complete at his weakest moments.

It's time that I reclaim who I am. You're mine, pet, in every way possible and I want to taste the thing you have become.

Fangs pulling forward, goosebumps trickled across his skin as he leaned in nuzzling her neck. Running his tongue across her skin, he enjoyed the wave of arousal that stirred inside her dreams. Inhaling, ignoring the pain in his chest, he took in the rise and fall of her scent, both salty and sweet from her natural perfume. Indulging in the fact she was still asleep, he playfully suckled at her neck, making her wiggle under him. Another wave of excitement flowed out of her, her hand grabbing the back of his head. Satisfied he had brought her to the verge of waking, he dug his fangs hard and deep into her neck. A wave of elation escaped him as he felt the familiar pop of skin breaking under the sharpness of his canines.

A scream from her lips was muffled by his palm and he tightened his bite. Keeping the weight of his own body on top of her, he was enjoying how she squirmed under him. He could feel her breathing under him, his other hand gripping her thigh to assure her it was indeed him. Biting harder, letting the heat of her blood boil up into his mouth, he rolled it on his tongue savoring the flavor. His mouth full, he took his first gulp. A shudder shook his shoulders and he paused. The flavor was sweeter than he recalled, but the magic was so much stronger than he remembered in the days when his own life depended on it for survival. Her magic was awake, and its flavor, its power more addictive than he ever thought imaginable.

Her fingers tangled in his hair, panting from the euphoria echoing between them through their bond. The emotions flooding him told him she had yearned for this moment, this ritual they had created during the medieval age of men. Curious by its taste, how her blood rolled deeper into his stomach, he took another long slow gulp. She hummed, her skin prickling, encouraging him to linger there. His lips pressing hard against her neck, suckling with tender affection despite the harsh tearing of fangs against flesh. Euphoria resonating between them, their bond feeling closer than it had ever been before. Wounds were healing, burning as the magic reached them and steaming in the cool air of the cave. She moaned, encouraging him to continue to drink more, but he pulled away.

Sorry, my love, I have achieved what I aimed to get from you for now...

Rolling onto his back, he felt the hot trickle of her blood run down the side of his mouth and cheek. He could hear her breathing, rapid and short. Raising his hand in view, just the two swallows had done far more healing than anything else he had ever killed. Even more thrilling, was he could feel an abnormal gain in power. If he was still struggling with his powers like when he last fed from her, he would have lost himself to the intoxicating flavor of it all. With the thudding of his heart in his ears, he covered his face with his palms, riding out the buzzed sensation fogging his mind. The magic from her was still pulsing through his veins, disorienting his mind and body. His head was spinning with a mixture of fears, excitement, and curiosity while her arousal started fading. After several minutes, she caught her breath, shifting to cuddle with him again.

"Is, is something wrong?" A wave of fear from her made him pull his hands away from his face.

"Nothing's wrong." His green eyes peered over at her, a toothy grin on his face. "In fact, I think we've found ourselves again, finally."

Rubbing her neck, sore and cold, she sighed. "I missed fighting beside you... being your pillar for healing. After so long, this is what I had already accepted as my fate."

Kissing the top of her head, he sighed, "We better gather our things. There's still a lot of ground to cover and now we have Barushka."

Nodding, they both pulled themselves onto their feet. Their gear had been repacked, waiting for them off to the side of the fire. Another shudder shook his shoulders, his body unnaturally light and he watched as she buckled her quiver on. Her magic was still tickling his taste buds and swallowing his concern, he marched past her to wait alongside Barushka and Nyctimus. Turning to face him, Nyctimus squinted his eyes as his nose twitched.

"Shouldn't you at least clean your mouth before Romasanta returns." He snorted, a clawed finger pointing to his own face where Angeline's blood had painted his cheek. "So, did you learn anything?"

Scowling, he wiped his face clean. "Yea... her magic is active."

Nyctimus' eyes widened, staring down as his own hand. "I wonder then..."

Furrowing his brow, Cedric scoffed, "Wonder about what?"

"Nothing." He shot him a toothy grin as if he received a childish secret. "I'll be able to figure it out in time at least."

"The longer you're alive the more you speak in circles old man." Cedric petted Barushka on the neck as Angeline walked out of the cave. "Let's not waste any more time."

***

There was about a day's walk left of the forest before they would find themselves in the open air of the mountain's summit. The sun was fading and Romasanta grunted, looking back at where Cedric and Angeline sat on Barushka. This would be their last chance to rest under some cover. Barushka sidled, his feet stomping the forest floor and ears folding back, listening to something from behind them. Romasanta and Nyctimus flicked their ears forward searching for the sounds that had unnerved the large shag foal. Somewhere in the trees the sound of claws against wood scraped ever closer behind them. Nose twitching, there was no mistaking the scent as the one Romasanta had picked up on by the cave weeks ago. It was on their heels, a sense of aggression in the scent this time. Romasanta rolled his shoulder, his body eager to give chase. Nodding to one another, Cedric watched the two werewolves split off, racing into the forest in opposite directions.

"Stay on Barushka." Whispered Cedric to Angeline, leaving the saddle.

"What is it?" Angeline was pulling her bow off over her head, ready to take any action needed. "Is it going to attack finally?"

"I think so, but..." Cedric stopped, listening and peering up into the trees. "I think we're not its target."

Angeline looked up, towards the direction Romasanta had ran to see bark and leaves twisting their way to the ground. "Romasanta is its target then."

Turning to catch the flurry of debris, he crossed his arms. "We'll wait here for the time being. The old man can handle this."

She shifted in the saddle, "Are you sure?"

He frowned, leaning against a tree. "Don't forget I still haven't beaten him in a fight, yet."

The weight of Romasanta's claws pounded hard against the ground. His nose sniffing, tracking the serpentine-scented beast that had followed him, scurrying in the trees above. Satisfied he was the primary target, he slowed to a stop and peered up into the trees. Leaves were knocked loose where it had rushed through the upper half of the towering firs. Spinning around, following the sounds of claws against bark, he again missed his chance to spot the creature. Growling made drool drip off his jaw in anticipation of a fight, frustration adding to his ire. He was tiring of this game of hide and seek it had played since he discovered its scent trailing behind them. The sun was starting to fade and he tensed, unsure who would gain the advantage.

Piercing pain ripped through the backside of his left shoulder, scraping across the shoulder blade. Barking in a rage, he spun around, swiping. His claw sliced through nothing but air and falling leaves. The creature had attacked to quick, he hadn't caught even a glimpse of it. Hot blood snaked down his backside, dabbling across the leaves at his feet. His eyes raced around, his ears flicking, desperate to find where the tiny beast had vanished. Another piercing pain ripped across his other shoulder, rattling him in agony. Foam dripped from his chin, growling. Anger fueled his failed attempts to catch his opponent, again he had failed to identify the creature.

Night had taken over, steam rolling off the heat of his own blood pooling at his feet. His back ached and throbbed. A branch snapped overhead, bringing his eyes back to the canopy. Fighting to check each branch he saw, he searched for any movement. A stabbing sensation dug deep into his lower left back. Dropping to his knees, he howled, engulfed by pain. Tiny claws dug into his sides, working their way into his ribs. Snarling, he failed to reach the tiny snake-like creature ripping apart his back. Blue and silver scales sparkled in the moonlight as the wildly twisted to avoid his grip. Pushing back the agony, he flung himself backwards, letting himself fall. Claws dug deeper into his flesh, but the tiny reptile squeaked. He threw all his weight between him and the ground. Roaring from his injuries, Romasanta continued to push hard against the dirt, trapping the beast. Fangs and claws nipped and scratched underneath him. The tearing of his flesh far lighter than the first three injuries he had endured. Rolling, cracking a few of the serpent's bones, he gripped it in the middle, pinning it to the ground under his claw. His eyes fell upon the thrashing tiny dragon, its head narrow and sharp like a javelin, the blue and silver scale reflective enough to hide it well from sight. Grunting, he flashed his teeth in annoyance, angry that something so tiny had damaged him so easily.

"I should have known," he growled. "A Jaculus."

The dragon paused, its tiny red eyes glaring at him, hissing to be released. He glared down his expression unmoved by its demand. Without warning, it rammed its spear-like head into the top of his hand. Tendons popped under the sharp edges of the beak. Losing his grip strength, he let go against his will. Dashing up a tree, he watched the snakelike reptile in frustration, unable to grab with his right claw anymore, his injury leaving it weak and unable to ball into a fist. It was the size of a large cat or dog, tiny arms with a long body reminiscent of a five-lined skink. Despite the weak looking limbs and claws, it uses its slithering body to move through the branches of trees with astonishing speed.

"Get back here!" His bark echoed through the forest.

He shook his fur, freeing himself of the trickles of blood tickling at his throbbing back. The muscles had been shredded and even his movement had become slow and weak. Wiping the dangling line of drool from his jowl, he brought himself to his feet. Looking up into the trees, he stumbled about, watching for any clues to where the Jaculus had gone. Breathing stung with each rise and fall of his shoulders. His wolven face tensing as he knotted his brow, spinning around, his frustration growing. Each step splashed in the thick warmth of his own blood still dripping down his spine and sides. Steam and fog tangled into one, making his task to spot the Jaculus impossible. His ears flicked behind him, he spun, but found nothing. Fur prickling, his muscled hardened in anticipation of another attack. Jaculus was a term implying 'javelin' belonging to the tiny dragons who hunted from above and would drop down from the trees like massive living spears. Their beaks and horns were reminiscent of a sword's edge. If he had been a human, the first attack would have cut him in half.

He couldn't manage a fist with his tendons torn, leaving him with only his fangs and one claw. Another round of scurrying from behind. Spinning, he found nothing. Debris floated down to the growing crimson lake at his feet, his head heavy from blood loss. Cursing under his breath, he envied the impeccable fast healing of Lillith and Cedric. He was healing, even now, but the rate was horribly slow compared to the insane speed an Incubus or Succubus possessed. Nose twitching, he could smell only the iron of his own blood, washing out the forest around him. A shudder rattled through him as a thought hit him.

It intended to spill enough blood in order to render my nose worthless. I was tracking it with my eyes not my nose, my first mistake. My second mistake was not killing it when I had it in my grasp...

Agony ripped down his shoulder and arm, muscles torn asunder. His other hand unable to grasp the Jaculus, he could only watch it hiss and leap from him. Roaring, he snapped his jaws after it, anger and agony becoming one and the same within him. A branch snapped from behind him, his ears shifted. His heart fluttered, turning on his heels to see what was approaching from the shadows. Nyctimus had paused, wide-eyed at the amount of blood dripping like rain from his friend. Sighing, ashamed to be losing this fight, he nodded upward. It was a silent signal to watch the trees for the next attack. Nyctimus lurked back into the shadows, the blood in the air more than enough to mask his own scent from both opponents.

The Jaculus was covered in Romasanta's blood and would be more careless thinking its next strike would succeed in killing the target.

Confident Nyctimus was ready, Romasanta opened himself up for a tempting kill shot for the Jaculus. Throwing his head back, exposing his neck, he grinned. Arms out, it was a silent shout for the Jaculus to go ahead and finish what it had started. Hissing and scurrying shook the branches above him. He opened one golden eye on the Jaculus on the branch high above him. The moment they locked eyes, it launched itself off the limb. It straightened its body, stiffening and tightening its physique like a rod as its arms waved out to correct its aim. It was a marvel to watch as it drew close, gaining speed. Heat and a blinding flash slammed into the Jaculus. Romasanta opened his eyes wider, surprised, following the flaming reptile. The tiny dragon slammed into a nearby tree, burning with a wizard's fire. The smell and look of it brought back harrowing reminders of his first encounter with Boreas.

Turning to Nyctimus, he stared with wonder at the flaming claw and toothy grin. He had mastered the offensive magic, his birth-right, that had eluded him all this time. Romasanta flattened his ears, unsure of the turmoil of emotions it stirred deep in his core. Romasanta slid to the ground on his knees, blood rippling across the red pool. With this amount of blood loss, his healing would set them back several days, possibly weeks. He had flustered over Cedric and Angeline's follies, but in reality he had been the careless one not considering how devastating to his journey it would be if he or even Nyctimus sustained injury. Lightheaded and dizzy, he let himself fall forward on his belly, feeling defeated.

Nyctimus approached, kneeling in front of his muzzle with a smirk. "Why do I have to save you from the small things?"

"I wasn't paying attention." He grumbled, a huff from his nostrils stirring the leaves between them. "At least I wasn't being eaten by a Jidra... again."

Chuckling, Nyctimus fussed, "but you let the little squirt tear you apart."

"I know," he whined. "So, by that attack just now, I guess the apple didn't fall far from the tree?"

"You can thank Cedric and Angeline for me figuring that out." Sighing, he called the flames back over his clawed hand. "But I suppose this is a good time to be able to use it."

Closing his eyes, Romasanta was still growing weaker, blood still oozing from his wounds. "Do me a favor and burn some of these holes closed. I know you don't want to have to carry me the whole way back."

Nyctimus huffed, working himself into a better angle to reach the ripped clumps of flesh. "This isn't going to look pretty."

"It won't feel pretty either." Clenching his jaw, Romasanta tensed. "I don't want to hear shit from you if I pass out from this."

Silence confirmed that he understood. Romasanta was experiencing non-stop pain and with the searing of flesh, it would drive anyone over the edge of not being able to sustain consciousness. Laying a flame covered hand over one shredded shoulder blade, Romasanta howled in agony. Nyctimus' nostrils were freed of the metallic smell of Romasanta's blood. The air was engulfed by the stench of burning fur and flesh, making him shudder. Nyctimus was working quick, moving from one horrifying wound to the next without hesitation. At one point in his life he had dabbled in medicine, but between the harrowing things they both had seen, experienced and even done, torn flesh was the least of his worries. Romasanta's stomach knotted, his jaw aching from the pressure in which he gritted his fangs. Nausea was building as one flesh melting handful moved to the next.

It's not the pain upsetting me... Romasanta's thoughts were sour, a tear sliding down his furry cheek. *This burn, this searing heat. Last I felt it in this way, Daphne... Daphne...*

Nyctimus paused. Only Romasanta's ravaged arm was left, but he had passed out. His breathing ragged from the torture of wounds cauterized in such rapid succession. Deep down, a sense of guilt waved through Nyctimus as he stared at the flame he called forth. This was a magic that had destroyed both their lives and yet here they both found themselves needing to use it for survival. Swallowing down his own unease, he refocused on finishing the work still ahead. It would be hours before he would be able to move Romasanta. The wounds might have been seared closed, but the state of them would be ripped open again at just tugging him out of the pool of blood he still laid within. Until he was certain of it, Nyctimus would watch over his friend, his savior who never once condemned him for the sins of his family's past.

**

Romasanta's head pounded, still weak and throbbing from the aching pain of his injuries. Nyctimus' hazel eyes shifted and met his own. The moon was high above them now, trickling through the trees like a phantom version of sunlight. Chills ran across his back, pain gripping him as he shifted. His fur was clumpy, caked in bloody mud and melted flesh. The stinging from the burns made his heart ache. As he struggled to get to his feet, he was failing to swallow back the memories this agony brought him. Looking to Nyctimus, he sighed, nodding it was time to travel back to where Cedric and Angeline were still waiting.

"Let's take this slow..." Romasanta's eyes were sunken, his energy low.

"I figured as much." Nyctimus picked something up off a nearby boulder. "Here, this is for you."

He dropped the half roasted carcass of the Jaculus in Romasanta's hands. "I don't think I have an appetite to eat this little shit."

Nyctimus chuckled, "And this is the part of you I think Fenrir liked best."

He managed a smirk as he broke it in half, offering it to him. "How about we eat in celebration to gaining your birthright?"

Nyctimus raised a brow, "You're not upset with me about that?"

"Why would I be..." He took an angry tear out of his piece like eating a stick of beef jerky as he gnawed it for a moment. "It just pains me to feel that sensation against my skin, that burn from a time when... You have every right to be able to use that power. Unlike your forefathers, you intend to use it in merit, not tyranny."

Staring at his half of the Jaculus, he sighed, "I suppose that is all true. Sorry to bring sour thoughts back to mind, but your wounds..."

"Eat." He gripped Nyctimus' shoulder and mustered a half-hearted smirk. "Because I'll need you to drag me back at this rate."

They laughed, gnawing on the Jaculus in the shadows of the night. Both felt drained by the haunting thoughts brought back by their pasts. At least they had traversed the passing time with someone who understood the savagery they had once lived through as nothing more than humans. Dropping what was left of his meal, Romasanta started stumbling his way towards Cedric's scent. Years of hunting down a key holding some of his bloodline had honed his ability to track him from anywhere. It was more a nuisance since the skill out served its intended purpose, making him feel like a bloodhound for hunting Cedric. Nyctimus trailed behind him, covering his blind spots while he lead them back. It took hours to walk the distance he had ran in minutes.

CHAPTER 18

A SOUR SIDE

The morning dew had started building upon the ground and plants before they stumbled onto Barushka. Braking from the nearby brush, the horse snorted in disapproval at the state in which he returned. Cedric shifted from where he sat on a boulder, his eyes widening to see Romasanta torn apart. His green eyes shot to Nyctimus, surprised to see he had no injuries and his brow folded in suspicion. Romasanta shot him a glare that made him hold his tongue. Angeline was still asleep in the sleeping bag on the ground, no fire had been made in fear of exposing their location. Sighing, Cedric slid off the rock, offering to help the old wolf to sit on the ground. Looking at the cauterized wounds painting his back and claiming the length of one arm, he shuddered.

This place was full of beasts that even took Romasanta down hard and we still have to face Delphyne... the mother of all dragons... but we're a man down...

"Can I ask what the hell was trailing us?" Cedric looked to Nyctimus.

"Jaculus. Luckily it was just the one. A tiny dragon, but it's like facing a living javelin." Nyctimus jumped up onto the boulder, perching where Cedric had been. "A very fast annoying spear falling from the trees on you without warning."

Cedric's jaw tensed, his muscles visibly twitching at the thought as he looked back to Romasanta. The old werewolf had allowed himself to drift back to sleep. The flow of the injuries made Cedric's own skin crawl. If he had faced something like that, it would have been hard not to relish in the pleasure the pain would have brought him. Regardless, they were at the mercy of how long it would take Romasanta to heal. Their strongest member rendered useless.

"Is there any way to speed up the healing?" Cedric and Nyctimus locked eyes.

"Not for us." Nyctimus' frustration was clear, muscles tensing and the anxious rate his breath flowed in and out of his large canine nostrils spoke volumes. "It takes time."

Closing his eyes, Cedric sighed. "I should have followed the moment I saw he was the target."

A chuckle came from Nyctimus. "And I assure you, Romasanta would have told you to stay if you had tried."

Cedric smiled, "I suppose that's true."

Romasanta shifted, snarling in his sleep. His wolven face distorted and twisted, his pain visible for all to see. Angeline stirred from within her sleeping bag. Blinking a few times, trying to comprehend what her eyes were staring at, sleep still fogging her mind. Sitting up in a rush, her hands covered her mouth, a pulse of panic slipping through her failed attempt to suppress it. Watery eyes shot up to Cedric who let his smile fall away. They were losing confidence in their ability to face the mother of all dragons. She had given birth to the Wyverns and Jaculus who had taken their toll on them with ease. This would be a dragon larger than a small house, smarter than all of them combined, and worse, older than Romasanta and possibly as old as Lillith. They were coming into this fight blind in hopes Gaea might intervene in order to get her own gemlike eye back.

Cedric's eyes slid away from Angeline's, his thoughts falling to a question he had failed to ask. *Does Gaea exist? Was she not the mother earth itself or some God created by the demons or humans to persuade others to fall in line to be commanded, controlled? Why would they venture this far for a stone that simply absorbed the side effects of Gaea's law, freeing its holder of recoils and curses.*

Barushka shrieked. Jolting their souls, they watched the shag foal snort, bobbing his head. He nipped at the saddle bag, his feet stomping, anxious. Looking, nothing seemed out of place as he tugged at it, his teeth pulling hard on the sliver of leather he managed to grab. A faint glow of red, the same magical aura from when they travelled through the Sibyl stone. Scrambling over to Barushka, Cedric wasted no time to cut the bag from his side. Nyctimus' eyes widened, realizing what Cedric had seen. He stood bewildered, holding the bag with the glowing of the Eye of Gaea increasing. A magical hum was building, all of them looking to Romasanta where he still laid.

"Shit!" Cedric rushed over to the incapacitated werewolf. "Romasanta! What the hell are we going to do with this thing?"

All he gained from Romasanta was a distorted face filled with agony. Dropping the bag on his chest, they all backed away, unsure what to do.

"Nyctimus?" The pain he had experienced from the stone was still sharp in his mind, making him pump the fist that last touched it. "I'm not touching the cursed thing."

"I, I don't know what to do." Fur stood on end down Nyctimus spine. "He lost the damn thing before I met him."

"Romasanta! WAKE UP!" Cedric roared over the magical sound now silencing the forest around them.

Helpless, they all watched the box burn through the saddle bag. Romasanta gritted his fangs, still unable to wake as the heat of the box landed across his chest. Power snaked from it, wrapping around the old wolf. Cedric's heart raced, sweat dripping down his temple. Fear was pulsing from Angeline as she held the sleeveless arm. She too could still feel the pain it had brought them. Cursing under his breath, Cedric took a step forward, but Nyctimus threw his arm out. The grave look made it known it was best to lose one of them, even if it was the biggest powerhouse.

Crimson flames from magical aura covered Romasanta's body. The blanket had been burnt away, leaving nothing but the ragged werewolf and a wooden box failing to contain the power it held.

Hearts were pounding in their ears as they waited for Romasanta's flesh to melt away, burn to ashes like the saddle bag and blanket. After several surreal minutes, it was becoming more noticeable what was happening. His face was falling into a peaceful state, his muscles relaxing. The burns across his arm were shrinking, slow in the beginning, nearly impossible to suspect. Relief waved between Cedric and Angeline, for once the stone was proving it had a gentler, more forgiving side.

"We may not have to wait weeks for him to recover..." Nyctimus looked to his fellow panicked comrades. "It seems Gaea is anxious to have her eye returned to her if she's going to assist him."

A large inhale hissed from Romasanta as he woke. The red from the box was dying away. A few flames rode out the last touches of the wounds and burns. He stared at the three terrified faces peering down at where he laid. Glaring to his chest, surprise rattled his face to see nothing more than the box. Blinking a few times, anger took hold him, snarling at them.

"It was burning through the saddle bag." Nyctimus interrupted the ire building at Romasanta's core. "We tried to wake you, but..."

The rage faltered in his golden eyes. Peering back to the box, he gripped it in a clawed hand. "What did it take in return, then?"

Cedric looked around, "Nothing that we are aware of."

"It always has a sour side." Grunting, Romasanta rose to his feet, shaking off the last of the magic. "There is always something taken in return..."

Swallowing, Nyctimus replied, "I pray it was not a high cost."

"W-what could it possibly want in return?" Angeline's shuddered.

Everyone shifted, tension building as they all awaited Romasanta's answer.

Romasanta frowned, nose twitching. "The cost this time was higher than any of you could have imagine. The last shag foal has fallen."

An ache like no other swallowed Cedric and Angeline. The agony of grief echoing into one another as they spun on their heels. Barushka laid dead on his side. His eyes white and foam dripping from his nostrils. Cedric's stomach twisted. The hum of the magic had made them deaf to his dying screams. Angeline was sliding to her knees, but Cedric gripped her arm, yanking her back to her feet. Tears rolled down her cheeks as she whimpered at the sight. Barushka's body was sunken in as if he had been starved to death, every ounce of him missing. What once had been a muscular horse larger than a Shire, now laid as a dried up corpse. Cedric's grief was evolving into rage as he looked at the frail husk of the only companion he had after Angeline was stolen. Barushka had even been a pillar of comfort when Wylleam died.

"Can you two bury him?" Cedric refused to face Romasanta or Nyctimus, his hand tightening on Angeline's arm. "I'd do it, but I know it would only waste time."

"It's the least I can do for Barushka giving his life, whether it was willing or not..." Stopping, Romasanta watched Cedric march off to the woods with Angeline.

Nyctimus scratched his chin, side-eyeing Romasanta. "What do you think he's about to do? I could smell the anger running through his veins."

Growling, Romasanta stared at the box in his grip. "If I were him, I would remind her that death comes to those who lose themselves in sight of the fallen."

Cedric marched on, dragging Angeline behind him. She whimpered, sobbing and failing to dig her fingers under his own. Her arm ached and burned from the tight grasp in which Cedric held her. Confident they were far enough from prying eyes and ears of the werewolves, Cedric slammed Angeline back against a tree. The jolt made her gasp and her crying stopped. She looked up at him bewildered. Searing heat drowned her as he opened the floodgates which held his emotions. Her face mottled. Struggling to swallow back fear, the hair on the back of her neck stood on end. His green eyes glowered down at her, a familiar animalistic look in them. Biting her lip, it brought back the past in an instant. Chills pimpled across her skin, his hand still tight on her arm as he leaned in, his eyes slicing through her soul.

"I can't protect you." The pain in Cedric's voice was loud. To confess this fact made his rage rise higher. "If your mortally wounded, I will not be able to come to your side until Delphyne lays dead."

She opened her mouth, but her thoughts failed to make words. The weight of his anger slamming into her through their bond kept her from finding the right response.

His jaw twitched, waiting before he continued. "I'm sorry I dragged you into this..."

Taking a deep breath, she retorted, "But you gave me a chance to back out several times..."

His hand let go, leaning in so that she could no longer see his face. The warmth of his breath against her ear made her shiver. Fear rose in her, his anger shut itself back inside him and left their bond void of any of his own emotions. She tensed, waiting for his next move, anxious of the hidden rage he had shown seconds ago. His fingers, warm and gentle, glided over her cheek and his thumb wiped away her last tear. Lips tickling at her ear, his whispered words fell hard, its tone deep and woeful.

"I'm sorry for the curse I've lovingly placed within you, my pet."

Before she could move or whisper back, he had turned away. Leaning against the tree, she stared at him in wonder. Her hand shook, reaching to her neck where he had hovered so tenderly. Something warm had hit her, and rubbing it in her fingers, the scent salty. Her chest ached, making her fight back the wave of tears that tore at her throat. Rushing after him, she wrapped her arms around him. Burying her face into the divot of his back, she shook her head, unable to say no. He had halted, looking up the forest canopy above, twinkling in all shades of green in the breeze. She squeezed harder, pushing harder for her voice to come to her.

"Don't you ever apologize for being what you are... and what I've become." Hot tears trickled down his lower back as she swallowed back the shaking in her voice. "I will never blame you for the life I live nor how it ends..."

He pulled her hands free, "Let me help them bury Barushka."

Covering her mouth, she couldn't stop the flood of tears streaking down her face. Knees shaking, the buckled under her weight. Watching him walk away, she was reminded this time Barushka was gone forever. Worse, Cedric had told her he may even lose her in this battle to come. There were no comforts left. Just the cold harsh reality of possibly watching each other obliterated in the battle waiting to unfold on the summit.

What could I do to even aid in a fight like this... Falling forward, she grasped at the leaves under her. *I am putting him in danger, putting everyone in danger. Delphyne is going to be so much stronger... how... how could I possibly join the fight knowing I couldn't put a dent in a wyvern?*

Biting her lip, she shook her head. Fear washed away under the siege of self-loathing invading her soul. The higher it climbed, the hotter the tears felt falling from her eyes. Clenching her teeth, fangs were growing, an outward sign of her new resolve.

If it means surrendering to Artemis... I will pull my weight in the fight against Delphyne... I am willing to sacrifice myself in order to stay at his side...

CHAPTER 19

CONTRACTUAL OBLIGATIONS

The cell phone in Tony's pocket chirped and buzzing tickled at his thigh. Sighing, Tony glared into his own eyes within the reflection of the mirror, sour faced at the time he had spent being idle. Pulling the phone out, the display was flashing *Lillith*. He silenced it, laying it on the bathroom vanity. Turning the faucet on, he splashed the cool water over his face. Again, he glanced up at himself as if the man in the mirror was a stranger. Each passing day was a struggle, much like his last time at the bar. His stay here in the apartment had proven to be a short term relief for the over-whelming spurs of body heat and arousal. Another rush of cold water and he felt the tingling on the back of his neck; Lillith was still calling him. The phone lit up and he turned the faucet off. This time it was a text message. Sighing, he wiped his hands off on the towel before throwing it around his neck.

Reluctant, he picked up the phone, reading the message: *He's here.*

Opening the bathroom door, he winced at the sight of Lillith leaning on the wall of the hallway. A scowl across her face, she nodded for him to follow her. His eyes dropped to the floor. He obeyed, grimacing as the sting of another episode of lust teased him from his own core. Walking into the living room, a man stood at the window rolling around what little wine was left in the glass in his right hand. He was tall and a polished looking gentleman from the way his business suit laid across his frame. The man's jade-toned glare turned from the city outside to Tony. Raising an eye-brow, a wicked smile broke the stern expression on his face, pulling his goatee and moustache wide.

"My, aren't we handsome?" There was a sparkle in his eye as he turned to Lillith. "You have been hiding him well, Lillith. Is this your new boy toy? If not, I'll gladly..."

"I'm not her boy toy." Huffed Tony, feeling agitated and more aggressive than normal. "Are you the guy who can read curse marks?"

He frowned. "Yes, I see. This is business after all."

Lillith remained silent, letting Tony take charge of his own situation for a change. "Tony, this is Mr. Nomius Panes Silvan."

"Please, call me Pan." He flustered, downing the last of his wine. "But in case I was not properly represented, I am the President of The White Ram Law Associates on Avalon."

"Law Associates? On Avalon?" Tony's brow knotted, tugging on the ends of the towel wrapped over his neck. "Exactly what sort of legal actions do you handle?"

A smile returned to Pan's lips. "We are tasked with record-keeping mostly. In today's world, it is in all of our interests to maintain a sense of privacy and secrecy that we are very much alive, being non-humans. Regardless, there are plenty of other services we provide, such as relocations, human legal system assistance, resolving conflicts without violence or in your case, curses."

Rubbing his wrist, Tony nodded, understanding the want to appear human in a world ran by them. "So, in my case, what can you do for me and how much will it cost?"

Pan shot a look to Lillith who waved her fingers in approval. "I can reveal information about the person who placed it on you, since in your case, you are not aware of who this individual is in connection to you. As for the cost, let's just call this Lillith cashing in on a favor and you don't have to worry about honoring-"

"No matter what, I will be turning into..." Swallowing back the wave of nausea, Tony started again. "I rather it be me who owes you a favor, Pan, since I am already indebted to Lillith. Stacking anything else on top of that seems too much. Not for someone as low on the totem pole as I am."

"Heh, aren't we quite the favorable gentlemen." He stroked his goatee, lifting an eyebrow towards the Queen Succubus.

Lillith rolled her eyes still tight lipped.

"Well, seeing and hearing no objections." His earth green glare returned to Tony. "I will call in a favor later. It will need to wait until Lillith fulfills her contract with you before I can make much use of you myself. Yes, I am aware of that part of this mess as well..."

Tony watched Pan place the wine glass on the end table and motion for him to sit. Without much prompting, Pan took his wrist into his hand. A burning sensation crept forward, as if the girl's touch was coming back to the moment she placed the curse. His skin turned black, marks of fingers and a palm wrapping around. The painful searing had him grinding his teeth together. He locked eyes with Lillith and pulled back the expression of pain forming on his face, not wanting to look weak. Something about the grave expression she was wearing was unsettling and he found himself absorbed by it. Her silence made him shift, the pain dulling from the sudden worry washing over him.

"This is a nasty one." Huffed Pan, letting go of his wrist. "A curse from the same bloodline is always the worst. Nothing good ever comes from them, for either side."

"Same bloodline?" Lillith interjected, her expression shifting to surprise.

Pan rubbed his goatee, his words falling out in a cautious tone. "I guess this only added to the complications. Research will have to be done. According to the ties and roots of the curse, they share the same lineage. I can't believe this fun fact... I'll need to hire help at this rate."

"Could it be someone in my own family?" Tony paled. "Maybe a cousin, aunt or uncle..."

"No, there's too huge of a gap. We're talking centuries apart on the line." Pan stood up, digging in his pocket. "And it's on the paternal side. Well, then again, there's two paternal sides involved in there if we want to get into the technicalities of labelling those..."

"Paternal? As in my father's side?" Tony's mind was filling with more questions.

"No, nothing like that. You're so cute and clueless..." Pulling out a metal business card holder, he flipped it open and handed over a business card to Tony. "Here, for future needs. Anyhow, when I say paternal side, I am referring to the first male demonic entity the blood can be connected to and then there is a second. Curses are only applicable to a magical being, both in terms of giving and receiving one. As close as humans get, are those of crossed blood or dormant magical powers who still have the right to invoke a curse. In fact, both the caster and victim have to be of magic or strongly connected by blood somehow."

"Let's get back to the point, Pan. Paternal?" Lillith sighed, voicing her assumption. "Is it safe to say its Cedric and not Merlin?"

Snapping his card holder closed, he frowned. "Both."

Lillith and Tony glanced to one another and shot a look back to Pan who was fumbling in his other pocket. He raised a finger, making them wait in their confusion. He pulled out a pack of cigarettes and zippo featuring a rose etched into the metal frame. Sliding one cigarette from the pack, he walked back to the window lighting it. His lips smacked a few times, smoke rolling from his mouth as the cherry on the cigarette came to life. From the window, they could see his gaunt expression which matched the tone of the fading sunlight. Taking a few drags, he shuddered, thoughts contorting his lips. Snorting out a rim of smoke from his nostrils he turned back to them both.

"This is a favor you may not ever be able to finish paying off if I disclose the details." His eyes locked with Tony who flinched. "Your curse is quite a clever device. I can confirm this was meant to hurt the caster and less so you, the victim. This person needed someone who carried both lines, they had an ulterior motive and you were their ticket to making it happen."

Lillith started across the living room at him, her heels clacking with authority. "Exactly what the hell did you see, Pan?"

"Whoa, Nelly!" Giving her a toothy grin, he threw his hands in the air, ashes flaked off the cigarette between his fingers. "First I want to know whose owing me my favor. Tony, you, or are we going to split this one since it will be worthwhile for you to hear it, Lilly. This is not your average curse reading like I thought I would be doing. There's complications and legal authority I have to respect on this one. This is high grade lawyer work and contractual obligations that need to be honored beforehand and even after the fact. Privacy and rights and-"

"I'll owe the favor." Tony interrupted. "It's my curse, I want to know who and why."

Lillith turned away from Tony, her face hidden as she addressed Pan. "Does this involve the one we call *brother?*"

Pan lifted both eyebrows high, his jade eyes looking up at her as the smoke fell from his lips. "Yes. This does involve *Kronos.*"

Her shoulders dropped and she walked out of the room and into the kitchen. Pan and Tony looked to one another in confusion by the sudden exit. There was banging of cabinet doors and she came marching back out with two large bottles. They were dust-covered deep green wine bottles, the labels barely existent. Pan's eyes sparkled, a grin crawling across his face like a child seeing presents under a Christmas tree. He reached his arms out to her, his fingers flicking to rush her. Grabbing the bottles, his cigarette dangling in his lips, he giggled looking them over. Lillith took the cigarette from Pan's lips and took in the last drag of it. Marching back to the couch where Tony sat, she put out the last of the cigarette in the ashtray on the end table.

Smoke streamed out of her pursed lips. "Of course, that's not enough for him to be out of doing you a favor."

"No... Gods No, but definitely weaseled yourself out of owing me one. You and I are even now." Clearing his throat, he hugged his wine bottles with a smile on his face. "Now that payment has been settled, I can properly provide my *legal intellect and counsel.*"

Tony tensed. This so-called payment in the form of *favors* was not sitting well with him, but Lillith seemed to trust this man enough to let him in her apartment.

"The girl who placed the curse on you shares the same blood-line as you, but in an interesting manner in regards to length of time. Please understand, Mister, er, Tony, that demon blood waters down in each generation, but one. Those who come directly from two magical beings are as strong and have a chance to be stronger than their parents. In short, first and second generations fair better chances, third and fourth generation begins to mutate and eventually fades off to becoming obscure or nonexistent." Lillith sat on the couch, leaning forward on her knees with her face tight muscled. "Not only did she share a first generation connection with Cedric, but she seems to have a connection to the Titan, Kronos. I believe you know him by Merlin. Unlike the time span difference, this is where you are marked a blood relative and the curse acts as if Kronos himself has placed the curse. This is why I believe you were solely targeted for your bloodline so they may activate a recoil. The mark is black, a sign of Kronos' touch, but ironically there is something laced within it that suggests..."

He paused, eyeing Lillith who retorted, "I thought the payment and favor was enough."

Sighing, he nodded in agreement. "Considering when the curse activated, it seems Merlin is alive and well... possessing the gypsy girl we know nothing about, except that she is immortal. Even that is now explained with her being related to both Cedric and Kronos."

"But, what of her relations to me?" Her hands clasped together, her tone quiet and her forehead creasing with worry.

Pan popped the cork on one of the bottles, making Tony jump. "None."

Sour faced, Lillith watched him chug back the ancient wine. "Do I want to even know who the mother is? What maternal lineage that may be causing the whiplash?"

"Oh, his mother is human as they get." He laughed, pointing at Tony. "As for Mysterious Gypsy girl, I cannot disclose that information."

Anger seeped forward in her voice, "Why not?"

Another long swig, thumping his lips free, he winced. "She's a long-term client of mine."

"More long term than family?" She lifted an eyebrow, twisting answers from him.

"Wait a minute." Tony was still grasping at all the names and information flying between the two. "So the Gypsy girl and I, we're related through both Cedric and Merlin?"

"Yes." Nodded Pan. "And she was aiming to curse Merlin via the whiplash, not necessarily you... so I suppose she used the word *bloodline* at some point in that phrasing."

"Yea, but am I understanding that this gypsy is technically Cedric's..." Lillith's gasp interrupted Tony's words, a wave of heavy sorrow waving into him from the mark on the back of his neck.

Jerking up and off the couch, she clutched her chest. She was panting, cold sweat glistening across her skin. Tears were falling from her shocked expression, her voice lost as her lips trembled. Stumbling a few steps, she gasped again, breathless. The tears were falling faster, her hand reaching out for some means to brace herself. Tony chased after her, gripping her arm before she lost her balance. Waves of despair slammed into him as their skin made contact, making his own breath catch in his throat. He let go, falling back onto the floor bewildered.

"You're, you're so hopeless…" Lillith watched a tear crawled down his face. "You can't take this love from me, you naïve fool. But, then again you haven't a clue on what you tried to do for me, did you?"

"I didn't mean…" Tony could breathe again, but the sensation was still echoing through him, clawing at his soul. "What is that?"

"It's Lillith's Mark, my curse." Swallowing, her maroon eyes looked to Pan. "Open a portal to Delphyne's temple."

Pan paled. "She'll kill you for showing your face there."

"I don't care, I must fulfill my promise." Lillith smirked, tears still dripping across the floor, her body trembling. "It's either I go, or you two watch me die here for not keeping true to a pact I made. It is Gaea's law, after all."

"You spiteful daughter, you…" Sighing, Pan slammed a hand against the glass window.

The glass rippled like water before the scene outside the pane shifted to a blinding white light. Layers of red petals unraveled from under his palm, blooming outward until the entire light had been drowned out. A robust smell of flowers and meadows blew on a breeze that tip-toed across the apartment. Pan looked back over his shoulder, a frown on his face. Lillith sighed, looking down at Tony a moment. A smile came across her face, her eyes soft for a second. As if the pain faded away, she stood tall and marched into the rose and it folded over her in a flash. Tony found himself sitting in the living room floor alone and lost in the waves of sorrow still stinging at his core.

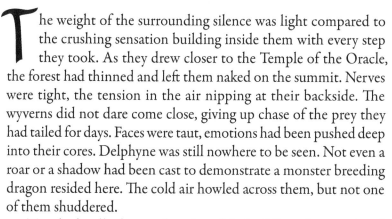

CHAPTER 20

DELPHYNE

The weight of the surrounding silence was light compared to the crushing sensation building inside them with every step they took. As they drew closer to the Temple of the Oracle, the forest had thinned and left them naked on the summit. Nerves were tight, the tension in the air nipping at their backside. The wyverns did not dare come close, giving up chase of the prey they had tailed for days. Faces were taut, emotions had been pushed deep into their cores. Delphyne was still nowhere to be seen. Not even a roar or a shadow had been cast to demonstrate a monster breeding dragon resided here. The cold air howled across them, but not one of them shuddered.

They had walked up to the edge of the building, the temple columns towering high above them like thin elegant skyscrapers. The white marble was free of decay or signs of being weathered as if it too were an immortal being. Standing in awe, they peered into the temple with wonder at the sheer span of square footage it hid. A brazier in the center had an eerie fire blazing, the oil unmoving within the bronze dish with the heat of it hitting their faces. Flames rose high, lashing up at the center skylight in the center of the ceiling. The orange arms reached for the sun in eighteen foot tantrums, no wind could make it sway off course. Below this, it sat upon a central multi-tiered fountain in the midst of a Romanesque public bath house complete with statues and adornments from an era long forgotten by humans and demons alike.

Cedric and Angeline came to a stop between two columns, looking back at Romasanta who had walked far behind them. He hadn't spoken a word after burying Barushka, guilt visible in his amber eyes. Nyctimus shot Cedric a silent look of concern. Their strongest member was compromised by his emotions at the very moment they intended to engage in battle with their greatest foe. Taking in a deep breath, they watched the large black were-wolf march between them and enter the temple first without ever losing pace in his march of regret. Angeline shuddered, goosebumps across her skin while Cedric's words still echoed in her mind, *I can't protect you.*

Funneling down the steep decline of stairs, they descended into the marble garden. The endless rows of steps added to the aching in their legs from climbing the soft ashy earth of the summit. There was no mistaking the forest had been burnt back so many times to the point that nothing grew. Here on the summit, everything was choked from the sun, the water, even the air. Cedric took one last look at the grim and grey landscape before following the others into the temple. Inside, the marble was white and clean. The reflection of the brazier's flames sparkled off the floors and fixtures, making the inanimate objects move as if alive. Their footsteps echoed off the towering ceiling, making their presence known. Hearts fluttered with each loud pound of footsteps shouting back at them from all around, hitting their ears like Death knocking on their door.

The water from the large fountain fell heavy over the layers beneath the bronze dish. A spring bubbled up from under the bronze brazier and spilled in thick sheets into the second layer, cas-cading further to another tier, and another, ever taller. After three layers, the water found peace, a chance to rest in a square lake edged by white marble stairs leading into its depths. The clear liquid cooled the breeze that competed with the fire that once had been eye level when they first stepped foot through the columns. Drowning the crackling of the flames far above their heads was the caressing sound of the water, whispering like the gentle rustling of a bride's skirt. At the corners of the pool were statues of women. Each one grasping different items in their cold stone hands, all with chiseled Roman letters at their bases to signify a meaning, or perhaps to declare who these lifeless vixens had once been.

"They are all names of Oracles..." Nyctimus squatted at the closest statue, looking over it in hopes of some clue. "You think there's a hidden entrance?"

"*The Oracle of Delphi resides under the Castalian Spring on the summit of Mt. Parnassus...*" Romasanta spoke, reciting what he had learned from Badbh. "*...guarded by Delphyne, daughter of Gaea and mother to dragons and beasts of the world.*"

"I suppose that's a yes." Cedric huffed, starting to walk the parameter of the pool.

"Who are you..." A female voice came from the edge of the temple where they had entered, "...and why have you come to this place?"

The fur on both Nyctimus and Romasanta's spines stood on-end making the werewolves look like overgrown razorback boars, fangs flashing. No one had heard anyone follow them, let alone seen any signs outside as to where they would have hidden themselves. She was a tall woman wearing a gown made of loose curtains of white and red silk, draping across her body in large swaths from her shoulder to over her hips and across her thighs before falling to the floor. Her skin was a warm color of clay and bronze, shimmering where the sun hit her bare shoulders. From where they stood, she appeared to be a goddess with the blinding sunlight filtering in behind her like the golden aura of a lost deity. Her eyes cut across them, the color an unforgiving black that hinted it had once been brown or even some other earthy tone long ago. The scowl across her thin lips was powerful enough to make them shift their weight in response. Her head swung back to Romasanta, the first person she had landed her sharp stare upon. He returned the glare to her, unflinching.

The hair on her head stayed its course, looped and braided with ribbons and golden ornaments. At first glance it had appeared to be a spiked crown of gold, red, and black, but as she descended the steps, coming ever closer, the black strands of hair had been skill-fully intertwined as part of her grand crown. Gold bands and chains dangling from her ornate hair held pearls in spurts of three at the ends or in the middle sections stretching from one spike to another. The gentle chiming of it with each barefoot-to-marble step added to the uncanny aura waving from her. Instincts were screaming inside all of them. This was the point of no return. She clutched the skirts of silk with angry hands, the muscles tense in her arms, twitching with the tightness in which she held them up and out of the way of each stern movement towards them.

Romasanta rolled his shoulder, rubbing his chest with nose twitching. "You are Delphyne, the guardian here."

A smile crept across her lips, slow and bone chilling in nature. "Why yes."

Angeline shifted, tightening her grip on the bow. A pulse of fear thudded against Cedric's emotions from their connection and he shrugged it off. He too was on edge to see Delphyne so amused to hear her own name spoken by strangers. Regardless, everyone was looking to him to keep his focus. He wasn't their greatest power, but sadly, Romasanta would have to fall back to being the target. As they dug Barushka's grave, Nyctimus and he had worked on a plan seeing the toll of Gaea's Eye had on the old man. The Jaculus had caused them unwarranted consequences, but what it had revealed was that Delphyne was aware it was Romasanta who travelled to the temple. With two werewolves racing through the forest, the tiny dragon had taken no hesitation in aiming to kill only Romasanta. After the wyverns would no longer give pursuit, they should have seen it as a sign they were sent to confirm who had arrived. Cedric and Romasanta took in deep breaths in unison, prepping themselves for what would unfold.

"And who are you to call me by my name?" Stopping, she dropped her skirts, her chin raised in pride. "Speak, wolf."

A grin came across Romasanta's snout, staring unmoved up at her. "Do I truly need to speak my own name after your children have already informed you of my arrival?"

The intensity between them could stop time itself. "In that case, why have you of all beings come to this place?"

"I wish to speak to the Oracle."

Her eyes narrowed and she took one more step closer. "Why would you have a need to see her?"

"I have something that belongs to your mother."

There was a long silence, eyeing the group of warriors before her, she returned her cold glare to Romasanta. "I'll return the eye to her. Do that, and I will overlook you ever came here."

"I can't do that. This was a task given to both Fenrir and I alone. Not you."

With a sneer she spat, "And I see only the man remains of the two."

"And it was Fenrir who took pleasure in eating Aitvaras." Romasanta's tone remained calm and level, responding without hesitation to the rise of anger in her voice. "Were you hoping Fenrir was still here so you could send him to the afterlife yourself? As he had done not once, but twice, to your beloved son?"

Her lips tightened, pressing into one another, almost puckering from the sour thoughts in her mind. "Are you implying I am taking pity on you, Romasanta?"

A smile crept across his muzzle, his golden eyes flashing bright, "Since when do you let anyone leave the temple alive, Delphyne?"

"You are no fool." A red glow was building in the center of the black irises, her tone pulled back from her anger and made stern. "You do realize I still have the upper claw in this matter."

Romasanta side glanced, earning a knowing nod from all of them as muscles tensed. "We are painfully aware of this."

"You came to fight me, then?" A toothy grin broke out between her lips, her eyes glowing red with excitement. "I will not give any of you an easy death."

Romasanta shook off the last of his regrets, his ears flapping against his skull before he snorted, "Nor will we."

"So be it!" Laughter boiled out of her, echoing throughout the temple in an endless taunt.

She crouched, glowing eyes peering down at them with her wicked grin. Her teeth were shifting, the pristine crease where they met distorted into endless rows of canines. More fangs fell into view as the corners of her mouth reached back to her ears, wide and consuming a large portion of her face. Arms, slow and graceful, reached downward. The skin splitting like cracked clay into metallic copper scales and her fingers elongating into massive claws. Following the contortions of flesh pushing outward, the scales across her arms were growing larger than that of the wyverns. The transformation happening as fast as Romasanta's own, the distance in proportions were inconceivable even to the inhuman audience below her. Eyes fell back to Delphyne's face, no longer did it resemble a human's. A massive reptilian head looked down at them with eyes so large they could hide even Romasanta behind them. Marble snapped and popped under the explosion of weight she had unraveled. Magic flowed off of her, the weight evidence she was indeed a daughter of Gaea herself.

Fear slammed Cedric. The bite of it was Angeline's own, but it sank its fangs deep into his core. Rushing back down the length of the pool, his heart pounded hard against his chest. Burying the sensation, his rage devouring her fears, he needed no distractions in the fight unfolding before them. The sting of his grasp broke her from her shock, bringing her to a battle-ready mindset again. Delphyne continued to unravel into a dragon on the steps above, the shifting of her human body to reptile surreal. Catching his eyes, Angeline swallowed. This was the only time he would be able to aid her.

Dragging her to the far side of the spring, he turned his back to her. Grimacing, he was ashamed of the action, but he was trying to give them some tactical advantage. Compared to him, Angeline had next to no battle experience, let alone against monsters like this. She was their only long range attacker, at least he could justify the urgency to keep her out of direct harm. Delphyne's overall bulk was ginormous. Angeline started climbing the stairs on the opposite side to have enough distance to read movements for her shots, let alone be high enough to be eye level with their opponent. Cedric locked eyes with Nyctimus and shuddered. They would be waiting on Romasanta's first move before acting.

Cedric's throat tightened, his thoughts leaving his chest aching. *We're going to be lucky if any of us can land a damaging hit on her before she decimates two of us.*

The tingle of Lillith's mark came to life in Romasanta's chest, and for once, he was thankful for it. Eyes locking onto the metallic mountain in front of him, he regained his focus. He took in every detail of the copper-scaled mother of dragons, desperate to find a weak point in her armor. Much like her hair, horns crowned the dragon's head with gold and pearl ornaments. The horns were streaked in black and red lines, making them menacing to look at. Anger seeped from her eyes, glowing red as she flashed fangs as tall as he was. Her claws sharp and large, dug into the stairs under them with nails long enough to impale any who got too close.

Laughter was rolling out of her belly, turning the tone into something deeper and demonic in their ears. Sunlight from the entrance was darkened by the height and width of her wingless body. Her tail coiled around her hind feet, bunched close to her front claws. Stretching herself out in a more comfortable position, her rump knocked into the low ceiling between two columns, making the dome above them groan. Dust trickled down like phantom curtains, adding to the unsettling setting they found themselves.

Romasanta dropped down on all fours, fur ruffling as his tail swung in excitement. He intended to fight in a manner that Fenrir had done. After all, he was the only being Romasanta knew to ever take down a dragon, twice. The scar in his chest stung from the grief weighing in his heart. He had never forgotten when Fenrir left him and it was this shift in nature that brought him back to the times when he had taken over his body so long ago. Prying the fingers of humanity from the lid of Pandora's Box deep within his core, he let himself fold to the wolven instincts. Whether he would be able to pull himself out of this animalistic madness after the fight didn't matter. They had to take Delphyne down. His muscles felt electrified as his teeth chattered in response to his growling. Drool tapped loud against the marble floors and the black pupils in his eyes faded under the glow of amber.

Nyctimus stepped further back from the pool, making more distance between him and both, Romasanta and Delphyne. The last time Romasanta let himself go, he went on a cannibalistic rampage, eating everything and anything in his path. In this state, there was no more friend or foe, but only a wolf and its prey. Eyeing behind himself, Nyctimus saw Angeline stumbling up the stairs, trying to get herself in a better position. Despite Cedric failing to hide his concern, they needed her to be in a location to give them support. There was no need to shout to one another. Everyone knew their roles in this battle. Angeline would be trying to disrupt any of Delphyne's attacks, Cedric would come at Delphyne from her left, he would cover Delphyne's right side, and Romasanta would be trying to stay alive in a frontal attack.

Snorting, a sour thought crossed Nyctimus' mind. *That's if Angeline can shake the fear and even attack.*

Delphyne reared back, her nostrils wide with a deep inhale whistling like the wind through a long tunnel. Stretching her neck back towards them, a deafening roar set loose from her maw. Ears ringing, Romasanta barked back, slinging drool from his snapping jaws. Delphyne shifted, sending another barrage of marble snapping and popping. A massive claw swung out, slamming into Romasanta who did nothing to dodge the attack. She had misgauged the distance and Romasanta's claws caught her left arm, just below her wrist. The marble floor was too smooth, his hind feet slid as she pushed him into the statue where Nyctimus had been standing.

Her red eyes shifted, the other claw reaching out and swinging in from the other side. Missing Nyctimus, it came all the way around, clapping into the other. Wind exploded from the feat, sending marble crumbs and dust with it. The statues and Romasanta disappeared between the dragon's hands, no room left for either to exist. There was a long pause. Nyctimus had struggled to stay on his feet from the force of the missed attack and its wave of wind. Delphyne's head peered from Nyctimus on her right then to Cedric on her left who had stopped his approach along the pool. She snorted, her top lip curling in annoyance. Peering back to her clasped claws, she opened them. There was nothing left of the statues, they had been pulverized to dust floating on the surface of the water between her palms. A smile crept across Cedric's face. Romasanta was nowhere in sight, but there were also no scent of his blood in the air. His ability to dodge her was astonishing.

"Where did you go, wolf?" Her voice rattled from between her growling fangs.

Stepping out of the waterfall from the fountain, he shook the water from his head. "You blew me into the fountain, Delphyne, how careless. I thought you wanted to slay me, not bathe me."

Another roar screamed out from her jaws, her claws slamming down on top of Romasanta. Water exploded from the impact, falling throughout the temple like rain. The brazier hissed at the touch of the larger splashes, but the water did nothing to lessen the flames within it. She moved closer to the pool, swiping at the water. Left, right, left again before smashing downward once more. Cedric shook off his admiration of Delphyne's physical power and started into a run. Romasanta was giving them the perfect distraction and they were wasting time. Pulling Boreas' Silver sword from its sheath, Cedric let his horns and wings free. If he was going to be remotely successful, he would have to take advantage of his ability to fly. She was three times the size of the wyverns in mass. Though she lacked their length and wingspan, the muscular weight she carried was uncanny.

Satisfied with Delphyne's distraction towards the pool, Cedric took a large leap. Two strong strokes of his wings put him high enough to land on her left shoulder. Gripping the hilt in both hands, he raised it high above his head, the point facing downward. His hopes were on penetrating pass the massive scales. Tucking his wings in, he let gravity add to his assault. Slamming against her shoulder was like hitting a concrete wall. A loud pinging sound stung in his ears and he was slipping. His hand went numb from the vibrations rolling through the metal sword, his fingers almost failing to hold the hilt. Hitting her scales with the sword was like smacking rebar against a block of iron. Her shoulder shifted, the scales smooth as metal shields gave him no traction to keep his position. She spun around, her eyes glowing brighter with rage. Seeing the right claw reaching for him, he kicked off her ribs. Wings pushing hard, he managed to get out of her reach, a burst of wind aiding his ascension to safety.

A howl came from the pool, Romasanta wet and shaggy still showed no signs of injury. Delphyne's scales rattled with frustration, bringing her attention back to the black werewolf and his toothy grin. Another claw slammed down on top of him, but again he dodged. Romasanta was moving himself up towards Delphyne, taking advantage of the dip in her wrists. Another visible snort came from her. Both claws rose and fell, but as they neared Romasanta, her fanged mouth lunged forward. She had caught on to the game!

The temple glowed in a bright orange, making Delphyne flinch, interrupting her attack. A huge ball of fire slammed into her right cheek, stopping her from chomping down on Romasanta. Peering over to Nyctimus, she broke away from the pool and gave chase. Up and across the stairs of the temple, her steps pounded and shook the ground at their feet. Nyctimus was in full stride, but he was far

DELPHYNE

more agile than the copper-scaled lizard on his heels. He turned, tossing more fire at her face, making her flinch again. The moment her eyelids closed, he darted between her front arms, dashed under her belly and ran full steam out from under her side towards Cedric on the far side. She snapped her head towards them, hissing as scales were chipping and cracking off her right cheek. The fire made from a magic user was somewhat effective. They had caught a glimpse of hope, but there was no way to know how long Nyctimus could maintain his magic use. It was like adding extra stress on the body, eating away at the stamina and endurance.

Delphyne twisted her body around, the temple rumbling from her movements. With each step, her claws left behind craters of crushed marble like pools of sand boiling away the stairs. She ignored Romasanta's barking, still after Nyctimus with snapping jaws. Seeing a chance, Cedric dove in towards her face. The blackened scales were brittle taunting him with a chance to draw first blood. Again, he let gravity pull him down, his wings aiding only in his aim. The sword tight in both hands, he focused on the scale with the most damage. If he was going to break through, the half-missing plate would have the best chance.

KA-POW-PIIIIIIINNNNNGGG!

"DAMMIT!" roared Cedric, releasing the hilt.

Slamming against her cheek, the sword broke in half. The sound of metal snapping and clattering against the marble stairs was echoing throughout the temple. Determined to do something, Cedric swung a clawed hand towards her right eye. Inches from making the hit, claws tightened over him, tossing him against the marble stairs at the far end of the temple. Angeline watched wide-eyed as he drew close, connecting with the marble stairs a few feet from her. His back slapped against the steps with a series of loud cracks and pops. Arching his back, blood splattered from his lips, failing to muffle the roar of pain exploding from him. His wings were shattered, taking most of the hit, but he couldn't keep himself from tumbling down the stairs. Sweat dripped from Angeline's chin as she panted from the waves slamming into her from their bond. She had forgotten how taxing it was for one of them to be hurt, even if the sensation came to the other as pleasurable.

Swords were useless against a dragon like Delphyne, even on damaged scales. Grimacing, Angeline swallowed and broke her stare of Cedric's heap at the bottom of the steps. There was no time to worry about saving each other, Delphyne was clawing at Nyctimus still. Standing tall, she slowed her breath, pulling back on the bow string. Words trickled through her mind, whispers from two entities that had been thrust into her were making themselves known again. Lady Ann was directing her body, straightening posture and sharing secrets of a dragon's weak points. A firm grip on her shoulder from an unseen hand was taking her attention to chant the words buzzing in her ears. Artemis was their only hope if they were going to pull through.

Evlógise aftó to skáfos...

"Bless this vessel..."

stin panoplía tou íliou...

"In the armor of the Sun..."

Boreí na trypitheí kai na kápsei...

"May it pierce and burn..."

ólous ósous vriskótan stin poreía tou.

"All who lay in its path."

Breathing out the last word, her fingers let the arrow fly. Her eyes followed the silver arrow, the world slowing for her as she watched in anticipation. The silver flashed to life, flames swirling around the shaft as they poured out of the tip. Delphyne's arm was in full stretch, her claws lashing towards Nyctimus who had a column at his back. She had cornered him. The arrow dove into exposed nook under her right arm, flames exploding out. Time hit full stride again, the pain of the attack pulling her attack short, saving Nyctimus. Delphyne screeched, reaching for the arrow with her other claw, she rolled on her side, desperate to slap out the flame burning at her in such a sensitive location. Nyctimus darted away and down to where Romasanta stood howling. A wave of blood hit their nostrils, nerves tightening in response.

Coughing came from Cedric who had sat up, wheezing. "Dammit, you got first blood."

A weak smile crossed her lips, "I was tired of watching you fail."

He grunted, watching as the dragon rolled down the stairs and into the pool of water. Steam rolled up and out, the magical flames Angeline had summoned proved hotter than the Brazier's and Nyctimus' own.

"Where was that trick when I was being crushed by a Wyvern." A wave of arousal hit her and she refused to acknowledge it.

Romasanta and Nyctimus were taunting Delphyne, trying to get her back up on the steps, away from the blocked views of the fountain that limited her own ability for a solid effective shot. Cedric was out of the fight for now, but the excitement growing inside him through their bond said her actions would fuel his healing. She sprinted to the corner of the temple, her eyes catching the burnt spot she had made. Blood oozed and dripped down Delphyne's arm. Drawing back the bow, she was searching for an opening. Delphyne was keeping her arm tucked over the weak spot, and despite Romasanta snipping at her hind quarters, she refused to spin around to expose the other.

At the same point, the dragon was tactful enough to keep Nyctimus focused on dodging to the point he no longer had the energy to spare for magic. Frustrated by no clear shots, Angeline bit her bottom lip, thoughts flying. Looking around, she could try sprinting to the opposite corner or move closer along one side. Delphyne's eyes flickered back to Angeline, locking stares with one another for a few seconds. The dragon snorted, annoyed, she kicked a back leg out at Romasanta who barked, foam dripping from his chin. Daring to traverse the sides would be dangerous and put her within Delphyne's reach. She was far slower than Nyctimus and Romasanta, the pools of crushed marble making her shudder. Worse, running back and forth from one corner to the other to get clear views on either side of the large fountain and brazier would cost too much stamina.

Clenching her teeth, Angeline gathered a solution. *I need to take out the fountain.*

She pivoted her aim from Delphyne to the fountain, whispering the incantation once more as her fingers let go. A roar rung out, the temple shaking with the speed in which the dragon flung herself between the flaming arrow and fountain. Nyctimus and Romasanta found themselves staring across from one another, a burst of flames connecting with the backside of the dragon. Angeline stood, her breath caught in her throat, wide-eyed. Red eyes looked over the copper-scaled shoulders, Delphyne growling in her direction. As the smoke and steam started to rise, something slammed hard into Angeline's side. With a yelp, she found herself rolling down the stairs.

KA-POW!

Marble was raining down on her, still bouncing down the steps with arms tight around her ribs. They tightened with each bounce against the steps, the fall picking up speed. A cracking sensation made her wince in pleasure on her left side, the pressure of the muscles wrapped around her proving too constricting for her frame.

"Shit!" Cedric's voice caught in her ears, but the chaos kept her eyes closed.

KA-POW! KA-POW!

Delphyne's tail was slamming across where she had stood only seconds before. Water rushed around her, there had been no time to inhale her breath. Side stinging, she burst from the pool amongst the stone-filled rain and before her eyes gained their focus, a hand gripped the back of her shirt. Her feet were yanked up and out of the water, a clawed foot smacking the pool where she had been. She was Delphyne's new target. The collar of her shirt was choking her, gasping for air her eyes were rolling back against her will.

Knees smacking into the marble floor, she inhaled deep, coughing. Wincing, her cracked rib cutting her attempts for air short. She was fading between pain and pleasure, adding to her confusion. Her eyes refocusing, she realized Cedric had pulled her out of danger. Biting her tongue, she fought back the anxiety. Her aching fist reminded her she still had her grip on her bow. Shoving Cedric, bruised and bloody, to the side, she aimed to return the barrage of attacks. Delphyne swung around, hissing to see she was too far to reach from where they had landed. Pulling back, again she repeated the spell, the arrow slamming the dragon in the face.

Delphyne backed away, putting the fountain between them. Screaming at Angeline, voicing her annoyance and frustration. Her claws scrambled to splash the water over her face, dousing the flames biting at her. Despite the sky fading to a deep purple, her copper scales adorned a crimson glow in the light of the brazier. Romasanta and Nyctimus leaped onto the dragon's back, ripping away the loose scales from Angeline's previous attack. Delphyne bucked and threw herself around like a dog rolling across the ground. Nyctimus was still showing no signs of calling his flames forward, leaving Angeline the only one able to .

Cedric flopped down again, panting as he looked over at Angeline. "I guess I lied. We'll need me to protect you at every cost if you are going to kill her by sun rise... sorry about the rib."

Ignoring his comments, unable to face him with tears of shame sliding down her cheeks, she focused on aiming for her next opening on the dragon. Angeline was still hunting for a shot, but Nyctimus and Romasanta had taken a beating in just the last few strikes. Delphyne was growing less predictable, her swings and moves more desperate than before. Angeline tensed, recalling the odd block of the fountain she had made, and she aimed again to the fountain. Letting the arrow fly, Delphyne broke away from the exhausted werewolves, diving towards the arrow. An outreached claw grasped the spellbound missile a few feet shy of slamming into the brazier. Clawed fingers ripped outward and away from the palm they had once been attached to. Shrieking erupted from Delphyne as she slammed her shoulder to the ground. Angeline had rendered her right hand useless.

An excited yelp burst from Romasanta. On all fours, he charged at the downed prey before him. Jumping onto the massive heap of dragon scales, it looked like a demonic version of hounds on a fallen boar. Blood splatter in every direction as wolven fangs bit into the wounds covering the reptile. The once clear spring ran deep red, no longer showing what laid under its surface. Nostrils stung with the rich smell of iron and the dank smell of the sizzling blood lining the outside of the brazier. All through the night, the fire still held true, burning on despite the fountain crackling and pieces falling to the pool. Not landing a direct hit, the stress of Delphyne's sudden movements and the shock waves of the spell were chipping away at the marble masterpiece.

"I bet the door to the Oracle has to do with that fountain." Cedric was pulling himself off the ground, ready to rejoin the fight. "Keep it up... she's destroying herself protecting it."

Grimacing, she retorted, "And your destroying yourself protecting me."

Wiping blood from his chin, he smiled, his fangs red with his own blood. "I'll stop worrying about you now. They need help keeping her down at this point."

Cedric leaped off the steps, aiming to slam down on Delphyne. She was snapping her jaws at Romasanta, her tail slamming and slapping at Nyctimus. A fanged grin crossed Cedric's face. Crashing down on the first wound Angeline had made, he clawed into the bleeding flesh. Digging deep into the heat of the muscles, he tore the wound wider, the popping of fibers intoxicating against his claws. Copper scales clanked against the marble, splashing into the red lake below with each wild stroke he made to pull her apart. Blood painted his arms and face, adding to the animalistic expression on his face. Arousal from the violence hit Angeline and her skin prickled. Fear slipped from her, a sense of terror towards Cedric she hadn't felt since the time she saw him eating the Orm.

Flinching, Cedric looked to Angeline on the stairs, the horror pulling him from his demonic indulgence. Delphyne smiled, the pause told her all she needed to know. Her tail slammed Nyctimus against the fountain, she had lost her interest in keeping it intact now that they had caught on to her duty to protect it. Romasanta faltered in his next rush, her tail still snaking through the air with immaculate speed. Fur prickled, his gut twisting with instincts. His body shifted, he found himself racing up the stairs faster than his mind could comprehend. Pain ripped through him, staring down at the glowing red eyes of Delphyne, he knew the sparkle in her eyes. She had caught her prey. It had been an unexpected reflex, somehow his instincts had taken an unpredictable shift.

Blinking, shocked as his abdomen burned, he peered down in a look of confusion. Delphyne's tail pulled away, blood and his own guts spilling forward from the gaping hole it had left behind. A scream rattled his ears and they folded back in annoyance. Looking over his shoulder, Angeline stared wide-eyed, her hands over her mouth, the bow clanking against the floor. He reached down, his fingertips so close to gripping the bow, *Artemis' precious bow...*

"ROMASANTA!" Cedric's anger turned to the smiling dragon he stood on. "YOU BITCH!"

The world tilted before he could touch the object at his feet. Angeline's fingers gripping his arm, laying his head gently on the hard marble floor. He tried to sit up, but his body was heavy and refusing to react. The taste of his own blood was boiling up his throat, rolling across his tongue before the warmth of it dripped from the corners of his mouth. Staring at Angeline, her sobs frightening him. His heart should be racing, but he felt the thudding slowing, weakening.

The light in his eyes failing, his breath not coming to him. Despite the agony throbbing through him, each pulse grew colder. He felt himself smiling, his thoughts musing over it all.

And here we were worried about Cedric getting himself killed. Artemis, you knew she needed to be more in order for us to face Delphyne. I suppose I will soon get to thank you in person. After all, I was nothing more than just a man who even now makes foolish mistakes...

Delphyne gripped up Cedric with her good hand, tossing him into the marble steps next to where Romasanta lay bleeding. It was a lucky hit, marble dust pluming up from where he had smashed into the soft crushed marble from earlier. Angeline was scrambling for her bow, but his eyes were on the old wolf laying lifeless. The stairs were lined with trails of red below the black furred beast, fueling Cedric's rage. He managed to sit up, his left eye squinting as blood slid across and streams of crimson dripped down his chin. Angeline was racing pass him, her bow in her hand to start a wave of rebellion. He reached out, jerking her to him.

Fangs ripped into her arm, the arousal exploding from Cedric making her freeze and shudder. Fear and excitement pulsed from Angeline, the spot identical to where he had ravaged her arm so long ago for the first time. Wicked grins crossed their faces as they stared into one another's eyes. Wounds closed, bruises vanished, and their exhaustion faded. Releasing his bite, he ran his tongue from her wrist to her elbow enjoying the salty tang of her sweat. A clawed hand gripped the hair on the back of her head, pulling her closer. The soft warmth of his tongue across her neck slithered to her ear. Intoxicated by the voluptuous motion, she was enjoying the reprieve from her terror. Angeline was breathless and panting, their bodies waving heat into one another as they ignored the roar of the dragon below them.

He bit at her ear lobe, his breath whispering, "Let's finish this as Lady and Lord, my pet."

As if a phantom, she was slammed by the cold night air. Eyes wide with renewed excitement, Angeline turned back to Delphyne who was clamoring up the steps after them. The lustful waves had drowned out any hesitation. Cedric came smashing down on the hissing snout, smashing her into the marble steps. Pinning her there, he looked to Angeline with a crazed grin.

"Do it!" He demanded. "Fucking finish her."

Her heart fluttered as the wave of desire took her breath from her. The fingers on the arrow releasing, magic pulled from them no longer needing the words she had spoken so many times during the fight. She could feel it, feel how to summon the sensation as Artemis had carved into her mind would start to happen with each use. The arrow flew ever closer, the heat of the sun evaporating the sweat across Cedric's body in wafts of steam. Satisfied he had held Delphyne long enough, he took to the air with a great flap of his unbroken wings. She lifted her head, her mouth wide with a roar. The arrow had been too close for her to turn away, to even close her jaws.

The heat exploded out, blowing off the top of Delphyne's coppery head. It landed with a great splash in the red pool of water down below. Rolling, still aflame, it smashed into the fountain. Nyctimus scrambled to escape the tilting brazier above him. Cedric dove in, dragging him up and away. The temple shook and roared from the thrashing death throes of the dragon's body and the sizzling steam of the fountain and brazier falling into the pool. Without warning, the body disappeared, flames and water falling into a gaping hole where the marble floor crumbled away. Below awaited a cave, but their attention shifted to the black heap of fur on the steps.

CHAPTER 21

LILLITH'S MARK

A ngeline threw her bow across her body, rushing back to Romasanta's lifeless body. Her ears were ringing from the rumbling bellowing up from the dark unknown below them. Some place down there was the Oracle and the passage to return the stone that had sent the old werewolf to his death. Wiping the tears from her eyes, she slowed, taking the last two steps left before her legs buckled next to his body. The blood from him all around her was still warm as her tears fell from her jaw and splashed into the lake of red.

The last of the splashing and crumbling of the central pool settled some place below. Vibrations through the marble fell silent at last. Cedric helped the now limping Nyctimus over to his fallen friend. Angeline's bottom lip trembled, a scowl across her face as she gave Nyctimus a mournful glare, her choking sobs consuming her.

"Why! Why did he save me?" She roared, anger and sorrow tangling in her voice. "I could have survived that... I would have survived that!"

Cedric let Nyctimus sit down on the steps next to Romasanta's body before he sighed. "He knew that. He saw the fight with the Busse... he knew as well as I did you could have taken that hit."

Her hand pulled away, her brown eyes bloodshot and wide with disbelief.

"Please understand..." Nyctimus wheezed, holding his broken ribs. "As werewolves, we sometimes have no way to control the instincts deep within us. From his expression, he had no idea he had become your shield until it was too late to correct it."

"Good God." Lillith's voice echoed from high above them from outer edge of the temple. "You'd think there was a funeral going on down there."

Cedric gritted his teeth. "If this is your idea of helping, you're too late. Delphyne took down your precious wolf."

"Still your tongue!" Her voice boomed, echoing several times as she marched down the steps. "You know nothing about why I am here."

Cedric opened his mouth to continue his complaints, but faltered as the glistening of tears on Lillith's face caught his attention. Behind her was a man he hadn't met before, adding to his curiosity. The stranger sat down at the top edge, lighting a cigarette and unmoved by the devastation laid out before him. Nerves were tightening in every person as the crack of her heels stopped at Romasanta's body. Kneeling, she placed a hand on his chest in the exact spot she had left her spell so long ago. She glared up at Angeline who stood there shell-shocked.

"I need your help with this next part." It was enough to make her blink and Angeline awaited Lillith's request. "Shove it all back in."

"Wh-what." Swallowing, she peered down at Romasanta's body where his entrails had fell across the stairs.

"I said put them back." She hissed in a heartless tone. "Before I do this... it'll hurt less if they are where they need to be. Shove them back."

Nodding, she pulled and pushed the slimy lines of intestines back into the hole where they had come from. Her stomach twisted. The smell of death teamed with the mixture of cold and warm sections made her light headed. Lillith petted the lifeless wolven head with affection, staring down at him like a true lover would be expected to do. Angeline sobbed louder as she struggled to tug the last strand out from under the weight of his body. Lillith scoffed, lifting him up enough to free the last loop of intestines. Shoving them into the bloodied hole, Angeline backed away. She covered her mouth with the only dry spot left on her forearm, desperate to keep herself from vomiting.

"Now it's your turn, my wolf." Lillith leaned over him, kissing his cheek. "Now for you to know what my promise truly means. Know that I have always been willing to sacrifice myself for your love and affection… but this can only happen once. You'll be free from my mark, unable to ever receive it again."

Wiping a tear from her cheek, she let it slide off the tip of her finger and fall into the opened jowls of Romasanta. Everyone watched with wonder, waiting for what was to come. At first it seemed like a grim good bye, an odd and ancient ritual. Cedric felt something shift within Lillith, his incubine instincts revealing this was something only Lillith was capable of doing. His eyes danced from Romasanta to Lillith and back again until he saw her tense. A wave of pain whispered from her, the skin on her shoulders prickled.

"You can't be serious…" Furrowing his brow, Lillith turned to face Cedric as he spoke, "That mark… the legends about the tears of a Goddess being the elixir of life… they were all about you."

A smile crept across her face, blood trickling down the corner of her mouth. Grimacing, she leaned forward coughing up blood as bruises and scrapes bloomed into existence. Wrapping her arms around her midsection did nothing to hold in the rush of blood soaking through her shirt. Horns poured forward, her teeth clenched as she screamed from the pain of it all. With each wound blossoming to life across her body, the mirrored injuries vanished on Romasanta's body. Another scream erupted from her, bone chilling as it waved through everyone baring witness to the spell taking place. Angeline looked down to her blood soaked hands. The pain Lillith spoke of was for her own sake, not Romasanta's. Angeline twisted away from the torturous scene, no longer able to hold the nausea at bay as the contents of her stomach splashed across the lower steps.

A great and deep gasp rose out of Romasanta, his chest rising high with air once more. The hole long gone as if from a nightmare and the flesh like new. Lillith was struggling to breath, blood dripping down her chin yet she smiled to see him jerk awake. His golden eyes were wide, meeting the maroon irises of the Queen Succubus. Grabbing her shoulders, terror rocked through him as he peered down between them. Where he had seen Delphyne's tail slide out of him was no longer there and blood poured out of Lillith.

"Why? How?" He rasped, wrapping his arms around her. "I know you can live through this, but I don't understand..."

Her arms snaked around him, her hands gripping the fur on his back. "I told you I loved you, my wolf. Not just anyone receives a mark from Lillith, the promise of taking away even death."

Swallowing, he could no longer feel the tingling at his chest. "What a dangerous creature you are..."

Tears rolled down his wolven face, tapping against her shoulder making her fuss at him. "It is my greatest curse and blessing."

Lillith broke into another round of blood-filled coughing, pulling herself from Romasanta's arms. He rushed to stand on his feet, picking her up and marching up the stairs towards Pan. She was whispering to him, each flick of her tongue making his muscles tense in rhythm to his steps. Nostalgia was washing over them, a distant memory of when they had both lain together for the first time. Reaching Pan, he placed her on her feet, a speckled trail of red left in their wake across the white marble. Kneeling before her, ears flattened on his head with a look of remorse, she kissed his forehead. Lillith broke away, her posture showing no signs of the injuries wrecking her body. She and Pan fell away from the staring eyes marveling over the grace and compassion her actions held. They had all seen a side of the Queen Succubus that many were not aware existed under her stern exterior.

Romasanta stood, shaking his head and shoulders, peering out to the morning sky. It had taken them over twelve hours to take down Delphyne. Marching down the steps, Lillith long gone from the realm of Delphyne, he took an assessment of everything. The barrier remained intact, but Lillith had whispered the Oracle was the true keeper and guardian of Mt. Parnassus. There was more he was made aware of and he failed to keep his shoulders from shuddering. The Gypsy had returned, and worse, cursed Tony.

His fur prickled hearing her lips in his ears, *but I will resolve this matter in my own way. He is the last remaining living man carrying my mark, like you, he is mine to care for until I see fit.*

At least, in his own experience since he carried her curse, she had never done him wrong or even lead him astray. More times than his heart could bare to admit, she had come to him and salvaged what little remained of him throughout the passing of time. Regardless, he knew Tony would be in over his head having to deal with a demoness as sharp minded as she. Pausing, he looked over his companions. Nyctimus' condition was rough, but his hazel eyes showed the relief of seeing his friend alive and well. Cedric's eyes fell away, a sense of shame written across his twitching jawline. Had he continued to stay and protected Angeline, none of this would have ever happened. Then again, he had warned him -no insisted- he accept the inability to protect her. In the end, Romasanta had failed everyone and broke the laws he had laid out for them all.

Snorting at his own thoughts, steam rolled from his nostrils in the cool morning air. He walked through them, ignoring Angeline who buried herself into the small of Cedric's back, clinging to him like a child. Blood painted her arms and it made his abdomen tense to smell it was his own. Shaking it off, he squatted at the broken edge of the temple's center, staring deeply into the dark abyss of the cavern below. His ears fell flat once more, his nose twitching. Fur raised across the back of his neck with renewed excitement. Something smelled familiar, something from his past. The instincts rising in him brought a fear with it.

"Do you smell that, Nyctimus?" His golden glare looked over his shoulder.

Nyctimus closed his eyes, taking in a deep inhale. "I dare not say the name in which I associate this scent with. It has to be a trick."

More fur ruffled over Romasanta, "I fear what scene lies down below. How many times will my heart have to break…"

"What is wrong?" Cedric's voice cut into the conversation, his forehead folding. "Who or what is down there?"

Romasanta and Nyctimus locked eyes, both breaking it with a canine shake and shudder.

"Let's pray…" Nyctimus stopped, an ear flicking, nose twitching as a whimper escaped him.

"Let's pray they are still a friend." Snorting, Romasanta's lip curled. "I would have never thought *she* would still be alive, nor powerful enough to sustain such a barrier."

Nyctimus peered down into the darkness. "Is it wrong that I fear seeing *her* again?"

"No…" Romasanta's words were nothing but a whisper.

Cedric sighed, "Are we in for another big battle?"

"No…" Huffing, Romasanta looked to Cedric with eyes filled with despair. "When we get down there, don't make a move without my signal."

Chills ran across Cedric's spine. "I see… whatever happens down there, the moment I see any aggression, I will take them down regardless what you demand of me."

Silence fell over them, confirming Romasanta could not stop him if it unfolds in such a way. After several minutes, everyone stood side-by-side to stare down the gaping hole. Light trickling down from the skylight revealed a spiraling stairway carved into a monstrous stalagmite with water trickling down from the broken tip. This was where it had once fueled the fountain, explaining why Delphyne had defended it with her body several times. Deep below, the darkness was broken by random flutters of fires sparkling like starlight. The roar of cavern waterfalls rumbled up, a mist boiling up in the peachy morning light. Peeling Angeline's arms off him,

Cedric leapt out into the gap, his wings wide with air as he glided to the stairway. Landing with elegance, he folded his batlike appendages, testing the weight below him. Looking to Romasanta, he tilted his head with an expression to say, *it seems sturdy*. Another flap of his wings and he had made it back to the edge where he left Angeline.

Romasanta's nose twitched, his ear flicking. "You sure its sturdy?"

"Didn't sway or wobble." Cedric rolled both his shoulders, using his wings was still a new and sore feat for him. "Not even a crumble of a rock came off it."

Ears flattening, he eyed Nyctimus who still had a rattle to his breathing. "Are you even going to be able to make that jump? You sound like you have a broken rib or two."

Grimacing at the thought, Nyctimus sat down on the stairs with a huff. "Honestly, if I can rest a few more hours, I'll be more than ready to make the leap and even fight again."

"Then that settles it." Cedric sighed, sitting with his feet dangling over the edge. "No need to rush into the unknown without making sure all of us are capable of defending ourselves at best. We still don't know what will happen when we crossover to Gaea's realm."

Romasanta shook, his nose twitching as he glared down into the black hole. "Agreed. I'll stand guard. You three get some rest. We should be safe now, according to Lillith."

CHAPTER 22

ON THE EDGE

Tony was pacing alongside the length of the couch, anxious to know what had upset Lillith so much. The tingle at the back of his neck erupted as a red glow came from the pane of glass she had gone through. Stopping, he watched wide-eyed. The rose reappeared, opening in endless layers, and Pan came stumbling in with her arm thrown over his shoulders. Blood slapped against the black marble floor, the sound twisting his stomach. Tony rushed over to help Lillith. The moment his hands touched her skin, he was met with a choking amount of pain and pleasure. It was a confusing and exciting sensation making his heart race. The mark burnt like fire in response to everything happening to her. Biting his tongue, ignoring the sweat pouring across himself, Tony focused on getting her across the living room to the couch.

She grinned, though the grimace and pale complexion on her face let Tony know she was indeed in pain. Her arm pulled off of Pan, she made a panicked sound, cursing under her breath. Rushing to reach for her abdomen, her full weight making Tony stumble to a stop. They were almost to the couch, but more blood spilled forth, splattering at his feet. His eyes followed her frantic grip. Tony's body tensed, watching her fingers tangle with her entrails. They were threatening to fall from the circular hole in her belly. Pan grunted, taking off his business jacket and began maneuvering to tie it around her waist in hopes of aiding her failing efforts. She shrieked with each knot he tied, working the fabric tighter. With every whimper, a wave of agony mixed with sexual excitement made Tony nauseous. Her nails digging into the flesh of his shoulders with each movement added to the unnatural arousal filling him. At this point, Tony was far paler than Lillith.

Confident her insides would be kept in place, Pan grabbed her arm back over his own shoulder. Again they dragged her, finishing their trek across the living room and lying her on the couch. Her eyelids were heavy, her body growing cold. Tony's distraught look made her smile, laugh a little even. His lips parted, but there were too many questions flooding his mind to speak out loud. Lillith patted his cheek, wincing as she fought the urge to giggle. The wheezing and gurgling in her breath sent shivers through Tony. Grabbing her hand in his, he fought the urge to gasp from the erotic sensation it added. Swallowing, the realization of what it meant to be an incubus rattled inside Tony's soul. Eyes glazing over, his mind started to recall Cedric's own story and struggles. Lillith gave a labored sigh, her face rolling away, her hand pulling free as she let herself drift asleep.

Pan lit another cigarette, making his way to the arm chair across from the couch. Sitting there, he crossed his legs. The green glare teamed with the grin was menacing. Tony sat on the floor, leaning his back against the couch, lost in the moment of the chaos. His eyes broke from Pan and fell on the red fluid painting the floor. A coppery scent mixed with the salty sweat of the bodies who occupied the room. Never had Tony been so in tune with the exact scent of every new object. The dried musk of the cigarette cut across his nostrils, making him aware Pan rolled them. Tony dug deeper into the smells, they were helping him escape the weight of the erogenous desires pouring into him from Lillith's own injuries. Cinnamon, apples, and a hint of a summer's breeze threw Tony's eyes back to Pan. He had placed his cigarette down and blew Tony a kiss.

"Ah, so that was what you were doing over there." Pan leaned back into his seat, taking another drag off his cigarette. "It's a clever way to distract yourself from that. In fact, first time I've seen one of you do that. Most can't come back from the height you were at, especially with her unable to keep her own power in check."

"One of us..." Tony repeated dryly, his cheeks hot with embarrassment.

"You are almost a complete incubus, yet you're doing better at keeping those urges at bay." Pan scratched at his goatee, thinking before he continued. "So what did it smell like? I'm curious now. Rumor says you can smell as sharply as a werewolf when you want to."

Tony lifted his eyebrows, feigning ignorant. "What did what smell like?"

A toothy grin responded, "My kiss. Surely you realized it's magical, hm?"

Tony looked down and away. Over his shoulder he found Lillith's sleeping face. "What happened to her?"

"She kept her promise to protect someone she loved." Sighing, Pan finished the last of his cigarette before smashing it into the ashtray. "You know, you can fix her right up in a matter of a minute, if that."

Tony refused to look at Pan, his voice getting closer to him, his footsteps patting soft and slow on the floor out of his peripheral. "I find that hard to believe."

"Did Cedric not share that secret with you?" Cooed Pan.

"I..." Tony's stomach tensed, *Could he be suggesting...*

"Shame you weren't in that meeting." Pan's voice was closer, chills rippling across Tony who refused to look in his direction. "Rumor has it, Romasanta shared their first time together. It was a lot like this, you know? Cedric and Lillith were never... loverly between the two. As for you, there might be a chance..."

Grimacing, Tony could feel the heat of Pan's breath trickling across his shoulder and neck. "I'm not one to pry into her personal life. She's hurt and in pain. You can't be suggesting we have..."

"Sex?" Tony flinched, staring at the blood trickling from the corner of her lips. "You can't tell me you don't feel those instincts stirring deep in your body... isn't that why you were sniffing out distractions?"

Pan whispered in Tony's ear and he bit his tongue.

"My, you are a special one..." Pan's lips tickled at Tony's ear.

Turning, Tony aimed to shove him back, tiring of Pan's game. Lips locked with his own as he opened them in protest. A boiling heat filled Tony while the flavor of cinnamon and apples licked across his tongue and teeth. Blood boiling, a hand gripped a fist full of Tony's hair, breaking the intrusion. Pan frowned.

Pan back stepped to escape Lillith's claw swipe. Arousal erupted across Tony, yet no pain came from the tugging on his scalp. An explosion of intoxicating arousal poured out from where Lillith's claw had stopped, fingers deep in the flesh of Tony's abdomen. Warm lines of blood tickled his skin, dripping into the puddle of Lillith's own blood. Panting, Tony could feel himself spiraling out of control, the mark on his neck failing to phase the heat of passion and want burning through his soul.

"What the fuck were you thinking, Pan?" She hissed, her grip on Tony's hair tightening.

"How much I would regret not kissing him before I left, my dear sister." Like a bubble, Pan burst into rose petals, his laughter lingering in the room.

Tony panicked, Lillith's claws popping through his stomach muscles. He should have felt the sting and agony of flesh forced apart. Instead, Tony shook with the building excitement and Lillith hadn't moved at all. Chills and waves echoed from her into him, and much to his surprise, the reverse was happening within her. Her labored breathing carried the fading scent of blood. The claws tightened, cutting into his flesh until he released a moan. His head jerked further back, arching so his ear reached her lips.

"What do you feel?" She shoved her claws deeper, another moan of pleasure escaping him. "Tell me, Tony? Is this what you expected?"

His eyes rolled back, every movement delightful yet unnerving. "It's... it's terrifying."

She licked the sweat from his cheek and he panted, breathless. "I can't let you go, not yet."

"I... I..." Closing his eyes, he focused on the smells again, slowly edging away from his ferocious sexual wants.

"No you don't..." She dragged her claws across him, ripping open the wounds that had started to heal. "What do you feel?"

Heart pounding, Tony fought his urge to cry out as he said, "Like the best sex I've ever had, but... but I can feel my body healing with each wave. I can feel... I feel you healing, and that, that's more intoxicating than what pain I should be experiencing."

She let go, a coldness slamming him as the last of their touch broke away. Tony fell on his side, his shoulder welcoming the icy marble floor and the sticky red pool. Rolling over, he found her sitting up, untying the jacket with an annoyed expression on her face. As the coat fell away, he could see her stomach healed as if nothing happened. Rubbing his abdomen, he found nothing. Bile rolled up into his throat and he swallowed it down. She stood, he flinched, unsure of what came next.

"I'm taking a shower." She snorted, peering down at him.

Sighing, he refused to meet her gaze. She tapped his ribs with her foot. Opening his eyes, he turned his head, reluctant to meet her gaze. A smile crossed her face and his stomach tightened.

"So what did it taste like?" A toothy grin broke through her red lips.

His face flushed, "The next time we meet, he'll be kissing my fist."

"You realize why he kissed you?" She lifted an eyebrow, sharpening her tone. "There's a reason why Pan was stirring you up your incubine desires."

Rubbing his stomach again, Tony's eyes dropped to the trail of red. "It was his way to heal you..."

"But knowing Pan, he wanted to steal a kiss." Laughing, she started to walk away then stopped. "You want to join me?"

"Join you?" His eyes widened as she shuffled out of her clothing with each step towards the hallway. "In the shower?"

She paused at the hall entrance, looking over her shoulder, her silhouette glowing in the filtering sunlight. "Yes, in the shower. We're both covered in blood, don't you want to rinse off?"

Breaking his eyes from the curves of her body, he swallowed, squeaking his response. "I'll use the other shower."

Chapter 23

The Oracle

"So what else was Lillith whispering about?" Angeline and Nyctimus had been asleep for hours before Cedric couldn't resist asking Romasanta. "There was more to it, was there not?"

"We should get going..." Romasanta dodged the question, but before he could walk to Nyctimus, Cedric stepped in the way. "It's all taken care of."

"What is?" The scowl deepened on Cedric's face, the horns still framing his face and the folded arm-like wings making him far more intimidating. "Or should I say *who* is taken care of *what?*"

Romasanta's ears flattened, snorting his reply. "Tony."

"Tony?" He blinked, an answer he hadn't expected. "What could be going on with him for Lillith to intervene?"

Romasanta lifted an eyebrow, "You caught that much?"

A fanged grin exploded across his face. "I'm too old not to eavesdrop when I can, old man."

"I can't deny that notion." A short chortle led into muscles relaxing. "He's been cursed at some point, by the gypsy girl. Regardless, Lillith's tone and intentions seem to have his best interest in hand."

"Even so..." Cedric turned to see Angeline's face crumble from a nightmare, possibly a memory. "Her idea of *fixing* a problem isn't always pleasant to those involved. Any idea what sort of problem a watered down halfling could be in?"

"True, but she's made the same contract with him. She never revealed what that might be." Cedric peered back at Romasanta who gave a grave expression. "He is now the sole carrier of the mark she had lain across my chest. Her ability to resurrect me broke, or fulfilled her obligation to me. I never knew what it meant... at least we can be confident he will still be breathing when we return with that much information."

"Tsch," hissed Cedric. "We will deal with when we get back, then."

"Agreed." Satisfied with Romasanta's reply, they turned to wake their counterparts.

Angeline woke with a gasp, a cold sweat painting her skin. Sitting up, her arms wrapped around him and she buried her tear-soaked face into his chest. Without hesitation he wrapped his arms around her, his wings unfolding around them like a curtain to hide them away from prying eyes. Her fingers were digging into his back muscles and her body shook. It was always hit and miss whether she would have a hard time snapping out of her sleep. Kissing the top of her head, he broke her embrace, raising her chin to him. Tears were rolling out of her eyelids, a never ending motion.

Cedric's face was emotionless glaring down on her. A sparkle in his green eyes, like she had remembered seeing so long ago. His lips broke away, his fangs calling the attention of her eyes, stopping her tears. The fingers on her chin tightened, making her wince from the aching discomfort it created. A brick wall made of anger and jealousy made her heart flutter. The potency of it made it hard to breath, filling her to the point she shook out of fright. His eyes glowed with a animalistic desire, bringing her back to the days where she was his new bride. No longer would he cuddle her, she had proven far stronger than he could have hoped her to become. His own regret eating at him drove his rage ever higher. Leaning in, his breath boiling against her neck, he made his promise to her and himself

"Listen well, pet." His whisper was sharp, the words leaving his tongue like arrows hitting her heart. "No one will die for your life except me. Any who dare to threaten it..." Lips and fangs graced her ear, the deepest tone she had ever heard from him rattling her. "Know I'll devour their souls."

Before she could grasp the depths of its meaning, he sunk his fangs into her neck. Wings tightened around them and she found herself moaning in ecstasy. Her sleep hadn't done much to recover her from the exhausting fight, but the vicarious suckling and digging of fangs at her neck filled her with energy. Satisfied they were both recovered, he released his bite and licked up the blood. Each soft warm stroke heated her entire body. Panting, she couldn't breathe. The arousing thoughts and sensations invading her, wanting him to play with her more. Snorting, he grinned at the ease in which he excited her. They didn't have time to indulge in one another.

He opened his wings wide, breaking the sensations resonating between them. Gripping her wrist, he dragged her to stand on her feet, impatient. Wrapping an arm around waist, he squeezed her tight. Before she caught her breath, he had pulled her to the ledge. A yelp escaped her as he stepped off with her in tow. Her hands clawed at him, holding on for dear life. His wings filled with air, flapping twice to bring them level with Romasanta. He gave them a disapproving stare, his golden eyes flashing. Huffing, gripping tighter onto Angeline, Cedric broke into a dive into the unknown darkness. Howls broke the roar of the wind, both Nyctimus and Romasanta racing down the stalagmite after them.

Cedric circled the base of the stalagmite, giving his eyes a chance to adjust to the light of the braziers leading away from the massive monument. On the backside lay the copper scaled heap of Delphyne's body and chunks of the marble fountain. Confident there was nothing dangerous, he splashed down in front of the base of the stairs. Angeline's ribs and hip throbbed from the roughness in which she had dangled in his arm the whole way down. Pulling her bow off, she watched the two werewolves gallop down the last stretch of steps with tongues dangling from their mouths. She couldn't resist the urge to smile at the doggish appearance they took on for a change, far from her first impression.

Nyctimus splashed down into the cool waters, rolling to his side to catch his breath. A claw was gripping his ribs, he was still recovering and the run down had been painful. After several rounds of coughing, he stumbled on two feet, shaking the water from his golden brown fur. Nodding to Romasanta, they waited for him to decide what to do. There were no signs of danger, no alarming smells besides the fragrance of flowers and burning incense on the draft pulling over and up through the gaping hole above their heads. Romasanta stared somewhere into the darkness where the braziers fluttered. His nose twitched and a shudder rattled his shoulders. There was still one scent mixed with it all still nipping at his soul.

Huffing, he gave one sharp glare to Cedric. In response, Cedric's jaw twitched, rolling both shoulders aching from his flight and added weight. Despite the silence, the message was loud, don't take any action without his say so. They fell in line behind Romasanta as he marched between the braziers, following him further into the underground abyss. With each passing row of flames, the massive hole became less noticeable and the stalagmite shrinking, fading into the distance. The air grew colder, the heat of the braziers more welcoming. Shivering, goosebumps prickled across Angeline's pale skin and her teeth chattered. No one had anything to offer her and Cedric's eyes and mind would not break from where his instincts pointed.

The black foreground broke away to a circle of braziers. In the center, one sat high, larger than those surrounding it. This pillar of flame and warmth was in the hands of statue, a werewolf deity, perhaps another Apollo reference. Instincts were sending stomachs tighter, noses picking up on the shift in the air. Breaking through the pungent scents of floral and herb incense was a distinct human ambience. Angeline swallowed down her nerves, it was the first time she had realized how strong a human smelled to a nose of a demon. Biting her bottom lip, her shoulders shuddering as she looked over at the glowing green eyes of Cedric. He stared at her, a coy smile across his lips, knowing all too well what she was thinking, sensing.

Chains clattered and they halted their approach. A skid and slosh of chain, stone and water, made Romasanta and Nyctimus flick an ear. Another round of raised noses and tiny spasms of sniffing. Fur ruffled. Romasanta turned to them, the fur around his head, neck and shoulders on end like a lion's man. Drool dripped from his jaw, anxiety and anticipation building at his core. He was failing to hide the panic gripping at his soul, stiff and unnerved. Cedric lifted an eyebrow, he wasn't this worked up over Delphyne.

Exactly who is the Oracle to unravel the old man this much?

"Stay here." Shaking his head, the mane flattened and drool spider webbed through the air. "This is my business and I don't need prying ears or lips."

He was marching away when Nyctimus spoke up, "Are you sure about this? It may be her body but..."

Stopping, he gave an angry glare over his shoulder. "It's her. There's no mistaking it. Though, we may be in luck. If it proves she is possessed, we should be thankful Fenrir no longer resides within my body."

Nyctimus took a step back, a sign of his submission and falling in line with Romasanta as his master. Cedric snorted, his jaw aching from the tension he felt with the thought this old man knew the Oracle. The whole situation seemed planned. Watching the were-wolves, Cedric couldn't help but speculate on everything this journey had revealed.

How much of this situation was prepared in advance for us coming here? The stone, Fenrir, even my own creation and my bond with Angeline... who could be powerful enough to pull the strings? Artemis? Gaea? Even Lillith seems to be a step ahead of us on the situation...

Looking to Angeline, he thought back to the time Romasanta revealed their blood relation through his witch of a sister, Artemis. Every memory was making his heart thud ever louder. Artemis planned for Angeline to have this, interfered with Badbh's spell, and even forced him to be her protector. Here at Gaea's Gate, they stood to face the Oracle to ask for passage. Here they stood with Apollo and his wolf Nyctimus as well as a Daughter of Artemis and her demonic knight. Someone was writing their lives into some sadistic fairy tale... but could they really afford to turn tail after coming so far?

Marching forward, Romasanta had lost focus on the whistling from Nyctimus' breathing. Flattening his ears, he paused, turning to look back to where he left the three companions. He could see Cedric's movement, pacing impatiently as expected. Another slight draft crossed his nose, bringing his attention to the familiar smell of a woman from his past. Taking in a deep inhale, he marched quick and confident into the circle of dancing flames. Under the warmth of Apollo's brazier chains clanked and slapped the rocks. She stood, tall and strong like he knew she would, like she had always done.

Pausing, he took in her strong shoulders and back muscles from under the thin veil of red and white curtains of her dress. Her black hair fell in large wet strings, disappearing into the rocks, chains and water at her feet. The rock under her, where her pedestal and collection of herbs, fruits and dishes of offerings, was the only dry spot within the circle of dancing flames. All around the Castalian springs bubbled up through the cracks, wafts of cool smoke drifting between them. The largest pool of water laid between her and the werewolf statue. She was far paler than his last memory of her and the crown on her head was an unexpected accessory. Ears flicking forward, he waited for the voice to enter them, but none came. After gathering his nerve, he braved to voice his conclusion to who stood here, who had earned the title of Oracle.

"Rhea." Her shoulders slumped, chains skidding as she hugged herself. "If... I had no idea you were... perhaps I could have braved coming sooner... fought harder..."

The words were catching in his throat. Agony tore into his soul staring at the silent back of a woman he cared for, the wildling Fenrir had adored, and the mother to the only children he had ever had. Another wave of despair clawed at his heart.

Does she know what sin Fenrir and I committed? Is she aware Remus met his death on these very claws? Looking down into the beastly palms, his tears splashed across like the blood of his son. *How could I ever forget something to horrific. How could I ask forgiveness...*

Pale fingers glowed bright through the blurred vision. Heaving with sorrow, ears flat, he was afraid to look her in the eyes. Her hands were gentle, opening his clawed hands wider. Thumbs ran across the creases, but still he refused to look her in the face, terrified of the expression he would see there. The silver cuffs had been on her wrists for so long they were calloused where they rubbed and pulled. His golden glare followed the shining grey snake in and out of the water, up and over the rocks and found where they disappeared into the rock under the statue's feet.

Her hands floated up, cupping his cheeks where her thumbs wiped away the tears. Reluctant, he forced himself to face her eye-to-eye. What he saw made the tears flow heavier. Her silence had not been of her own choice. Lips and eyelids had been sewn together. Anger and guilt brought a claw to the caged mouth and broke each line in half. She smiled, her hands gripping his claws before they could free her eyelids. Shaking her head, she hugged him and he wrapped his arms tight around her fragile form. A twist in his chest, like that of a knife, filled him with misery to think how long had she been in this tortured state.

"I don't understand..." He gnashed his fangs, still lost for words.

"My eye sight belongs to the premonitions now." Her raspy voice made the knife of his emotions twist further. "I've been waiting a long time for you to come here, Romasanta."

"Waiting... here for me..." His stomach knotted. "Chained to this place, for me?"

Pulling away, she smiled as her hands glided over his wolven face. "Don't be sad. I chose this fate for the ones I loved more than life itself. Nothing would do me more honor as to be the one to let you through Gaea's Gate and put you in reach of getting your dear wife back."

"But to be here... in this prison..." His voice trembled with the heartache squeezing his soul. "I would have refused to let you live out your days like this... you deserve so much better Rhea..."

"He tells me that every second he gets..." The words made every nerve tighten.

"Fenrir."

Nodding, she gave him a hearty pat on his head, the chains clanking loud in the cavern. "Yes, my beloved Fenrir. Here the veil is thin and we can talk to our hearts' content. I see his gift has served you well over the years. Though my own curse vanished when he crossed into Gaea's plane."

His knees gave out. Splashing to the ground he let out a lonesome howl. All this time he had thought he failed Rhea and his dearest friend Fenrir had abandoned him. How far from the truth his mind and heart had painted his memory of them. Centuries passed and the whole while he struggled with who and what he was, these two had made sure to secure his way to Gaea. Another round of howling and soon the splashing of Nyctimus, Cedric and Angeline approached.

Nyctimus threw out his arm, stopping Cedric in his tracks. "There's no threat. Just the howl of a broken heart."

"Nyctimus?" Her eyebrows lifted high, her bound eyes looking in the direction she had heard the voice.

"R-rhea." His hazel eyes glimmered in the light of the braziers. "I thought when they dragged you away you... you were..."

He rushed across the distance, gripping her in his arms. "Delphyne showed not even a day after I was imprisoned by my enemies. She made an offer to me, with a need for an Oracle to maintain a barrier in Delphi and serve Gaea directly. I left everything behind, knowing you would watch over things, knowing I would outlive my children and the world as I knew it. I'm so sorry I did not have a way to tell you, even tell Romasanta."

"I am so sorry I was not..." Her hand covered the front of Nyctimus' muzzle, silencing his unwanted apologies.

"I can't believe you are still suffering with the curse." Her face twisted with worry as her hands wondered across his face and arms. "Why were you not freed like me when Fenrir passed on?"

A chuckle rolled from his chest. "Because my magic adopted this ability and made it its own."

Cedric shuffled in silence, shooting a glare to Angeline. The Oracle posed no threat, but Nyctimus' words told him volumes about what was happening to Angeline. This was her magic adopting his ways, his powers, and using them to its advantage to shield and protect her. The idea of it made him proud yet made his stomach twist to know what else did it take into her. She would struggle for a long time before she would master it. Even then, he had his own powers he still didn't grasp or fully comprehend. How much did he blindly push into her without knowing the consequences? Or was her magic simply taking what it pleased...

"The Lykoan tribe were indeed gifted in the arts." Reaching out as she spoke, Romasanta grabbed her hand to help her back to her perch on the dry rock. "Give me a few minutes to prepare the way for you."

She knelt on the cushioned pedestal. A chant flowed from her lips, an archaic language unknown to even Romasanta. The smoke of the incenses swirled around her, reacting to the flowing movements of her arms and hands. As if she could see, she reached down, raising a bronze dish high and towards the statue, imitating it. Reaching into it, she pulled out a smoldering bundle of herbs and began drawing on the air before her.

Nyctimus placed a heavy hand on Romasanta's shoulder, both of them relieved Rhea had not become a foe. She was here because she had chosen to be close to Fenrir over everything else. Her desire to return the sacrifices Romasanta had made to allow their love to blossom would be atoned with her ability to grant them passage. Cedric stood behind them, watching from afar. He hadn't interfered nor offered rebuttal to the events unfolding. Instead, he glared at Angeline, his emotions tangled with the unknown.

Rhea's voice echoed throughout the cavern like a million enchanters humming the same spell on a mountain top for all the world to hear. A wind was building, flowing out from where she stood. The words heightened, shrieking as they vibrated the air from their lungs. Angeline had gripped Cedric's arm, afraid it would blow her away. Rhea's hand dropped away, but the dish floated in place. Kneeling again, her voice fell deeper, lower until a mumble was all that remained. The dish tilted above her, an endless supply of smoke pouring down into the core of the springs. A mixture of blue and green light swirled and murmuring of voices came from beyond it. Gaea's Gate was open.

Panting, Rhea had finished the incantation. "Hurry, it will not stay open for long."

Without hesitation, Nyctimus, Cedric and Angeline dove into the swirling pool. It swallowed them whole, no signs of even a splash or disturbance to the spring itself. Romasanta paused, looking to Rhea, unsure what to say.

"It's ok. You can leave me here." She laughed. "Delphyne is the undying... she'll be revived in a day's time."

Shuddering, he grumbled. "She makes for bad company."

"So did Fenrir at times."

Closing his eyes, Romasanta let himself fall into the springs. Unlike the abrasive crossing through the Sibyl Stone barrier, this one was warm and inviting. The voices were becoming more articulated, and many of them were familiar. He did not feel himself fall or land, but a shake to the shoulder made his eyes open. Nyctimus gave him a toothy grin, but his wolven form had vanished. Romasanta found himself laying on his back. Bringing his hands into sight, he could no longer change skins, he too was human once more.

Sitting up, before him knelt a massive demon with green eyes. Cedric had taken on a monstrous size and form. He was double Romasanta's height as a werewolf. Muscles dove in and out of his arms and stomach. The fangs in his mouth no longer hidden behind his lips while the wings at his back shadowed over them all. Horns curved out thicker and more aggressive from his skull, a second set spiraling out and behind like that on a gazelle. His tail swiped side to side. He stared at Romasanta and Nyctimus who had been reduced to their human forms. Peering around, the muscles across Cedric twitched with anger.

"Where's Angeline?" Cedric demanded.

Before Romasanta could process their surroundings, something large was approaching. Rustling of the underbrush and trees called them all to attention. A massive godlike wolf brushed pass Cedric and headed straight for Romasanta and Nyctimus. The fur was thick and silvery white like a phantom. Romasanta scrambled to his feet, on edge, but the body language from the animal gave no signs of being a threat. Sitting on its haunches, its golden glare looked over Romasanta. Snorting, its lips curled into a toothy snarling grin.

"You look well, Farmer." A familiar voice fell from its muzzle.

Romasanta's heart and soul stung at the very presence of the godlike entity before him. The golden glare was all too familiar. The smug expression the animal held was like the hardy pat on the back from an old war companion. Gripping at his arm, phantom pains from fangs from so long ago echoed through Romasanta. Staring at the size of the teeth within the massive muzzle brought back his past and the start of his own journey. Relief washed over him, the muscles in his shoulders and body letting go. Romasanta willed himself to speak the wolf's name.

"Fenrir..." Romasanta's face flushed, grinning. "You look old, whatever happened to your black fur?"

"I gave it to you." He chuckled and then nodded in respects to Nyctimus. "You've grown quite a bet, Nyctimus. I am glad I spared you from your namesake's fate."

"They deserved the punishment you bestowed on them." Nyctimus sighed, but shifted his weight to peer at Cedric who sat behind Fenrir. "It seems we are missing someone."

"No..." Sighed Fenrir, standing on all fours. "Artemis took the girl. She is in safe hands and will meet you at Gaea's throne."

"I don't like it." Cedric stood eye-to-eye with Fenrir whose lip curled in response to the aggressive posture. "She belongs with me."

"Calm yourself, my friend." Cedric paled at the voice cutting into the tension. "Fenrir is right, she is in safe hands or I would have accompanied her."

From behind Romasanta and Nyctimus approached another familiar form. Cedric's chest ached to hear the clack of the staff against the ground. The blinding light that had masked where they stood was fading at last. Blinking, they found themselves in a cave much like the one they left behind. Speeding pass everyone, Cedric wasted no time to wrap his arms around the old Cynocephali. Wylleam groaned from the sheer strength behind the bulk of Cedric's monstrous form. He paused from pushing him back, realizing how much he had been missed.

"I never thought I would be so lucky as to see you again..." Cedric whispered so only Wylleam could hear him. "So many times I have found myself yearning to hear your words of wisdom... and the guilt of never paying you back..."

"Honestly, this embrace is payment enough. You were a friend, and when I called upon you, you never failed to come to my aid." He laughed. "I never expected you to grow so large in my absence..."

Pulling away, Cedric snorted. "This is not what I normally look like. In fact, we are baffled by the state we find ourselves in within

Gaea's realm. I think someone forgot to give us information about how this place effects our bodies."

Scratching at his canine jaw, Wylleam looked over everyone. "I see. No one explained the way spirits are reflected in this realm."

"Spirits?" Cedric glanced over his shoulder at Romasanta and Nyctimus. "So, they carry human spirits... and I..."

"A rather unique demon." Interjected Fenrir. "It reflects you are a King Incubus, but some of it expresses something else..."

Cedric watched as Fenrir paced around him like a circling predator. "So this is what I am when there is no body left to contain it?"

"Yes..." Fenrir dropped his head, taunting Cedric. "The green eyes, the overall size and the wings all remind me of what the soul of a moroi looks like."

"Moroi." A smirk came across his face. "I suppose moroi are monstrous souls, and the reason they were driven into extinction, hunted at every turn from the moment they come into the world."

"They break Gaea's Law being born, but you on the other hand..." Fenrir stopped, his eyes burning into Cedric's own. "You are one of the few who are capable of competing with myself or even a titan."

Romasanta patted the side of Fenrir's forearm. "And he's adopted your son's name for himself."

Fenrir snorted, "He'll prove to me if he's worthy of keeping it. Gaea has granted us the honor to serve as your guides, but she wants you to prove yourselves worthy of seeing her."

"Downing Delphyne was not enough?" Cedric licked his fangs, pride swelling. "Making it through the barrier, climbing Mt. Parnassus, none of this was not impressive to the Mother of Gods and Earth?"

"Let's first get you all clothes, we have quite the long journey walking to the throne on foot." Wylleam clacked his staff towards a lit exit. "We'll have time to explain what this place is and what is unfolding in both realms..."

CHAPTER 24

TONY'S DECISION

Tony woke, his hand gripping his chest. The agonizing ache and tightening in his body left his limbs numb. Panic soared through his mind, shaking the thoughts screaming *heart attack*. This was something surfacing from deep inside him. Lillith's mark was tingling, but after the incident on the couch, it did nothing to govern the demonic tendencies stirring within him. He pulled the sweat soaked covers off, feeling choked and tangled, wishing to be free. He stood, took a few steps and fell. Wincing, he panted from the pain rattling his entire body, desperate to catch his breath. A burning sensation was blossoming from his heart and flowing into the rest of him as if his blood was boiling. Clenching his jaw tight, he pushed himself back to his feet and stumbled down the hall.

The burning was taking over, sweat steaming off his bare shoulders as the fever spiraled out of control. Stumbling, leaning against the wall, he managed to make it to the bathroom. He misjudged his reach for the vanity. Losing balance, his body numb, his feet slipped out from under him. Cracking his forehead against the corner, he rolled on impact, landing hard on the tile. Gripping his forehead, the blood trickled from the throbbing cut like hot wax. His soul was on fire and it was threatening to burn his body to ashes. Rolling off his back, he crawled into the shower on all fours, red dribbling across the floor like drool. The pain from the hit made his eyes roll back.

Where is the intoxication sensations of pleasure? Why does my body feel numb and painful?

Groping overhead, his palm found one of the shower knobs. Squeaking it on, the cold water seemed to sizzle as it hit across him.

Relief was rained down on him. He managed to sit, leaning against the wall. Feeling his forehead, he hissed, the knot swelling, still bleeding. He looked down at the water swirling away the clouds of red and sighed. What made his body roar to life in such a violent reaction was beyond his understanding. His eyes fell to his abdomen, blood dripping across where Lillith's fingers had dug into his flesh. Chills rattled him, rubbing the skin, marveling no scars or marks had remained. Touching the knot on his forehead, his curiosity growing if a moment like that would take even something this nasty away.

"Good grief..." Lillith yawned, flipping on the bathroom light. "It usually helps to take your pants off when you take a shower."

He glared at her, unamused. "I was in bad shape, but the blood across the floor and running down my face should say volumes."

She was in a tank top and yoga pants as she sat on the toilet lid. "I suppose you are wondering why you feel like you're on fire so suddenly."

Again, he hissed trying to touch the angry knot of his forehead. "Once more, I am not shocked to hear you know a reason for yet another mystery happening within my own body?"

"Cedric and the others have made it to the Oracle and crossed over." She propped her chin in her palm, rubbing sleep from her eyes with the other. "Which means you need to make a decision. Take my deal or let the curse run its course."

Reaching over, he turned the shower off. "The curse seems to be doing this slow and painful."

"It is..." Another yawn broke her sentence. "That's just how a curse works. It will wait until the most inconvenient, inconceivable moment to blossom in full, all the while keeping you teetering on the edge. So I can't say it'll bloom today, tomorrow, or even next year."

"Next year..." He grunted.

"Or..." Stretching her arm high, his eyes falling on the silhouette of her breast and relieved to feel the familiar wave of arousal. "We can take it up a notch, one up the magnitude of your transformation and beat it into submission."

There was a long pause of silence between them.

"How exactly do I get my forehead to heal like this stuff did?" He managed to get back on his feet, rubbing at his abdomen, pushing a change in topics. "I mean, your fingers were really in there... so..."

Her eyes fell down to where she had clawed into him and she smiled. "Kiss mm-!"

Tony had caught her by surprise. She could taste the blood on his lips, sugary and sweet. His tongue licked at her own, his lips hungry to kiss and play with her. Her back pressed against the cold tank of the toilet. Icy drops of water dripping across her, off his chin and body. He towered over her without fear. She hadn't realized how much larger he was compared to her. The aggressive advance had aroused her. Her fingers ran down his stomach, sneaking their way under the wet waistband of his pants.

A firm grip wrapped around her wrist. His lips breaking from hers and the bottle green eyes hit her own. She was at a loss for words. The man before her peaking her interest in ways she didn't see, dissolving her initial impression of him. Heat waved off him, there was no denying he was in a full incubine lusting. Licking her lips, taking another taste of his blood, it still hinted he was human, not yet in bloom. Despite it, he had figured out how to control the overwhelming arousal building inside him.

"Thanks." His voice breathed before letting go of her hand.

Without further words, he marched away. The slam of his bedroom door told her he still hadn't decided which route he wanted to take. Peering down to the pool of blood, she followed the bloodied footsteps down the hallway. He was both angry and frustrated with his situation. The more his incubus traits come forward, the more curious his actions and reactions became in her eyes. Whether he realized it or not, the level of control he was exercising was impressive. So much so, he was able to defend, no, flat out counter her attempts to toy with him. Just now, she failed to pull his desires out further. Instead, he had jumped to kiss her, understanding at this point even that is enough to heal something like a concussion. What was flooring, was his ability to stop and pull away from her. Granted he fled down the hall, but it was alluring to watch.

Tony sighed, his back against the bedroom door. Touching his forehead, the wound had vanished with ease. Sliding to the floor, enjoying the cold his wet state brought, he knew his time of sitting on the fence had ended. He would have to make a choice, even though he had announced he would take Lillith's path over the curse, it still frightened him. Being with her, laying with her was dangerous. The stories he had heard of her promiscuous nature with the way she had overtaken Rusty, and even after Pan toying with him. She was powerful and dangerously obsessed. In that moment, he felt like she owned him, but just now, in the bathroom, he had proven he could be just as aggressive.

Closing his eyes, he swallowed everything down. His chest was trying to burn back to life and he rubbed at it like heartburn. Was there even a guarantee this would even stop? Get better? What or how could things even get "better" from where he sat? Cedric was gone, he had no one between him and this new dangerous world he was joining. From here on out, he was on his own and the next steps would fall onto him to decide and follow through. He thought of himself as strong before all of this. Why not reclaim some of what he was before the world of monsters invaded his life?

Time to embrace the power, Tony. He rose to his feet, the fever creeping back out from his core. *Time to take what this bloodline offers on my own terms.*

Swinging his door open, he marched back down the hall. Lillith was stepping over the blood in the bathroom floor, but the slapping of his bare feet made her freeze. She glanced up, his lips rushing her own once more. Stumbling with each hungry lick and suckle sent chills across her skin. Provocative waves were drowning her as they pushed out of him and through her. Tony had made up his mind and he chose to take matters into his own hands. His hands were hot, surfing across her hips, tugging her pants off. Musing over his actions, she dove her hand into the front of his pants. Her fingers reached the object only for him to pull away from her.

Breathless, he moved to suckling at her neck, relishing in long hard sucks, leaving his mark across her elegant neck. His hands squeezed her bare ass cheeks, lifting her off her feet. Yelping, the icy vanity smacked across her bottom. Pulling away from her, he tugged the yoga pants free from her legs. His prowess was intoxicating, her heart racing. She rushed to relieve herself of the constraints of her shirt, wanting him to have full access to every inch of her. Squatting before her, he shoved her legs wide. The heat of his silky tongue pressed its way from her knee, across her inner thigh, and at last suckled between her legs.

Lillith's back arched as she moaned. Each lick and suck toying with her own pleasures. Both hands gripped the hair on his head, demanding he eat more. One hard long suck sent her thigh squeezing around his head, wiggling where she sat on the bathroom vanity. Letting go earned another moan from her. His tongue dove inside before rubbing its way back to the gem where he teased her further. Another dive, aggressive and hungry, her back arched. Screaming, the sensations resonating between them orgasmic. The bathroom mirror shattered, horns smashing it as he worked her over, making her arch further. She tugged at his hair, trying to pull him away, overwhelmed for the first time in her life.

"St-stop..." The pounding of her heart throbbed in rhythm with the heat invading her body. "No more.."

Pausing, he rocked back onto his heels. Panting, she stared down at the glowing green eyes between her legs. A fanged grin stretched across Tony's face, horns starting to peak out from under his hair. Swallowing, she gauged the man before her one last time.

"Are you sure you want to go through with this?" Lillith was failing to hold back her arousal, his own pulling her into an endless want of desire. "There is no turning back…"

Sighing, he furrowed his brow. "This makes me into a King Incubus, right?"

Smiling, she shivered as he stood, creeping closer. "Yes. I see you figured it out…"

"It was the only possible way to upgrade above just a normal incubus." His fingers were sliding up her inner thigh, his eyes locking her own. "But I'm not doing this your way."

"Oh?" His lips were a mere few inches from her own, enticing they may take a kiss from her again. "I thought this was you choosing me…"

Fingers rubbing and teasing in and out, his lips breathed at her ear. "I want you to come in the palm of my hand…"

Gasping, he threw a wave of sexual desire through her. "I never expected…"

Nibbling on her ear, he whispered. "I thought this is how incubus are supposed to work over their prey."

Her hand gripped his wrist where he teased her between closed thighs. "I think you misunderstood… I'm supposed to be working you over…"

Grunting, he ignored the desperate pull on his arm. His strokes were fast and aggressive. Glass was falling off the shattered mirror, the vanity shaking with the power of his movements. Lillith's eyes squeezed tight, he dominated her own surges of pleasure, overpowering her physically and magically. She lurched forward, gripping his arm, squealing as her orgasm began to reach its climax. Her thighs tensed and shuddered, squeezing his arm, announcing she had did as he commanded. She panted, hearing her own liquid drip across the tiles.

"Was that so hard?" He cooed, warranting a heated glare.

"Where did this vigor come from?" Swallowing, she was trying to catch her breath, wincing as he slid his hand free. "I didn't think you'd have it in you to be..."

"Dominant?" He caught a glimpse of himself in the shards of the mirror. "Is it normal to have two sets of horns?"

Her face flushed. "Not when you're the Incubus King. It is the first time one has asserted sexual dominance over me to claim it for themselves."

Grabbing up her wrists, he slammed them high above her head. Broken glass dug into his knuckles, slicing her arms as pieces clattered across the counter behind her. Leaning in, he kissed her deep and slow. Her breasts pressing against his chest hot and enthralling. Opening her thighs, she invited him in and he wasted no time to tease her further. Sliding her wrists together, a single grasp of his palm pinning them into place. A wave of arousal vibrated through him from Lillith and he knew what she wanted from him. Dropping his pants, his fingers toyed with her for only a moment before he pushed his way against her. The cold vanity pressing across his thighs added to the excitement shared between them.

Breaking their kiss, he gripped up her breast, suckling at it as he dove in and out of her slow and hard, and back again. Teeth teasing her nipples, the new sensations waving in and out of each them was invigorating, urging him to keep her on the edge of her next orgasm. Her back starting arching, he was pushing deeper, faster. Thighs tightening around his waist shuddered with anticipation. Letting go of her wrist, he moaned at his own peak, hugging her closer. Claws dug into the flesh of his back, inside she tightened and he let himself ride out their climaxes together. Squealing with delight, the last of the mirror fell away, clattering across the vanity and shattering on the tiles at his feet.

Steam rolled off his shoulders and she hugged onto him, not wanting to break their union just yet. Her lips began to suckle at his neck and collarbone, sending excited shivers across him. He stood up straight, tried to pull out, but she locked her ankles, pushing him back. Locking eyes with her, she licked her lips. Finger shushed his lips, stopping him from interrupting where she planned on taking the moment. Her hand snaked down his chest, across the ripples of his abdomen. Slipping her fingers between them, she grinned wide. He could feel her tighten as she began to play with herself. Leaning in, he aimed to assist, groping both breasts, teasing both with tongue and teeth.

Humming, he could feel the wave of her next climax. His own excitement building, realizing he could feel her pleasures as if they were his own. Slow and in rhythm with her own playful surges. Again, she lurched forward, tightening, he pounded against the vanity. His hands slid behind her, her climax starting to fall. Gripping her hair, he yanked her back into an arch, opening her further to him. Again, she tightened, horns scraping across the drywall once hidden by the mirror. Her scream was more primal than the first and he couldn't hold off his own second elation. His moaning was joined by the hot sliding of his tongue across her collarbone and neck.

One last push, his breath was hot against her neck. "Why did we wait so long..."

"I have never..." Her legs unwrapped and she pressed him against the wall. "You make me question everything I've ever known about myself..."

He tried to run his fingers through his hair, but raked his knuckle across his horns. "Are you telling me it's not normally this amazing?"

"N-no..." Lillith's face mottled, sliding to the floor she stumbled, her legs weak. "Christ..."

"No as in good or bad..." He mused over her second attempt to walk before turning to lean on the vanity. "We beat the curse to the punchline, right?"

"Y-yea." Lillith frowned, looking at the tiny broken reflections of herself with him towering from behind her. "I am supposed to overwhelm you... but you keep matching it, maybe even throwing it back in my face..."

"Good..." The warmth of his hands gripped her hips. "I'm not done."

She gave a toothy grin over her shoulder, finding the assertive attitude alluring. Chills rippled across her as the heat of a hand slide up her spine and gripped her by the back of her neck. Pushing her down, her breast and cheek aching from the weight. The other hand glided across her stomach, rubbing between her thighs as he pushed himself against her from behind. Moaning, she melted under him, no longer willing to deny her new mate.

"I believe I owe you from that time in my office." His body was boiling hot on top of her, his knees spreading legs wider so he could push ever deeper. "We haven't broken the vanity yet..."

She laughed, hearing the wood creak through the granite counter. "You're not trying hard enough..."

He laughed, pausing a moment. "If you insist..."

Crushed under his weight, each slap against her backside sent the plywood creaking. She gripped either side of the vanity, squealing, hot with lust. Letting go of her neck, she arched, her horns hugging either side of his cheeks. Clawed hands covered her own, both groaning with the next orgasm, pushing their weight against the counter. Snapping and a crackled erupted, the vanity buckling. Collapsing on top of the debris, the panted. Tony's arms hugged around her, both of them humming with the wake of their sexual feats.

"Ok..." He could hardly catch his breath. "We broke it, I'm done."

Laughing, she shook her head. "Normally I'm the one breaking, not the room."

"Times have changed..." His voice lowered. "That's not me, I may enjoy being in charge in the sheets... but not in the form of ripping the girl apart."

"What was that then?" Fussing, she was pulling his arm, wanting to be free.

"That's how someone shows they care..." Pulling her closer, he whispered in her ear. "That's how I show that I really do love you."

Letting her go, she scrambled to her feet. Kicking him in the ribs, he grunted, both knowing it was more pleasurable than what it had meant to be. Grimacing, she shook her head, stepping over him. Sighing, he knew he had spoken his admirations of her too freely, but could she really deny what had happened between them...

To Be Continued...

Ready for Book Four?
Artemis: Eye of Gaea

Is waiting for you here on Amazon:
http://mybook.to/CedricSeries

Reviews are my tip jar!

I f you enjoyed the book, or something really nagged you about the story, I encourage you to speak your mind about my book in the form of a review. Both authors and readers depend on them to know if they will like the story and characters within the pages.

Where can we leave the reviews? There are a lot of places! Amazon and GoodReads are great places to leave them, but feel free to visit your favorite online venues and leave them there. Whether it's a one-liner that sums up how you feel, a in-depth review of breaking down the book and characters, or a spoiler warning of the rant to follow – ALL ARE ENCOURAGED.

You may leave reviews here:

Amazon
http://www.amazon.com/Valerie-Willis/e/B00FQMV8SU

GoodReads
https://www.goodreads.com/author/show/7822183.
Valerie_Willis

About the Author

Valerie Willis is a Fantasy Paranormal Romance author based out of Central Florida. She loves crafting novels with elements inspired by mythology, superstitions, legends, folklore, fairy tales and history. She received the Reader's Favorite Bronze medal in 'Fiction – Mythology' and FAPA's President's Silver medal in 'Fantasy/Sci-fi.' You can find her hosting workshops or a guest speaker at many events sharing her expertise in self-publishing, novel writing, research in fiction, worldbuilding, character development, book design, reader immersion and more.

Her Award-Winning Dark Fantasy Paranormal Romance, 'The Cedric Series,' is a wonderful blend of genres that appeal to a wide-range of readers described as "dramatic, lustful, and fantasy fulfilling." The motto here is: "No immortal is beyond the ailments of man" and that includes powerful creatures, demons, witches, and Gods. Many of the monsters present in the content is derived from Medieval Bestiaries and adds a fun flavor of new yet deeply rooted assortment of creatures such as Coin Iotair, Shag Foal, Cynocephali, and many more.

For Young Adult readers look for her Dark Urban Fantasy filled with coming-of-age and beyond life lessons, the 'Tattooed Angels Trilogy.' Hotan is a failed reincarnation and is becoming immortal against his will. Life is complicated and often we withdraw within ourselves and shut others out when life becomes hard. As the story unfolds, we learn the importance of opening up and asking for support in all its forms even beyond friends and family. Each immortal controls powers of nature like fire and wind or elements of humanity such as fear and judgment.

You can often find Valerie hosting workshops about writing and self-publishing in the Orlando, Florida area or working on the next novel. She loves to inspire other writers and creative minds. Be sure to visit her blog for some of the writing advice she has to offer. Uniquely, she brings in a perspective that has influences from Game Development and Graphic Design.

www.WillisAuthor.com

THE CEDRIC SERIES
Adult Fantasy Romance
Cedric the Demonic Knight
Romasanta: Father of Werewolves
The Oracle: Keeper of Gaea's Gate
Artemis: Eye of Gaea
King Incubus: A New Reign
ON GOING SERIES!

TATTOOED ANGELS TRILOGY
Young Adult Urban Fantasy
Rebirth
Judgment
Death

As Honey Cummings
Erotica & Steamy Romance
Sleeping with Sasquatch
Cuddling with Chupacabra
Naked with New Jersey Devil
Laying with the Lady in Blue
Wanton Woman in White
Beating it with Bloody Mary

Beau and Professor Bestialora
The Goat's Gruff
Goldie and Her Three Beards
Pied Piper's Pipe

ANTHOLOGIES & COLLECTIONS
A World of Their Own
Work of Hearts Magazine Release
How I Met My Other: True Stories, True Love
It Was Always You: A Thrill of the Heart Anthology

Demonic Wildlife: A Fantastically Funny Adventure
Demonic Household: See Owner's Manual
Demonic Carnival: First Ticket's Free

The Hunted – Thrill of the Hunt 3
Urban Legends Reimagined – Thrill of the Hunt 4
Buried Alive – Thrill of the Hunt 5

PUBLIC DOMAIN REMAKES
Bulfinch's Mythology with Illustrations
Book of Werewolves
The Fairy Faith of Celtic Countries

BOOK CLUB
DISCUSSION QUESTIONS

1.   How has the emotional connection between Cedric and Angeline changed in book 3 compared to book 1?

2.   Who do you feel is having the most trouble dealing with Angeline's emotions: Angeline or Cedric?

3.   Why was it important for Tony to see Romasanta's transformation?

4.   Who benefited the most from Angeline's battle against the Golden Stag?

5.   What is the significance of the sword being passed between Romasanta to Cedric?

6.   How does Tony's curse reveal more about Lillith's own struggles as a Succubus?

7.   Does Cedric feel guilty for his actions towards Angeline, both past and present?

8.   What is the significance of Lillith dragging Cedric into the hallway?

9.   Was it necessary for Angeline's character development to discover Cedric's journals?

10.   Inside Delphyne's realm there is no technology. How will this aid Cedric and Angeline's relationship? Is there or will there be any detriment?

11.   Who is the voice of reason for the party as they prepare and traverse Delphyne's realm?

12. Nyctimus has joined the party this time. How does he hinder/detract from the dynamics of the group?

13. Delphyne appears as a Greek Goddess to the group. How does this imagery prepare the reader for the battle to come?

14. How does the past decisions/actions of Cedric/Romasanta affect the current situation or each other? Does this affect the rest of the group?

15. The Oracle is someone Romasanta knew. Why do you think the author decided to place Rhea here?

16. Can any speculations be pulled from the fact that Pan and Lillith are siblings? Mythology? Within the story?

17. Was Pan's kiss for Tony out of want, desperation, or both?

18. Who's the better werewolf? Nyctimus or Romasanta?

19. Lillith's mark is powerful. How did you feel seeing it's use throughout The Oracle?

20. What is the significance of Tony bearing this mark?

Printed in the USA
CPSIA information can be obtained
at www.ICGtesting.com
LVHW041759031123
762990LV00004B/636